MISSION CHURCHILL

ALEX ABELLA

Inspired by the Warren Adler and James C. Humes Novel

Target Churchill

To Armeen

Senza dubbio, sempre diritto!

CHAPTER ONE

1933
La Habana, Cuba

"¡NARANJA DE CHINA DULCE!"

The melodious cry of the orange vendor under his window woke Marcus Riley with a start. He'd been dreaming he was back in County Cork, the Black and Tans hot on his trail, him running as fast as his brogues would let him, down dusky copses and through scummy green bogs. Then, as in that bad movie with John Gilbert he'd just gone to see with some Cuban cailín, he'd tripped and fallen and risen again but still the bloody English Auxiliaries drew closer and one of them fired and . . .

He opened his eyes. He was back in Havana, in the small apartment in the heart of the old city, with the constant clamor of street vendors, laughing housewives, harried workers, and dazzled tourists. The smell of the powerful coffee brewed by his next-door neighbor had already seeped under the front door, accompanied by the sad yelping of their doggie begging for breakfast.

Up and at 'em, Marcus, he could still hear his father in the early morn, back when they were all in the Londonderry flats. *Ya believe the world owes ye a living? Off with ye, my boy, show the world what you're made of.*

Riley smiled at his recollection, eased out of bed. Throwing aside the thin bedsheet, damp with night sweat, he walked over to the window. Opening the louvers, he gazed at the many-gabled roofline of La Havana Vieja and, beyond, the limpid vast bay shimmering like a silver platter in the morning sun. Five years and counting, he told himself. O Wilderness were Paradise enow, take the cash and let the credit go, he recited to himself, and went to take a shower.

An hour later, Riley stepped out of his building and into the crowded narrow sidewalk. Tall and ginger haired, he towered above the Cubans who hustled alongside him as he walked to the garage by Chinatown where he kept the De Soto that had come with his job at the brewery.

Funny job that, Da, he continued with his mental dialogue, looking at a billboard displaying his employers' stellar product —a golden glass of lager hoisted by a hooded Eskimo in a field of snow.

¡Cerveza Bru—deliciosa, refrescante!

Bru Beer, he thought. Now, in what other country would such a name be possible? Only in Cuba, so close to America, so ignorant of the language.

On Obispo Street Riley stepped around a lottery boy loudly hawking el gordo of ten thousand pesos to be drawn that coming Friday. Years later he would think back as to how his life would have been different if the boy hadn't blocked his way and he'd just kept on walking blithely down the bustling street, unaware of the presence in Havana of the man who had caused his bitter tropical exile and brought so much tragedy to his family and his country.

But aware of that presence Riley did become when he accidentally cast a glance inside a jewelry shop. He stopped in his tracks and peered intently through the window, uncertain he had glimpsed the right man. After all, his physical type was not uncommon among the English—on the small side, plump, rosy cheeked, given to early baldness. But no doubt about it, that was him, Winston Churchill, with his pinstripe suit and perpetual cigar, jabbing at a jeweler who by the looks of it wasn't understanding his meaning. Standing next to Churchill was a taller man, of solid build and erect bearing, also in a suit, hovering over the discussion with the blank look of the disinterested observer.

Jesus, Mary, and Joseph, thought Riley, *I wish I had my gat with me.* A wave of revulsion swept over him, and it took all the self-control he'd learned from the beatings at Goldenbridge Children's Institution for him not to burst into the shop and strangle with his bare hands the man who'd been the ruin of Ireland.

Hiding his thoughts behind a mask of composure, he stepped casually into the jewelry shop. Two long display cases on either side of the room showed rings and watches in the ornate style favored by Cubans. At the far end, in front of a small display of fine filigreed silver chains, stood Churchill and his companion.

Must be his bodyguard, the hellhound they call Thompson, thought Riley, recalling the stories he'd heard of how Thompson saved Churchill's life when an IRA assassination team sprang an ambush at the Kensington Gardens in London. *He's got a gun,* he thought now, noticing the bulk by Thompson's left armpit. *Best be careful. But what are they doing here? Can't let them know I'm Irish, don't want to arouse suspicion.*

Adopting the supercilious airs he'd seen upper-class Englishmen flaunt all his life, Riley strolled about the store with a slight sneer, as though nothing in there was to his satisfaction. Out of the corner of his eye he noticed Churchill's walking stick, of dark mahogany with a silver handle, and how Churchill's right side was hunched over it, the man keeping himself upright by leaning on the cane. *Must have had an accident. A stroke? We should be so lucky.*

"Perhaps we should go somewhere else, sir," Riley overheard Thompson say to Churchill in the flat tone of the well-trained manservant.

"No, no, let me try once more, confound it. *Parlee voo fransay, mon bonhomme?*" said Churchill in his schoolbook French, his cheeks flushing pink as he flailed his cigar at the bewildered jeweler.

The man shook his head in dismay. *"Lo siento, señor, mi hija vuelve en un minuto y con gusto le puede atender, ella sí sabe inglés."*

Churchill glanced at Thompson. "Inglés, I've heard that before. It means Englishman. See, the man does understand us, he knows whence we came."

Riley saw his cue and before Thompson could reply, stepped in quickly between the two men.

"Actually, he wants to tell you that his daughter, who speaks English, will be back presently, Mr. Churchill," said Riley in the poshest accent he could muster.

Churchill turned and sized up Riley with observant eyes of the coldest blue, as calculating as a hussar picking his next pony for the final polo chukker.

"Perhaps I can be of assistance," continued Riley, with a nod.

"That would be fine," said Churchill. "Please tell this man I'm very much interested in that silver necklace, but that I don't want him to overcharge me. I know Cubans, I fought them in '95."

"Yes, Mr. Churchill, I read your memoirs," said Riley, who proceeded to tell the jeweler in fluent Castilian Spanish not only Churchill's wishes, but also that his customer was one of the top leaders of the mighty English empire. The jeweler's eyes opened wide, his mouth agog.

"*¡Coño! ¿De verdad?*" Damn, really?

"*Así es, mi amigo,*" confirmed Riley.

The jeweler, amid a torrent of praise for the many accomplishments of the English race, picked out two silver filigreed earrings from the display case matching the necklace and presented them to Churchill.

"What's this?" asked Churchill.

"He wants to gift you these. He says they will make a lovely present for your *querida*," said Riley.

"*Querida?* What is that?"

Riley hesitated, shook his head slyly, dropped his voice almost to a whisper. "Your lover, sir."

Churchill harrumphed, then chuckled. "Well, my wife will certainly be amused by that description, it's been a while since . . . never mind. Thank him for me. The price?"

The jeweler glanced at a sticker on the bottom of the velvet case holding the necklace, made a quick mental calculation.

"Fifteen dollars," Riley told Churchill. "That's for all the items, he says it's his own wholesale price."

"Very decent of him."

"But he would like your autograph, sir."

"That can be arranged."

LATER, back on the steamy sidewalk outside the jeweler's, Churchill faced Riley, shook his hand.

"Say, good man, what is your name?"

Riley was momentarily taken aback. When he'd entered the store his objective had been to get as close as possible to Churchill, but in the heat of the moment he had forgotten to prepare a false identity for his charade. He blinked twice, bowed slightly before the shorter man, a gesture of subservience he knew an inflated ego like Churchill's would expect, and offered the first name that came to mind that wasn't obviously Irish.

"Patrick Whitsett, Mr. Churchill," he said, borrowing the identity of a Canadian at the brewery, confident the man had never set foot in Churchill's rarefied circles. "If there's anything else I can do for you during your stay in Cuba, it would be my pleasure."

"You live here?" asked Churchill, cocking the still strong but fleshy head.

"I'm the operations manager at a local brewery, sir. Locals much appreciate our product."

"Not as much as I do your help today, young man. We're having a small reception at the embassy tomorrow night. I would like you to be there—not too many of our countrymen around these parts. Nothing fancy, you understand, just your usual dinner dress."

"It will be my pleasure, Mr. Churchill."

"Good. How long have you been here, you say?"

"A few years, sir. Left England after the General Strike of '26."

"Yes, nasty business, that. Well, we must be off. I'm still recuperating from a small accident in New York, can't walk around too much. I need regular naps. Doctor's orders, though mind you, I've never needed much excuse to take siesta. It clears the mind wonderfully. Good day," he added, vigorously shaking Riley's hand again.

"Before you go, Mr. Whitsett," interrupted Thompson, who had remained skeptically silent throughout the conversation. "What is the name of your brewery, sir? I ask so when I order a pint, I can give you my business."

"Cerveza Bru. Bru Beer. Odd name, isn't it? Bru is a not uncommon name in Spanish, from Catalonia, I was told."

"Bru Beer, that's a tautology if I ever heard one," said Churchill, impatiently. "Come along, Thompson, we need to get back to the Nacional. I've still to send those telegrams."

"Yes, sir," answered Thompson, nodding goodbye at Riley.

———

RILEY DROPPED his ingratiating smile when he saw Churchill and Thompson turn the corner on O'Reilly Street and push their way through the crowd. *Give me my business,* thought Riley, *I know exactly what you're going to do. You're going to check up on me, ain't ye? I best hurry and inform Uncle Brandon that the beast is in our midst. We should kill him while we have our chance.*

CHAPTER TWO

RILEY'S PLACE of employment was on the outskirts of Havana, in the melodiously named town of Cotorro, or parrot, thoughtfully situated on the banks of the meandering Almendares River—the source of the water for its famous product.

Built on what had been a twenty-square-mile farm, Cervecería Bru was renowned throughout Cuba for its gardens, baseball stadiums, and Olympic-sized swimming pools, but especially for the open-air pavilions used for the many festivities of the locals—weddings, birthdays, patriotic events commemorating the profusion of heroes of the decades-long revolt against the Spanish. It often seemed to Riley that Cubans, like the Irish, never missed an occasion to celebrate. And to drink beer, which of course was the whole point of the amenities.

Riley waved at the entrance guard, who tipped his cap and lifted the creaky wooden gate to let his car through. The massive De Soto rumbled down the enfilade of stately royal palms to the three-story pink masonry building next to the plant, the heart of the business. The sweet smell of toasted

barley reminded Riley it was Wednesday and that he still had
to finish the contracts for the upcoming Carnaval celebrations
sponsored by the Havana Kiwanis Club, which would engage
the entire grounds for a whole weekend. But that would have to
wait. For now there was much more important work to be done
—killing Churchill.

———

"NO, NO, NO!" said Uncle Brandon, slapping a hand on the
ornate mahogany desk he had inherited from the deceased—
and sorely missed—great uncle who had founded the brewery
thirty years before with a Cuban wartime general.

"Killing Churchill would be a waste of a God-given oppor-
tunity, Marcus, can't ye see that? That kind of thinking is
exactly what scuppered our chances when Michael Collins had
victory at his fingertips. I have a better idea."

"And what might that be, Uncle?" asked Riley, sitting in the
high-ceilinged office facing a leafy bower angling down to the
Almendares. An ibis flew by, its white wings noisily flapping in
the stillness of the early afternoon.

Now Brandon O'Connor—president of Cervecería Bru,
founder of the Asociación Cubana de Hijos de Eire, Riley's
distant relation, his protector, and most importantly, an equally
fiery Irish patriot—rose from his desk. He hobbled over to the
telephone desk, pulled open the drawer, ran a finger down the
name cards in the telephone index.

Riley observed him coldly. He would have walked out if
not for the fact that Uncle Brandon deserved his respect, not
just for sheltering Riley in Cuba, but for the sacrifices he had
made for the cause of Irish independence, his painful limp a
testimony of the bullets he took from the English.

"Here it is," said Uncle Brandon, pulling out a card. "I

recently made the acquaintance of a well-placed man in the Cuban Army who I am certain would be glad to lend us a hand in the project—in exchange for a fee, naturally."

"What is this project you're speaking of?"

"It's obvious, Marcus. Why, to kidnap Churchill and hold him hostage in one of the keys outside Santa Clara! We'd release him in exchange for Peadar O'Donnell and some of our other lads still in English prisons. Much better than just a revenge killing, my boy. That would only make Churchill a martyr, and who wants that?"

"Fine then, but who is this Cuban, Uncle?"

"*Un hombre de confianza.* He can be trusted. A great organizer but with little in the way of reserves. Our money will be of great help to him. The name is Batista, Fulgencio Batista. A sergeant. In the meantime, best be sure your cover is not discovered, what you say?"

Uncle Brandon staggered back to his desk, pressed a button on the black Bakelite intercom.

"Miss Gonzalez, please have Patrick Whitsett report to me right away."

"Yes, sir," replied the secretary. Uncle Brandon dropped his two hundred and fifty pounds of muscle, fat, and pain into his leather chair, which whooshed like an emptied lung.

"Now, my boy, did I ever tell you how we outsmarted the English in the battle of Galway?"

Riley grinned and shook his head no, even though he'd heard the story one too many times. The old man deserves to be humored, without him I'd still be rotting in some damned Belfast prison.

"Can't say I recall, Uncle."

"Well, then, let me tell you the whole story, once and for all," went on Uncle Brandon. His light gray eyes sparkled while he recounted his youthful escapades, and he was dissecting the degrees of consanguinity between the Rileys, the O'Connors, and their treacherous English cousins, the Johnsons, when there came a knock at the door.

A timorous, pasty white face peeked around the half-open entrance.

"You wanted me, sir?"

"Patrick, please come in."

The real Patrick Whitsett, a short man with the narrow, deep-set eyes of a not too distant Cree ancestor, entered the room still wearing the leather apron of his job as master brewer.

"Patrick, I have received your request for vacation time, and I've decided you are more than deserving. I am very happy with the work you have been doing on the new dark beer. Let's see what name the committee decides to give it before we put it out. Regardless, you have earned a bit of a breathing spell. You may take the next two weeks off."

Whitsett's face contorted in the agony of fearful embarrassment. "Thank you, Mr. O'Connor, but I had asked for a month off in June, sir, to visit the family in Ottawa."

"My boy, you have done such a splendid job, I'm giving you the two weeks off extra, in addition to your summer leave. It's with pay, of course. Starting right now."

"Am I fired, sir?"

"Not at all! We are like family here, and I wish to recompense talent when there's talent in the family. Tell me, what will you do with the time?"

"Well, sir, now that you ask, I have been wanting to visit the country's central mountains for a while. I am an amateur geologist. I believe the Escambray Sierra may hold some fine examples of Cretaceous igneous shales. I don't think that area has ever been explored. By white men, I mean."

"Hmm, you're probably right. Then off with you, my boy!

Bring me some samples when you return, I'll put them in our lobby display case!"

"Yes, sir, thank you, sir!"

"You're welcome! Before you leave, tell Towers to put Arriaga on your job while you're gone—the Cubans need more hands-on experience. Now flee, my lad! Go!"

Uncle Brandon stared the door for a few moments after Whitsett had left the room, deep in thought. He spun around to Riley, all bonhomie having flown from his face.

"That takes care of that problem. Tomorrow night you must be appropriately dressed. I will have my tailor call on you. When you go to the ambassador's residence, get as close to Churchill as you can. Find out his schedule, where he's staying, all the rest. Better yet, find out exactly when he's leaving. We'll grab him on the way to his ship. He'll never know what 'it him."

CHAPTER THREE

RILEY FELT CONFINED, trapped inside the narrow-waisted dinner jacket Uncle Brandon's tailor had found for him to wear at the British Embassy function. It had been a last-minute choice because, as always in Cuba, something went wrong—in this case, the one thing Riley could do nothing about, his size.

There were Cubans of Riley's height and weight, naturally, not many but a few; most were white men of means who had their suits custom made or specially selected for them in New York, London, and Paris. But rarely in Havana. With no off-the-rack suits that would fit his long, muscular arms and his ample back, and no time to make a new suit, the tailor gave Riley a bespoke tuxedo jacket that had been ordered by the owner of Cubana de Aviación, who had recently died in a car accident with his mistress before he could wear it. The man had been as tall as Riley but lanky, with shorter, thinner arms. The tailor had let out the sleeves and opened the back as much as he could, but there was little to be done about the waistline. Riley would just have to hold it in for the duration.

However, the jacket was ample enough at the shoulder and

front for Riley to slip in its left breast pocket the Walther .32 he'd bought when he first came to Cuba. A small and powerful automatic, the Walther was not very accurate for long distances but deadly at close range. Which was fine, because Riley intended to be very close to Churchill when he used it to blow the man's brains out. He'd never let the beast who had ordered his brother's death live. To hell with Uncle Brandon.

In his teen years, before he and his older brother Sean joined the Irish Republican Army, Riley had dreamed of being an actor. He had briefly performed as an amateur player in some theaters in Belfast, had a walk-on part in a revival of *The Playboy of the Western World*, and played the lead in one of Oscar Wilde's minor plays.

Riley's training in dissembling had come in handy when he joined the fight against the English, as he was able to penetrate the fanciest establishments and place his bombs and incendiary devices without drawing much notice. His experience served him well that evening at the ambassador's residence in Miramar, the neighborhood home to the mansions of the island's elite, a stone's throw from the murmuring sea.

Riley drove his De Soto Roadster himself, foregoing Uncle Brandon's black Cuban driver. Riley had had the car washed immaculately inside and out, and he was pleased to see it did not look out of place next to the Packards, Cadillacs, and Buicks of the other attendees. A young black servant in white uniform took the keys and parked it in the vast courtyard behind the residence—a two-story Mediterranean once owned by a minor member of the wealthy Zayas presidential family.

Riley had driven around the neighborhood the day before, taking note of the service alley behind the residence, the stop light at the corner, the distance to the nearest police station. He'd also checked into the Havana Yacht Club, a few short blocks away, and had parked there a black Ford Coupe for his getaway—as well as a launch with an Evinrude outboard motor at the dock—in case his plan and not Churchill went to hell.

The ambassador's butler, the sort of mealy-mouthed Englishman Riley had loathed all his life, stood blankly at the residence door. Riley gave him his name and the butler directed him to the reception already under way in the ball-room. As he entered the house, for a moment Riley wondered if he might be recognized, fearing some of those present might be aware of the Irish background of the brewery's president, or of himself.

Don't think about that, my boy, Uncle Brandon had said. I avoid all contact with the English. Besides, you know what a snobby bunch they are. Remember your job, get as close to Churchill as a girl's knickers, and you'll be fine.

The ballroom was vast, with wide glass doors leading to the gardens outside, a smooth parquet floor, stained-glass windows below a frescoed ceiling, and a sparkling chandelier that lent a soft butter-yellow glow to the wood-paneled walls. The effect was of that of being transported to some Ruritanian palace in the far reaches of a make-believe Europe.

That cosmopolitan feel was marred by Havana's pervasive humidity, the dampness of the nearby ocean augmented by a recent shower that had left the air laden with moisture and foreboding. Two large fans rattled at either end of the room in a hopeless attempt to lower the temperature; a trickle of perspiration began to run down the back of Riley's stiffly starched white shirt.

A buffet table had been laid out with all sorts of English dishes—cold roast beef, ham, tiny sandwiches, cheesy puffs. Riley swiped a glass of champagne offered by a passing waiter and reconnoitered the room, observing its many doors and windows for quick exit when the time came. He spotted Churchill at the far end of the room, expanding upon the grave

dangers to world peace that only he, the far-sighted if momentarily out of office statesman, could remedy:

"One of the things which we were told after the Great War
would be a security for us was that Germany would be a
democracy with parliamentary institutions. All that has been
swept away. You have dictatorship—most grim dictatorship!
You have militarism and appeals to every form of fighting spirit.
I believe we must do something now to stanch that evil before it
spreads to the rest of Europe. We must arm, arm, and arm some
more!"

Riley drifted along the edge of the crowd, the men in tails
and winged collars, the women in gauzy dresses clinging to
dewy skin. He spotted Churchill's bodyguard, Walter Thompson, dressed in a plain gray business suit, standing discreetly
behind Churchill.

"Nasty bit of weather we've been having, don't you think?"
said a voice behind him. Riley turned to see a man as tall as he,
with a receding hairline, large droopy eyes, and the snub nose
of the privileged, a sheen of perspiration on his pale face.

"One gets accustomed to it, eventually," said Riley, amiably
he thought, and nodded, wanting to brush him off, but the man
continued:

"How does one do that? I've heard Hindus drink warm tea
to cool down, you think that might work here?"

"It might. I'll have to try it sometime," said Riley, looking
around for an excuse to move away. He saw Thompson had
noticed him and was giving him a slight smile and a nod.

"Say, how long have you been in Cuba? Haven't seen you
at the embassy," said the man next to Riley.

"I don't work there. I hold a job at a local brewery."

"Rather! I wouldn't mind a pint or two right about now.
The champagne they've been handing out gives me a headache.
They saved the Dom Perignon for Churchill. Best they have

locally, couldn't find a bottle of his beloved Pol Roger. He may be out of office, but he acts as if he were still Lord of the Admiralty. I say, Miles Thurmond," said the stranger, offering his hand.

Reluctantly, Riley offered his. "Patrick Whitsett."

"Where in England are you from?"

"I'm not. I'm Canadian. From Ottawa."

"Splendid! I've just been reassigned here from there. Commercial attaché. Wonderful scenery in Canada. Did a bit of skiing too at Chalet Cochand. *Vous connaissez?*"

Mercifully, at that point Churchill, glancing at the room as he was about to make a point, spotted Riley.

"But enough of war, war, war. There's the man who may yet save my marriage! Come here, Whitsett, I want to introduce you to this august company!"

Chuckles from the crowd as Riley nodded goodbye at Thurmond. "If you'll excuse me," he said and moved into the ring of admirers. Thompson smiled and stepped back, giving Riley room to stand next to Churchill.

"I was out shopping for a present for Clementine at this jewelry shop, a small act of penance for not bringing her with me, and the jeweler was not understanding my English. This young man came in and saved the day. Not only did he faithfully render my offer into Spanish, he convinced the man to throw in a pair of earrings as well! Patrick Whitsett, Ambassador Sir John Broderick."

"Thank you, Mr. Churchill," said Riley, with a wide grin, shaking the ambassador's hand. "An honor to meet you, Sir John."

WHILE RILEY WAS ENGULFED by the appreciative crowd, Walter Thompson stepped out of the ballroom and headed for the mansion's kitchen. Earlier in the day, as part of his duties as Churchill's bodyguard, Thompson had made the rounds of the building, going up and down the marble staircase, inspecting the basement and the attic, the library and all the other rooms where an intruder might hide. Now that everyone was at the function, he thought it best to double check in case there were some nasty surprises hidden in the woodwork. After all, the kitchen was the likeliest place for an attacker—someone could enter and, posing as staff, could be armed with a gun, waiting only for the fateful moment to strike.

Thomoson had asked one of the embassy's security, a slender young man named Mitchell, to check up the staff and to be on the lookout for unusual changes or new people.

"Frankly, Mr. Thompson, we don't anticipate anything of the sort," Mitchell had said, annoyed by the task. "We've had the same crew for a year now, long before Churchill's arrival. Highly unlikely they would have foreseen him coming here, right?"

"One never knows," had said Thompson, ignoring the churlish response. "I've seen more unlikely things happen. Just be a good chap and keep your eyes open. Let me know if there's anything or anyone new."

Thompson stepped into the kitchen, a long cavern of green tiled walls with wide sinks, two stoves—one gas and one coal—a wood-burning oven, and one very small and rickety refrigerator. About a dozen servants bustled about, shuffling dishes with hors d'oeuvres, pouring champagne flutes, washing dishes and cutlery.

At one of the sinks, a black man with a pick was breaking up a yard-long block of ice with quick sharp blows. Mitchell was standing next to the other sink, chatting with one of the female staff, her back turned to Thompson. Distracted, Mitchell failed to see the detective approaching.

"Anything new to report, Mitchell?" said Thompson. Startled, Mitchell replied a tad too quickly to be believed, "Nothing at all, just practicing my Spanish with this señorita."

"Hmm," said Thompson, dismissing the obviously inefficient official.

"Yes, and you're terrible at it," said the girl, her back still to Thompson.

Thompson stopped, his attention as focused on the girl as if she'd whipped around with a revolver aimed at his belly. There was something extraordinary in the girl's voice, a musical quality that expressed itself unequivocally in those few words— a warm invitation to a world of delight, an inflection both childish and maternal that promised much more than he'd had for years—not since his courtship of his estranged wife when they were in their twenties in Manchester.

All of that crossed his mind in the few instants after he heard the girl speak and right before he said, "Who's this?" in a peremptory tone that surprised him when he heard himself.

Mitchell, embarassed and expecting some sort of reprimand, babbled, "A dishwasher. Never mind her, she has quite a tongue on her."

The girl turned to look at Thompson, and to his secret delight, he saw that the body matched the voice. A mass of black curls, tied back by a red kerchief, graced an oval face the color of caramel toffee, large sable eyes, a straight nose with slightly flaring nostrils telling of African ancestry, sensual lips, and a well-proportioned body that even her shapeless shift could not disguise. Thompson was immediately taken by the charming girl, but took great care—or so he thought—to disguise it.

"What is your name?" he snapped.

"Fabiana Nuñez," she said with a Carmen smile.

"How long have you been working here?"

"That's really none of your business. Who are you?" she said, her smile even more haughty.

"I ask the questions," he said.

"And who says I have to answer them?" she replied, still smiling.

"Told you she had a tongue on her," said Mitchell.

"No, that's right. She should know who's questioning her. We all have rights. I'm in charge of security, miss, for Mr. Churchill's visit."

"Oh!" she said, momentarily impressed, then added with a twinkle in her eyes: "You're Churchill's bodyguard?"

"Yes. Now, if you don't mind answering," said Thompson, fully aware that it was all just an excuse to hear her voice again.

"Ask, and you shall be given. The answer, that is," she said.

"Right. How long have you been with the embassy?"

"About six months."

"Where did you learn your English?"

"The nuns at St. Agatha's."

"Here?"

"Hardly. Queens, New York, where I was born."

"A Yank, are you?"

"If you say so. I like to call myself a New Yorker."

"What are you doing working here?"

"You may have heard there is something called a Depression going on in America. My mother thought it best to return to Cuba. At least here we wouldn't freeze to death."

"Of course. Well, carry on, Miss Nuñez. Pleasure."

"The pleasure is all mine," she said, and those few words sent Thompson's heart reeling. Careful, old boy, you're a tad too long in the tooth for this, he thought.

"Mitchell, come with me. I wish to inspect the gardens."

Mitchell grinned, noting Thompson's interest in the girl.

"Should I frisk her for weapons, sir? I'd like that."

"Never you mind, come along!"

"Goodbye, mister no name bodyguard!" cried out the girl, teasingly.

Thompson looked back and felt himself captivated by the girl's dazzling liquid eyes.

"Thompson," he said, "the name is Thompson," and walked out of the kitchen to still his heart.

"Thompson," repeated the girl to herself, softly.

A woman's voice shrilled in Spanish: "Fabiana, quit gabbing and finish doing those dishes!"

CHAPTER FOUR

THE GARDENS behind the mansion were hexagonal in shape and half a block long. In the soft darkness of the Antillean night, they seemed to Thompson as fantastical as the ones he'd seen in Brighton, at the park where some seaman had brought back samples of all the exotic vegetation he'd encountered in his travels.

Thompson had inspected the embassy gardens in the daytime, noting again how everything in Cuba was lush and colorful, with a vitality that far surpassed the tidy green of the British Isles. With Churchill Thompson had traveled far and wide, to France several times, to the Middle East, to Madeira, to Germany and America, to India even, yet nowhere had he seen such a profusion of lush vegetation as he encountered during their stay in Cuba.

There were palms, coconuts, oranges, lemons, alligator pears, all growing wild in such profusion by the side of the roads that the countryside to Thompson looked like some sort of Eden, a place where you could stick a piece of lumber in the ground, and it would throw roots to begin growing again.

Here, in the grounds of the ambassador's residence, previous owners had filled the lush gardens with palms, fruit trees, and exotic ornamentals, shaping the grounds so that the usual resting places along the pebbled paths—the stone bench here, the odd gazebo there—gave an impression of lushness, abandon, mystery. Now, at night, the place felt haunted by some dark tropical spirit, despite the scattered yellow light bulbs dangling from the handful of posts on the grounds.

The embassy had not wanted any extra security at the residence since, as the staff informed Thompson, nothing ever happened in the posh neighborhood. The German Embassy was to one side—shuttered, as the previous ambassador had just been recalled by the National Socialist government. On the other side of the residence, the manse of the mistress of Julio Lobo, the richest man in Cuba. Cuban police squad cars patrolled the area day and night. Who on Earth would think of doing anything in these gilded quarters? Only after much insistence had Thompson managed to have Mitchell and another man detailed for the night.

Veering off a path, Thompson conferred with the guard hiding in the bushes, who confirmed nothing untoward had happened, but that the smell of the cooking was making him very hungry. Feeling sorry for the man, Thompson sent him inside for a bite, then ordered Mitchell to walk around the far side of the garden while he scouted the northern portion closest to the house. They met halfway, at a gurgling Spanish fountain draped in moss.

"Everything is normal, sir," said Mitchell. Mind if I go in for a while? Mosquitos seem to love me, but I don't return the feeling."

"Fine," chuckled Thompson, "go right ahead. I shall stay here until you return."

Thompson sat on the lip of the fountain. Indulging in the

one habit he'd always found hard to break, he pulled out of his right breast pocket a thick Partagás cigar. He inserted a toothpick at its tip to open the leaf and lit the puro, savoring the smoke's chocolate richness.

The soft murmur of the ocean a few blocks away echoed in Thompson's ear like the soft refrain of a Cuban love song he'd heard on the radio—or the musical cadence of the voice of the girl he'd just met. His thoughts drifted to the intriguing, saucy housemaid, briefly wondering if there could ever be a future for him in Cuba, when he heard the snap of a broken twig.

Then another.

Thompson exhaled quickly, put down the cigar on the fountain's edge, and quietly scurried to a dark corner of the garden, hiding under a giant philodendron. He waited patiently for a few seconds, his attention as drawn to the shapeless mass of green before him as when he'd been in the trenches at the Somme, when a careless move meant instant death from German sharpshooters.

A figure stepped out of the bushes—a young man, with the typical Cuban dark hair and fair skin, of medium height and build, wearing all black, down to the rubber plimsolls covered with mud. He must have jumped the back wall and landed in the draining ditch, thought Thompson. I should have asked for dogs.

The intruder glanced about, sniffed the air, took out a small revolver from his waistband. Slowly he approached the fountain, pointing the gun straight ahead of him like an amateur with his finger on the trigger. The man stopped, looked around, and placed the lit Partagás in his mouth.

Absurd, thought Thompson. He's here on a mission and he's going to smoke a cigar? What kind of people are these? Never mind, here's my chance.

With a jump and two swift steps, Thompson surged out of

the darkness and fell upon the young man, quickly wrestling the gun away from him and delivering a powerful punch to his sternum. The intruder bent over, choking. Thompson struck him with the butt of the gun, throwing him to the muddy ground.

The intruder fell on his back, but then, quick as a rabbit, jumped back up and tried to run. Thompson grabbed him in a neck hold and turned him over, sweeping the man's legs from under him. He landed him face down on the dirt, Thompson's body weight grinding him down.

"Lemmy go, lemmy go!" shouted the man.

"Speak English, do you? Then you know this is British territory, huh? What the bloody hell are you doing here?"

Thompson grabbed one of the man's arms and twisted it back with all his might. He heard the bone snap out of its joint and the man yelled an agonizing cry. Thompson seized him by the shirt, yanked him upright to his feet.

"Start talking!" said Thompson, shaking him with barely restrained fury.

The man's yelling brought out Mitchell, who peeked out the kitchen door. He dropped the chicken drumstick he'd been nibbling on and ran to Thompson. The other guard also rushed out of the house, followed by a handful of servants, as the intruder struggled with Thompson.

"What happened, sir?" asked Mitchell

"Caught the bloody bastard sneaking in with a gun!"

"Lemmy go, lemmy go!" the man repeated in English, then broke into Spanish. "*¡Hijo 'e puta, me jodiste el brazo, coño!*"

"What's he saying, Mitchell?" asked Thompson, as the man struggled to break free.

"Says you broke his arm," said Mitchell.

"Tell him I'll break the other one unless he tells me who he is!"

Mitchell translated.

"Okay, okay!" said the man, gasping for air. *"Estoy con el ABC, movimiento revolucionario. ¡Esto es un acto patriótico para la liberación de Cuba!"*

"¿Que ibas hacer?" asked Mitchell.

"¡Matar a los imperialistas que apoyan a Machado!" gasped the man. *"¡Es la revolución!"*

"What's he saying? What's this Machado?" asked Thompson.

"Says he's a revolutionary, wants to kill imperialists who back Machado. That's the Cuban president," said Mitchell.

"Dictator, actually," said Churchill, drawn to the commotion along with the guests from inside the residence. "He rigged the last election, keeps going by force of arms."

"That's not quite the official story, Winston," cautioned the ambassador. "His Majesty's government has an interest in his government." Churchill ignored him.

"He wants to kill a few of us to make his point?" said Churchill.

"¡Pérfida Albión apoya a Machado, sus amigos son nuestros enemigos!" snarled the man, defiantly.

"Says Albion backs Machado, sir, therefore we're his enemies," said Mitchell.

"Ah, yes, perfidious Albion, a tired trope. Ask him when's the revolution going to happen," said Churchill, as unflappable as if questioning his cook for her omelet recipe.

Riley stepped out of the ballroom at that moment, along with other guests who followed Churchill. Witnessing the scene, he felt as if the Walther were burning in his breast pocket, urging him, do it now, before your chance slips away!

Riley looked to his right. The back wall of the garden was about a hundred feet away, a six-foot brick and mortar construction from the nineteenth century. It would take him mere seconds to dash through the bushes, jump the wall, and run the two blocks to his getaway car in the yacht club.

He knew Mitchell could not keep up with him. Thompson would be the problem. It'd be easy if he could kill both him and Churchill, but for now that seemed impossible. Better to let the scene play out and wait for something to present itself. He moved close to Churchill, as if protecting him with his hulking body.

"What's that, sir?" asked Mitchell, turning to Churchill.

"Ask him about the revolution. Ask him!"

"Really, Winston," said the ambassador, "perhaps we should call in the local police. This is not the moment; it seems to me . . ."

The ambassador's words were suddenly drowned out by a concatenation of explosions, a series of loud jarring blasts, from bombs going off in all corners of Havana. To the east, the west, the south, the entire city seemed to burst in a deadly symphony of destruction. The guests reeled back from the noise. Thompson, startled, released his grip for a moment. The captive broke free and took out of his pocket a hand grenade.

"Watch out, sir!" shouted Thompson.

Thompson leaped on the captive, who cried, "¡Abajo Machado! ¡Viva Cuba libre!" and pulled the tab on the grenade. Thompson, falling on him, turned him around, the man's body sheltering the company from the explosion. The man's head blew off, reeling like a football against the base of the nearest palm tree.

Riley saw his chance. Taking out his gun, he grabbed Churchill by the collar, but the blast of the grenade disoriented him—and he failed to release the safety on the Walther.

Thompson spun around from the bloody mess of the dead revolutionary and, in a flash, as if in slow motion, saw Riley fiddling with his gun, pointing it at the back of Churchill's neck. Instinctively, Thompson took out his revolver and fired a single shot at Riley, aiming for his head. The bullet missed and struck Riley on the shoulder. Riley dropped his gun.

"On him, Mitchell!" cried Thompson, as the guard wheeled about and jumped on the would-be killer. Riley threw him off and ran into the bushes, vaulting over the back garden wall. Thompson ran after Riley but lost him in the darkness. He came back minutes later, reluctant to leave Churchill alone.

Thompson found Churchill standing by himself on the terrace in the soft darkness of the night, the other guests having retreated into the residence.

"Well done, Thompson," said Churchill, lighting a cigar as the symphony of destruction in Havana continued its movement of terror. "We'll catch up with the man, eventually."

"Yes, sir, I expect we will."

"And Thompson?"

"Yes, sir?"

"Cancel our return to London. I wish to stay in Cuba and cover this revolution. I expect *The Times* will be happy to pay for the work."

"I'm sure they will, sir," said Thompson, wiping blood from his forehead.

CHAPTER FIVE

GETTING the approval from *The Times* was the easiest part of Thompson's sojourn in Cuba. No sooner had he sent a telegram to London offering Churchill's services and gone back to his suite than a bellboy appeared with a return telegram from the newspaper, offering Churchill the princely sum of a thousand pounds a week and an additional hundred per article. Naturally, he accepted, so then the next question was where to find the revolution.

"Elementary, my dear Watson," said Churchill, setting out from the Nacional, wearing the white linen suit that was de rigeur in Cuba at the time. "The revolution is everywhere, and everywhere we shall go!"

At first they hired a translator recommended by the Nacional's concierge, but his English turned out to be of the American variety, the bad Southern part, and there was mutual incomprehension. They could not understand his drawl over a Cuban Spanish accent, while he found it hard to comprehend proper British diction.

By the third day they dropped Señor García and, out of

desperation, recruited Mitchell from the embassy, whose Spanish turned out much better than expected, judging from their previous encounter.

The return to reporting—the reason why he'd been to Cuba in 1895 and South Africa in 1899—animated Churchill enormously, as though he were reliving his peripatetic youth. He and Thompson walked for hours every day, observing, note taking, interviewing. There were bombings every night, so every morning Churchill would report yet another tally of the destruction—shoe stores blasted to bits, government offices burned, even the local Bacardi rum headquarters attacked. He'd interview the survivors, or the afflicted owners, trying to gauge what he called the street sentiment, how ordinary people felt about the regime, which mostly was not laudatory at all.

Churchill interviewed the Cuban president, Señor Presidente Machado, a couple of times. The dictator was a small man, shorter than Churchill even, with two fingers missing from his right hand, a memento from his previous profession as a small-town butcher. Machado fawned over Churchill, seeing him as a representative of the English empire, which he greatly admired. At first the two reminisced about the Cuban War of Independence, where Machado achieved the rank of brigadier general, then the president launched into a philippic against Communist conspiracies. He blamed all the political unrest on Moscow agents and boasted of having ordered the execution of the young man, exiled in Mexico, who had founded the Cuban Communist Party. "Like a bug we quashed him," he said.

During their interviews, Churchill accepted quietly Machado's compliments, but then put the dictator on the spot for the many reports of murder and torture carried out by his private army, the Porra. To Churchill's amazement, Machado pointed the finger at England and said had not King George done the same, crushing revolts in India and Malaysia with an equally firm hand?

Churchill's report on the interviews, highlighting Machado's totalitarian rule and glaring political illiteracy, did not endear the Cuban president to *The Times*'s readership—nor Churchill to Machado, who refused any further contact with him. Which was just as well, given that what Churchill wanted to do next was penetrate the ABC, the terrorist organization that had planned to assassinate him. One afternoon, at the home of Señor Ferrara, Machado's foreign affairs minister, he found the way in.

Italian by birth and temperament, Orestes Ferrara had given up a profitable career as an attorney in Naples and come to Cuba to fight for its independence; for his efforts he had been rewarded with a long and highly profitable political career. Wanting to repair his president's reputation abroad, he hosted a reception for Churchill at his personal villa in Havana, a copy of a sixteenth-century Florentine palace.

Thompson was at Churchill's elbow, keeping close watch on those who approached him, when he was accosted by a beautiful young woman, tall, with an hourglass figure and wide wondrous eyes in an oval face surmounted by a waterfall of curls.

"Say, is that Churchill, the politician?" she asked Thompson, in fluent American.

"Yes, it is, miss."

"The same Churchill who's been writing the articles about President Machado?"

"He certainly is. Would you like to speak to him?" said Thompson, but the young woman ignored him and, slipping through the crowd, sidled up to Churchill and whispered in his ear.

Churchill's face lit up in surprise and delight. He nodded

vigorously. Thompson moved right after the woman, watching her hands to make sure she wasn't some sort of killer in chiffon.

"Miss, if you please . . ."

Churchill broke in. "Never mind that, Thompson. This young lady and I have something urgent to discuss," he said, and without bothering to excuse himself from the throng of admirers, took her by the elbow and guided her to a far corner of the salon.

Ferrara, the old diplomat, came up to Thompson, smiling.

"I see Lena has made another conquest," he said.

"Who is she, may I ask?" said Thompson.

"Magdalena Zayas, niece of our former president. She has quite a reputation, I'm afraid. Very forward. Just recently she was with left wingers. Antonio Guiteras, and before that with poor Julio Mella. Now it's Churchill. She has very catholic tastes," he added, approvingly, to Thompson's surprise.

"I'll say."

"I hope Mr. Churchill is prepared for her. She is like one of our rainstorms, comes on without warning and all at once."

Thompson nodded in agreement, watching their tête-à-tête become progressively more agitated. Churchill leaned in so close to Miss Zayas he seemed about to kiss her, then realizing the dangerous proximity, stepped back and hooked his thumbs in his vest, as was his habit when listening with great attention. When she finished talking, he nodded his assent. She smiled discreetly, gave him a peck on the cheek, and took French leave of the function.

"There she goes," added Ferrara. "I wonder what mischief she's up to now?"

"Your meaning, sir?" said Thompson, but Ferrara had turned his attention to a wizened old lady in black, sitting in a cane wheelchair pushed by a uniformed maid.

"Señora de Céspedes," said the diplomat with appropriate unctuousness, kissing the gnarly hand.

Thompson was about to march up to Churchill and inquire the meaning of his conversation, to make sure he had not agreed to another reckless adventure, when he glanced up at the old lady's maid. To his delight it was the saucy girl from the embassy, Fabiana.

Dressed in a starched black and white uniform with her hair gathered in a bun, Fabiana looked like a tropical version of a Parisian soubrette. Recognizing him, she raised her thin eyebrows and shook her head no to ward off any advance on his part. Thompson nodded, barely masking the sudden emotions she provoked in him. He moved across the hall to Churchill, who stood silently by the balcony, peering at the city skyline.

"Everything all right, sir?"

Churchill seemed to come back from some faraway place in his mind, shook his head. "Thompson, I'm not well. Let me say my goodbyes and retire to the Nacional. I need some rest."

"Of course, sir," said Thompson, somewhat surprised, as it was only five in the afternoon, and Churchill had already had his noontime siesta.

Ferrara lent them his HispanSuiza and his chauffeur, who drove them back to the Nacional. Churchill immediately secreted himself in his suite, claiming a headache. Thompson's suspicion grew when he heard Churchill click shut the lock in the connecting door between their rooms—a very strange state of affairs, as Churchill had no sense of modesty, walking around naked if the heat was too oppressive, and thinking nothing of giving dictation to a female secretary while in the bathtub. Still, not wanting to give Churchill any reason to carp about what he called his exaggerated sense of duty, Thompson walked down to the lobby for a drink.

He was enjoying one of the favorite concoctions of the

island, a refreshing mixture of lime juice, mint, ice, and rum, when someone walked up to him at the bar.

"Coming to Cuba is a busman's holiday, eh?"

Mitchell, the man from the embassy and Churchill's translator, in the arm of a brunette Cuban beauty.

"Always on the job, I'm afraid. But what are you doing here? Day off, remember?

It was a Saturday. Mitchell had spent the previous day accompanying Churchill and Thompson on an exhausting tour of a tobacco plantation in Pinar del Río.

"Precisely why I'm here, old man. Lily wanted to see, and I said I would oblige. Miss Liliana Nuñez, Walter Thompson."

"Pleasure," said Thompson, shaking the girl's hand. He addressed Mitchell, assuming his companion did not speak English. "I'm afraid Mr. Churchill is not well. He's in his room."

"That's no problem," said the girl, in American English. "It's you I wanted to meet. Politicians don't do it for me."

A pleasant surprise. Thompson recognized the accent, but most all, the unmistakable New York attitude. Before he could ascertain the fact, Mitchell broke in.

"Lily is Fabiana's sister. You remember her from the embassy?"

"Of course. In fact, I just saw her at a function. She was accompanying a lady in a wheelchair."

"Oh yeah, that old hag," said the girl. "I told Faby they'd dress her up in some fancy outfit. But anything's better than doing dishes—for a dollar a day," she added teasingly, looking at Mitchell, who blushed, shrugged.

"Not my department, I'm afraid."

"You Brits are always laying the blame elsewhere. Anyhow," she continued, "I told Baby I wanted to meet the man who saved Churchill. Faby was very impressed."

"I was only doing my job."

"Sure, but you're great at it. Doll, you got something to write with?"

Mitchell dug in his jacket pocket, produced a Parker Vacumatic pen. The girl took it, wrote on the edge of the week-old *London Times* Thompson had been reading.

"Listen, Faby would love for you to come over. Believe it or not, we have a phone in the neighborhood! It's at the corner bodega, but you can leave a message and . . . what am I saying, you don't speak Spanish! Tell you what, come by tomorrow for lunch, will you? Say, at one o'clock? We'll have a nice Cuban meal for you, how does that sound?"

"Sounds lovely," said Thompson, amused by the girl's vitality.

"Good, good." She crossed out the phone number and wrote down an address. "It's in El Cerro. Not too far. If you get lost, I'm sure Baby here can direct you."

She looked at Mitchell. "Can we go now, Baby? Don't want to miss Clark Gable smooching Jean Harlow. I loved *Red Dust*. I hope this is as good."

Thompson shook Mitchell's hand, then leaned over to whisper in his ear, "Baby? You lucky dog."

He shrugged, smiled sheepishly. "When in Rome, do as the Cubans. Toodles!"

———

THOMPSON HAD FINISHED READING the last paragraph of Churchill's article in the *Times* and was about to order a second lime drink when he spotted Lena Zayas striding through the lobby, accompanied by a short, handsome, dark-featured man in the ubiquitous white linen suit.

Thompson moved his chair behind one of the pillars to

better observe them. She spoke to the concierge, gave him an envelope. A bellboy was summoned and sent off, while Zayas and her companion waited nervously by the front desk. A few minutes later, the lobby's elevator tinkled and out stepped Winston, in a white linen suit as well, sporting a large Panama hat he'd pushed down, as if trying to hide his face. He shook hands with Zayas and her companion, and they sailed out.

Trouble, thought Thompson, and followed them out to the street.

For a moment Thompson debated whether to go after them in one of the many taxis parked outside the Nacional. Then the likelihood of having to translate his wishes to a cabbie who spoke little or no English made him change his mind. Invited or not, he would crash the party.

Thompson walked up to the trio, waiting for a car to be brought out from the back lot. They were so engaged in a whispered conversation, they failed to spot Thompson until he was right next to them. That's when it struck him that Lena was at least a good four inches taller than either man, or about an inch shorter than Thompson. Strange the details one notices when on the job, he thought.

"Going somewhere, sir?" he asked.

The three swung around in tandem. Churchill, flushed, snapped at Thompson.

"Damn you, man! Take the night off!"

"Sorry, sir, I can't. You are my responsibility. Unless you wish to discharge me right now, I must insist on accompanying you. For your own protection."

Lena quickly translated for the shorter man, who nodded urgently and asked a question, the words of which Thompson could not understand but whose intent was crystal clear, as he gestured with his hand.

"Are you armed?" she asked.

"I am. It's part of my duties."

Churchill shook his head no. "Under no circumstance will I allow . . ." he began, but was interrupted by the shorter man, who let out a torrent of quick Cuban Spanish.

"Mr. Churchill," said Lena, "Sergio suggests it might not be such a bad idea to have some sort of protection, in case the Porra shows up."

"In an army camp?" blustered Churchill, instantly forgetting about Thompson.

"They are everywhere," said Lena. The shorter man spoke some more as a valet in a black Ford coupe wheeled about and stopped the vehicle before them.

"All right, then," fumed Churchill, "but we shall have a talk afterwards, Thompson!"

"As you wish," said Thompson.

The short man boarded the car and eased behind the wheel. Lena sat next to him and Churchill by the door, the three packed tightly in the front seat.

"Well, get in the back, man!" barked Churchill.

"Where might we be going?" said Thompson, sliding in.

"To meet the leader of the ABC, Thompson. Why else do you think I would be venturing out like this?"

Thompson could think of a thousand reasons, but he bit his tongue and silently closed the car door behind him. The shorter man turned round, offered his hand.

"Mucho gusto," he said. "I am Sergio Carbó."

"You speak English?"

"A little. Now we hurry. El mítin finish soon."

"The what?" said Thompson, as Carbó stepped on the gas. The car lurched forward, then sped off down the Malecón, Havana's wide oceanfront boulevard.

"A meeting of the Army and the ABC, Thompson," said Churchill. "They are planning a coup d'état!"

CHAPTER SIX

ENTERING CAMP COLUMBIA, the headquarters of the Cuban Army, presented no problem, the sentry waving the car through after Carbó whispered a few words. Lena, playing cicerone, pointed out the various buildings—the barracks for the recruits, the armory, the commissary, and finally, their destination, what she called the relaxation center, a small two-story building housing a library, a small theater, and several classrooms.

The four went in and sat in the back of a study hall in the small desks of grammar schools, watching a dark-skinned man review the different symbols of the peculiar science of stenography. Thompson studied his sharp features and confident demeanor, the high cheekbones that told of some aboriginal origin, the wide almond eyes, the thick shiny hair, and the animated smile that put you immediately at ease, even if, like Thompson, you couldn't understand a word he was saying. What magnetism, thought Thompson. He must be the leader.

When the man concluded his lesson after writing a few more symbols on the blackboard, the classroom broke into applause. The room was packed with soldiers in khaki, not a man bearing officer's chevrons in the lot. Lena whispered to Winston. Thompson leaned in to listen, as the instructor went on.

"He's telling everyone there will be an advanced class following, and that those not taking it should leave. They will receive further instructions in writing."About forty men walked out, leaving behind a handful of noncommissioned officers. A corporal walked to the door, locked it. Carbó got up and gave the instructor the typical Cuban embrace of hugs and pats on the back. The instructor waved the three of them to the front of the room. He greeted Churchill with a vigorous handshake, saying, in passable English, "We are very grateful for your presence here today. I am Sergeant Fulgencio Batista. The future of Cuba is in our hands."

Batista introduced the different subalterns in his group, commanding different Army installations around Havana and the provincial capitals. All were to rise and take over their bases, stripping the senior officers of their charge, then send men into the Presidential Palace to wrest power from Machado. The exact date was yet to be decided, all hinging on the preparations of the different outposts and, of course, the whereabouts of the president.

"We wish also to apologize for the incident at the ambassador's residence and the attack on your person," said Batista, using Lena as the interpreter. "Some of our youngest members in the ABC misinterpreted our political guidance and took matters into their own hands."

"What is your relationship with that peculiar group?" asked Churchill.

"We are allies. They pursue a policy of political action in the city, striking at the enemy, while we prepare for a formal military action."

"You mean deposing the President?"

"Yes, a golpe."

"I see. If you succeed, what will you do once you achieve power?"

"Improve the living conditions of the country, end corruption, free ourselves from foreign interference."

"And what will you do with the president once you have him?"

"We'll send him . . . to Florida!" answered Batista to great laughter, obviously meaning a less sunny and considerably warmer place.

Thompson observed Churchill's attention intensely on Lena, as if her words were not just interpretation but a link being established between the two. Careful there, old chap, think of Clementine, he thought.

Churchill and his wife, Lady Clementine, had had an awful row before Churchill left for America on his speaking tour—as always, over money and Churchill's cavalier disregard for his expenses. Their marriage had been strained almost to the breaking point, and Churchill had embarked on the tour to calm their tempers and make enough money to satisfy his wife.

Thompson, whose own marriage was also on the brink, made a mental note to say a few words of sentimental caution to Churchill, possibly when they returned to the hotel.

———

NO SOONER HAD they left Camp Columbia in Carbó's ramshackle Ford than a black Packard surged out from a side alley. It halted right in front of Carbó's car, blocking the way, its left fender striking the Ford's bumper, which fell with a racket to the ground. The doors of the Packard slammed open and, as if in a scene from the movie *Little Caesar*, two men with submachine guns stepped out.

Screaming Carbó's name, they let loose a spray of bullets at Carbó's car. Carbó was a man with extremely quick reflexes and much experience being shot at. No sooner had the bumper fallen off than he was putting the car in reverse and spinning it round in a lighting-fast U-turn, hightailing it out of the intersection so fast only a few bullets managed to strike.

Churchill fell on Lena, protecting her. Thompson took out his revolver and fired at the gunmen, downing one of them, as the car sped away down the darkened streets of Havana, Carbó zigzagging around traffic, blowing traffic lights, hurtling through a neighborhood of dilapidated tenements, until they lost the attackers.

"Are we all right?" said Thompson.

"I'm fine," said Churchill, "bloody blackguards!"

"I've been hit," moaned Lena, clutching her arm.

"*¡Coño, cabrones!*" and many other curses flowed easily from Carbó. In the torrent of words out of his mouth, Thompson heard him say 'hospital.'

"No, no, Las Palmas, *¡Las Palmas!*" urged Lena.

Carbó nodded, swung around, and quickly drove out of the city, heading for the outskirts down a narrow country road under a winking moon.

"Let me see, ma'am," said Thompson, leaning over the front seat. The bullet had pierced her upper arm above her elbow, leaving a through-and-through wound, blood spurting out in gushes with every beat of her heart. Thompson took off his belt, cinched it round her arm to halt the bleeding.

"We should go to the hospital," he said. "It may have cut the artery."

"No, no, they will find us there," insisted Lena, trembling

from the pain. "My uncle's farm, they won't dare go there, my uncle knows what to do."

"Who was that shooting?" asked Churchill.

"La Porra," said Carbó, maneuvering around a passenger bus rattling in the new highway out of Havana. "They want killing me."

Carbó said something else in Spanish. Lena, grunting from pain, added, "Someone betrayed us," and fainted from the loss of blood.

"Well, go on, man, hurry!" urged Churchill.

"Yes, yes, I go fast, very very fast," said Carbó.

CHAPTER SEVEN

LAS PALMAS, Lena's family country estate, was south of Havana, protected by gates, stone walls, and half a dozen guards with guns. Carbó stopped his rattling Ford in front of the entrance gate, sounded his klaxon. Within seconds two surly men in khakis, bandoliers, and sidearms appeared.

"Is it safe?" asked Thompson, holding his gun to his side, just in case. Carbó ignored him, moved to exit the car. Thompson grabbed him.

"Is it safe?" repeated Thompson. "No boom boom?"

"*No, no, está bien,*" said Carbó, as the men approached. He conferred quickly with them; one of them opened the gate and picked up a phone to call ahead.

Carbó drove down a gravel road, lined with cypresses looming like sentries, to an ornate Spanish Moorish castle all lit up like Billingsgate at Christmas. An older, smaller man in formal clothes, with a trim Van Dyke beard, waited at the front steps of the mansion, surrounded by half a dozen maids and servants. Lena greeted the gentleman with a languid wave of her hand.

"Tío," uncle, she said, and something else Thompson assumed meant we need help, and passed out again.

"*¡Presidente!*" said Carbó, stepping out of the car and going around to shake the man's hand. The two quickly conferred. The older man snapped his fingers and ordered the servants to assist Churchill in getting Lena out of the Ford. They carried her into the mansion, followed by Carbó, the old gentleman giving further instructions. Then he turned to Churchill.

"Mr. Churchill, welcome to Las Palmas. Thank you for bringing my niece," he said in a clipped Yankee accent. "I regret my country's politics have proven so dangerous."

"Think nothing of it," said Churchill, shaking his hand. "You do have a doctor to treat her? I don't believe the wound is very deep, but she has lost some blood."

"He has been called for and will be here shortly."

"Good. Let me introduce my trusted companion, Scotland Yard Inspector Walter Thompson. Thompson, President Alfredo Zayas, fourth freely elected president of the Republic of Cuba."

"And not the last, I hope. I may disagree with my niece's tactics, but I agree with her objective. Machado must go."

Presently the doctor summoned by Zayas appeared, and Thompson followed the former president of Cuba to Lena's old room, pictures from women's magazines still pegged to the walls, girlish dresses draped on mannequins. After examining her, the doctor gave her a sedative and some plasma; he then assured Zayas that Lena would survive her wound, but that she would need bed rest for the next few days. Carbó retired to his room, exhausted.

Churchill was very concerned about Lena's condition and apologized for the incident to her uncle. "I should have never agreed to the encounter," said Churchill.

"Don't feel sorry, Mr. Churchill," said Zayas, handing him

a glass of Scotch in the mansion's wood-paneled library. He offered Thompson the same.

"Thank you, Mr. President, but hard liquor and I have never gotten along," said Thompson.

"You're a lucky man, then. To some people liquor is like the siren's song, irresistible, making you do all kinds of foolish things."

"Like a love of politics, then," said Churchill.

"Yes, politics too can be a drug," said Zayas. "I would say it is the Cuban people's drug of choice. Unfortunately, my niece is no exception. She is a woman of strong disposition and even stronger ideals—like many of our women, who have always played a significant role in our history. Anyway, sad to say, this is not the first time she's been exposed to these dangers, and I'm afraid it won't be the last."

"What of her parents?" asked Churchill. "Are they aware of her political activities?"

"They are no longer with us. Her father, my brother Mario and his wife died at sea."

"I'm terribly sorry," said Churchill. Zayas took another ship of his Scotch, drew a deep sigh.

"Thank you. Lena was seven years old, still at school in Havana. My children were already grown, so I brought her up as my own. We sent her to finishing school in New York and then to Cornell, my alma mater. You know, she's a gifted linguist. She speaks five languages, has translated from the Italian and the German. I just hope that this political situation will finally normalize, and that she will as well."

"My sentiments exactly, Mr. President. Now, about the local politics, sir, I have a question or two I'd like to pose to you," said Churchill.

As was his custom, Churchill proceeded to put the events of the evening in a universal political perspective, confirming the malady that Zayas had just warned about. Since Thompson did not share their common passion, he bid them good night and retired to his room, where, in a narrow but comfortable bed, he dreamed of vast oceans drowning out all life in the city.

———

OPENING his window the next morning, Thompson was stunned once more by the exuberant vitality of the Cuban countryside. Clusters of fruit trees spread out far from the back gardens, which extended as far as the eye could see. The stone wall, which he had noticed the night before, was surmounted by a gallery of royal palms, the whole surveyed by the estate's vigilant guards making their rounds.

After washing up as best he could in the adjoining bathroom, where the help had left shaving implements as well as fresh towels, soap, toothpaste, and toothbrush, Thompson went downstairs to the kitchen. There one of the staff indicated in halting English that they had prepared a special treat—what they called a plátano tortilla, which he soon learned was an unusual but very tasty banana omelet.

Thompson took a walk around the estate, hoping to run into Churchill, who was not in his room. Instead, he found Carbó saying goodbye to Zayas. The former president translated that Carbó, also a journalist, was returning to Havana to report on the previous night's incident—without mentioning Lena or Churchill's names, of course.

Thompson found Churchill in his bath, smoking a cigar while drafting a column for *The Times* on a piece of ancient stationery he'd sequestered from a drawer of his bedroom.

"Thompson, send this off to London by telegram. Tell them there will be more to come in the next few days, I still have some more investigation to conduct."

"Should I also send word to Lady Clementine?"

Churchill's face suddenly changed, his youthful spirits and swagger vanishing, and with a cold stare he shook his head.

"Don't bother. Now, off with you," he snapped.

Winston's peremptory command grated on Thompson, and taking offense at this, he answered back: "Sir, I remind you that I am your bodyguard, not your aide de chambre."

Churchill glared at Thompson. "Meaning?"

"That if I do any of these things you ask me to it is because I want to, not because I must. My sole obligation is to make sure you stay alive, not to be your manservant."

Churchill flushed, then seemed to melt right in front of Thompson. "I apologize," he said, shaking his head. "I have been wrong to take you for granted. I shall endeavor to be more polite and considerate. Please forgive my rudeness."

How can one stay angry at a man of such extremes? thought Thompson. He raised a hand, to assure him. "I just ask that you give some consideration to your language and your requests to me."

"I shall." Churchill stood in the bathtub, all his naked plumpness pink from the hot bath, and extended his hand.

"Friends again?"

"Of course," said Thompson, shaking his wet hand.

"Good," said Churchill, plopping back down in the bathwater. "Now take that . . . forgive me, would you mind sending that off, please? I would truly appreciate it."

Thompson couldn't help smiling. "My pleasure," he said, taking the damp missive. At least he's trying, he thought.

Thompson went downstairs and with gestures inquired of the telephone from the kitchen help. They directed him to a small closet by the library, where the single telephone line to the outside was located. With much difficulty he managed to communicate with the overseas operator and with Western Union, relaying the report Churchill had given him.

As he hung up, Thompson remembered the invitation to lunch with Fabiana and her sister. Their phone number, written on the copy of *The Times* he was reading, had been left behind in Carbó's car. He would have to somehow make it up to her when he returned to Havana.

Thompson had just taken a few steps away from the phone when it rang again. One of the household staff picked it up, spoke, then rushed to the library. Out stepped Zayas, who took the receiver and spoke forcefully into the phone.

"*Sí, sí, inmediatamente,*" said Zayas. He gave a quick order to the butler, then turned to Thompson. "Tell Mr. Churchill I must travel to La Habana immediately. President Machado wants to meet with me for consultation."

And with that, showing a vitality surprising for a man of his age, he rushed out of the mansion and into a black Cadillac waiting for him. He returned a few hours later with grave news.

"There's been a change of diplomats," he told Churchill, who had been writing in the mansion's library. "A new US ambassador, Sumner Welles, is pressuring Machado to surrender power."

"Is there anything His Majesty's government can do?" said Churchill.

"Not for now. Cuba is dependent on the dollar, and the American ambassador's voice carries a lot of weight. I came back to pick up some things, then I must return to Havana. Machado wants me as intermediary between the factions."

"Well, then, thank you for your hospitality. We too shall be leaving for Havana presently," said Churchill, walking out to the hall with Zayas.

"No, please," said Zayas. "Stay here for as long as you wish. Keep my niece company, she's prone to . . ."

"You are leaving already, tío?" said Lena.

They turned to see Lena walking slowly, painfully, down the tiled staircase in a robe, holding on to the banister. Zayas stepped up quickly, gave her a quick kiss, the two of them exchanging a hurried conversation in Spanish, then Zayas hurried out to his waiting car and drove away again.

Churchill looked up at Lena. "How are you today?"

"Much better, thank you, but still, a touch . . ."

She fell into a swoon, fainting, almost tumbling down the stairs. Churchill raced up, caught her just as her head was about to hit the ground. Thompson went up to help, but Churchill pushed him aside.

"I have her, Thompson," he said and, lifting her in his arms, carried her back to her room.

The house butler, who had witnessed the scene, called out for the help and in seconds all the staff was trooping up to assist. Thompson went up behind them. Going into Lena's room, he saw Churchill sitting reverentially by her bed, looking like a man in the grip of an unexpected and tender emotion.

Lena came to and, opening her eyes, smiled and dismissed the help. Churchill was about to go as well, but she called out to him.

"No, please, stay here with me, Mr. Churchill. I wish to hear all about your adventures," she said.

"Oh, good, I shall bore you to sleep, then," he said, walking back.

"I doubt it, but try all the same."

"Fine, then. But call me Winston."

"I will. And you can call me Lena," she said.

He sat at the foot of her bed. "Shall I begin where I was born, in Blenheim Palace?"

"If you must."

"I do. You see, I have the most splendid recollection of my

childhood there—and of a set of lead soldiers my father gave me when I was six."

The two were so wrapped up in each other that they failed to notice Thompson as he tiptoed out and softly closed the door behind him, Churchill deep into the details of his story.

"Those soldiers served me quite well when I fought in the Sudan. How, you might ask. The formation of the troops, you see. I had read how my ancestor, the Duke of Marlborough, when fighting in France . . ."

CHAPTER EIGHT

LAS PALMAS WAS EERILY quiet when Thompson
returned late one night a few days later. The lights were down,
with only a bare bulb illuminating the stairs leading up to the
second floor. He went back outside.

A guard was posted in the shadows, a surly fellow in a cane
rocker smoking a cigar, a shotgun on his lap. He informed
Thompson in broken English that everyone had been given
permission to go to a fiesta in the neighboring town of Artemisa.
Only he and two other sentries were around.

"Señor Churchill?" said Thompson.

"Arriba," he said, jerking his chin up.

Thompson's sense of imminent danger immediately flared
up. Was this a trap? Had the Porra somehow sneaked into the
house? In fact, who was this guard? He had never seen him
before. The silence was so still Thompson could hear the
distant hooting of an owl over the throbbing of crickets, the
croaking of frogs in a nearby creek.

"Gracias," said Thompson, and putting his hand on his
holster, he entered the house. There he took out his revolver

and proceeded cautiously into the hall. He looked right and left. No one hiding in the shadows.

Then a thump from above. A moan.

Churchill!

He raced up the stairs, down the corridor to his room.

Still no one around.

Another moan, now clearly from inside.

He backed up to his door, gun held high, then in one swift move turned the knob, slammed the door open, and strode into the room, index finger on the trigger, ready to shoot. In the bed was Churchill, naked, portly, pink, and pale, vigorously thrusting into the equally naked Lena, writhing underneath him. The slap of the door on the wall alerted the two. Churchill jumped off, hollered at Thompson.

"Get the hell out!"

"Sorry, sir," mumbled Thompson, and holstering the gun, he stepped back. "Do you wish the door shut?" he added, in a dumb daze.

"Of course, you bloody idiot! Be on your way!"

He closed the door and stood in the hallway, stunned. He could hear the two of them laughing at the incident, and a few seconds later, the bed squeaked, and the moaning resumed, softer this time.

This is not good news, thought Thompson, retiring to his bedroom—although the truth was, he had to smile when remembering he had been doing precisely the same activity just hours before with the maid, Fabiana.

———

THAT MORNING CHURCHILL had summoned Thompson to his room and presented him with a block of typed pages. "Thompson, here's my finished report. If you could please take this to our embassy and have them send it by air diplomatic pouch to *The Times*. It has confidential information and I do not trust the Cuban postal service. Tell them the *Times* will cover the cost. Now please hurry up, this is for the Sunday edition and it's Thursday!"

Thompson was glad to be out of Las Palmas for a while, thinking even Paradise must come to be boring for souls facing endless happiness. Variety is the spice of life, both earthly and eternal. Beyond that, he had been wanting to see Fabiana again to apologize for not having shown up to that luncheon.

But there was something else.

One of the reasons why Thompson had agreed to accompany Churchill on his tour of America, and now for his stay in Cuba, was to give his own troubled marriage a chance to heal. Due to his prolonged absences as result of the demands of police work, and the sporadic requests of Churchill to accompany him on this or that journey, not to mention protecting him while he was serving in Parliament, Thompson's wife Eleanor had found a more constant companion.

It had been painful for Thompson to accept that a village auto mechanic could hold more attraction for her than he, but such was the case. Thompson and Eleanor had had a good run —twenty years, three children, the oldest about to finish his schooling—but evidently she needed something else that Thompson could no longer give her. What that was never was very clear to Thompson, but he assumed it had something to do with his emotional reticence, an innate suspicion of appearances compounded by an ineptitude at demonstrating affection, especially with the effusiveness Eleanor had come to desire.

They had agreed to put off a final decision until he returned, even though he had the feeling when they parted that she had already made up her mind. Fabiana then to Thompson was not just a temptation but an open door, an invitation to another way, another life.

Or perhaps nothing. He wasn't certain what his expectations were, other than he wished to see Fabiana again, to hear her musical voice once more. Yes, all men, even policemen, can be such fools.

———

FABIANA LIVED IN EL CERRO, a neighborhood that, for the moment, was free of political violence. Sited on a hill, it was once a wealthy quarter but had fallen out of favor years before. The few remaining aristocratic mansions, with their large gardens and riotous greenery, were cheek by jowl with row houses built for the help of the mansions. Thompson knocked at the tall door of one such modest dwelling—a solid slab of weathered mahogany, no peephole, no knocker.

"Well, well, well, if it ain't the mystery man himself," said her sister Lily, opening the door. "You packing today, doll?"

"Excuse me?"

"I'm asking if you have a gun with you, mister bodyguard."

"I do."

She opened her hand. "Give it up, honey. Faby might just take it and shoot you for standing her up."

"I'm sorry, I'm afraid I can't do that."

"Just joshing with you, doll," she said, laughing. "Come on in, take a load off."

She turned and screamed at the back of the house, "Faby, your favorite hero's here!"

She added something in Spanish, which made Fabiana break into gales of laughter that rippled down the narrow hallway, sounding to Thompson like the peal of a silver bell. He sat on a rattan and wood couch, in a vast living room furnished only with the couch, two rocking chairs, and a round glass coffee table bearing a stalking black panther figurine.

"So," said Lily, looking him up and down. "You look rested. Got some sun, too. Were you in Marianao? Varadero?"

"Pardon?"

"The beach, doll, where have you been?"

"Well, I was out in the country . . . " he began to say when Fabiana appeared, a dish towel in her hands, a wide welcoming smile on her face.

"Yeah, Mr. Thompson, just where have you been?"

He was momentarily speechless, stunned by her beauty. She wore a flouncy apron over denim pants and loose cotton blouse, all of which served only to further accentuate her full figure. They stared at each other in silence for a long moment.

"Okaaay, I guess this is where I make my exit," said Lily. "I think I'll go see what's on sale at the market. Or the pharmacy. Maybe I'll pinch some oranges from the neighbors, they're never home. Anyhow, you two lovebirds behave. I'll be back later."

She picked up her purse, threw her sister a kiss, and walked out, closing the door behind her. Fabiana and Thompson were left staring at each other, still smiling, as if they had been waiting only for her sister to leave so they could defrost and return to normal.

"You're cooking?" said Thompson, finally finding words to say.

"I was doing the dishes—we just had lunch."

"Mitchell says you're quite the cook."

"Oh, that guy thinks everything's good. Eats like a pig. He's so skinny, I don't know where he hides it. You hungry?"

"Now that you mention it, I haven't had a thing to eat all day."

"Well, c'mon, let me get you something."

———

IN FABIANA'S kitchen a full pot of black beans simmered on the stove, their aroma pervading every corner. Another pot held a meat and sweet pepper stew she called ropa vieja, and another, a glistening mound of white rice. She ladled it all on fine China—"the only thing my mom left us"—and sat with Thompson at a small folding table, talking while he ate.

Thompson found himself beguiled by the eyes of the vivacious girl, entranced by her laughter, by the slight defect of her lower teeth, where one tooth fused with another, creating a crooked smile. Everything about her was fascinating, from the slight maculation of her plain fingernails to her rebellious curls that had a will of their own, to the way the first buttons of her blouse were left undone, affording him a peek of her lacy brassiere.

And so, after the meal and a cigarette and two or three lime and rum drinks, he found himself in her arms in her bed with a joy he had not experienced in many a year. Was it wrong? He could not say, but it was certainly ecstasy—and that night, when he returned to his bedroom at Las Palmas, Thompson could only grin at Churchill's fling and wish him as much enjoyment as he'd had that very same day.

———

THE NEXT MORNING at breakfast Churchill and Thompson avoided looking at each other over their ham and eggs, neither one willing to say a word about the previous day. Lena came down dressed in a rustling red robe, sat at the table. She lit a cigarette and watched them warily over her café con leche. After a few moments of quiet, she said, "What are we going to do?"

Thompson raised his eyebrows. Churchill harrumphed, blushed, pushed aside his plate.

"Well, my dear, I was hoping to spend more time with you and . . . Thompson, would you mind?"

Politely, Thompson moved to get up, but Lena grabbed his arm, pushed him down.

"No, stay. Let's talk about this like grown-ups, shall we?"

She looked at them with hazel eyes as calm as those of a bookkeeper tallying up the day's receipts.

"I don't regret what happened, or what you saw, Walter, but I don't want either of you to give it any more importance than it deserves."

"My dear," Churchill began, "I do believe that when a man and a woman engage in . . ."

"Don't start giving me any of your old-school morality!" she snapped. "I don't care about that, never have, never will. There's a revolution going on out there and I am a part of it. I might not live to see it through."

"Excuse me, but how involved are you in this revolution?" asked Thompson.

She looked around, as if trying to discern some hidden presence. "I'm glad my poor uncle is not here right now, but I'm sure he's probably convinced."

"Of what?" said Thompson.

"I am a member of the Communist Party. I've been one since meeting Julio Mella, who founded the party here in Cuba. He was my lover and Machado had him murdered."

"You're a Bolshevik?" exclaimed Churchill. "My dear, how could you have fallen for such a mendacious doctrine?"

"When you see the poverty of Cuba, and the wealth that you gentlemen are the guests of, the chasm is so extreme only a socialist solution is possible for the problem."

"Miss Zayas," Thompson broke in, "is your involvement merely rhetorical or are you willing to do more for your cause?"

She shook her head in frustration. "I can't believe you two are talking this way. I'm Cuban. Something has to be done! And of course I'm involved. I'm telling you all this because in fact I'm about to deliver weapons to the ABC, weapons I've stored in our garage right here. Oh, men are so blind!"

She got up, gathered her robe close, bent down and pecked Churchill on the cheek. "I'll always remember last night, Winston, but that was the end of that. You're married and your home is far away. I'm not and this is my land. I have a fight to finish."

A servant walked into the room. "Teléfono, señorita."

"That must be the call I've been waiting for," said Lena, dashing out of the room. Churchill looked on, sheepishly.

"Well, that settles that," he said as he and Thompson were left alone in the room. "Fortunately." A pause, a frown. "Or not."

"Lady Clementine?"

"A telegram will suffice."

Lena rushed back, all aflutter. "The ABC is about to take over. They need the weapons. I've got to go!"

"You're barely able to drive," said Thompson, but she raced up the stairs to her room.

"Thompson, please go with her. Do your best to protect her."

"I shall."

CHAPTER NINE

THE DAY THOMPSON left with Lena turned out to be the start of a whirlwind revolution, with things unfolding so fast it was hard to know who the players were, although the game was always clear—to gain power.

By the time they reached Havana, the clear loser was President Machado, who, under pressure from the American ambassador, had resigned, and flown to Florida along with Lena's uncle and half of Cuba's gold reserves. On hearing the news, mobs spilled out all over the city, celebrating the dictator's downfall by ransacking the Presidential Palace and bashing in the brains of his followers with hammers, shovels, whatever implements they could find. Ferrara, the foreign minister, barely avoided being shot by the revolutionists when on his way to a waiting seaplane in the harbor, destination New York.

Thompson and Lena were carrying a full load of armaments in the trunk of a Cadillac she had commandeered from her uncle's garage—Winchester shotguns, Colt revolvers, Thompson machine guns, ammunition. At any time the rioters could have stopped them and, finding the weapons, accused them of backing the dread Porra and attacked. To prevent this, Lena stopped at a side street once they reached city limits and, taking off her light green blouse, drew with her lipstick on the blouse a modified Star of David with the letters ABC in its sides.

"Pardon me, miss, but do you feel safe like that?" asked Thompson, after she pinned the improvised flag to the car's radio aerial.

"It's the emblem of the party. It shows we're with the revolution."

"I meant going about half naked, miss," said Thompson, pointing at her silk undergarment, which clearly showed the shape of her generous breasts.

"Walter, women in Cuba wear far less than this in the heat. We'll be fine, I assure you."

She gunned the Cadillac and made her way through Havana. As she predicted, every time the car would turn a corner and run into another mob, the rioters would cheer and gladly wave them through when they saw the improvised flag, shouting "Viva ABC!" and "Death to Machado!" as their victims bled to death on the sidewalk.

Lena and Thompson reached Carbó at his newspaper, *La Prensa,* in the outskirts of Old Havana. Unlike the streets surrounding the nearby Capitol, besieged by the vengeful mobs, all was quiet by his office. Lena sounded the klaxon. Carbó rushed out in shirtsleeves, his typesetter's cap still on.

"Tengo las armas," I have the weapons, she said. He responded quickly, shook his head no, then ran back inside the building.

"Where does he want us to take the weapons?" asked Thompson.

"He says they're not needed anymore. He's got bigger fish

to fry. He's been named war minister by the new government and is about to make his first appointment."

"What is that?"

"He's making Batista the head of the Army."

Presently Carbó returned, dressed nattily again in his white linen suit, and jumped in the back of the Cadillac.

"¡A Columbia!" he said, then added something in rapid Spanish that made Lena blush.

"What did he say?"

"He says I'm very sexy with just my slip on."

"Did I not warn you?" smiled Thompson in satisfaction on being proven right.

"Men!" she fumed.

———

AT THE COLUMBIA ARMY camp they received the same clamorous welcome when they entered—cheers of Viva Cuba Libre, Death to Machado, and one that Lena translated as "down with the high command." They stopped at the main barracks, where hundreds of soldiers in khaki welcomed Carbó as he got out of the car. Short as he was, he had to climb on the hood of the car to address the crowd, with Lena translating for Thompson's benefit.

He and the other members of the interim government, which he called the Pentarchy, had drafted a new guiding plan for the country, which was being printed at his newspaper even as he spoke, and soon would be distributed to all. As the newly named minister of war, he had come to award, honor, and promote the man who had made it all possible, with the patriotic help of the Army's enlisted men: Fulgencio Batista.

The crowds opened and from the midst came Batista, beaming a wide grin. Carbó got down from the hood and shook hands with Batista, then announced he had been promoted in rank from sergeant to colonel in recognition of his services to the country. Carbó and Batista hugged, Batista wiping his brow with a white handkerchief, like a tenor on a stage, and grinned his widest Cheshire cat grin—he had maneuvered his way not just to a promotion but to decades-long control over the levers of power of his country.

The crowd dispersed after that and Lena, as a representative of the Cuban Communist Party, left with Carbó and Batista to decide the future of the country. Thompson headed back to Las Palmas, to see about Churchill—he was his charge, after all—the load of undelivered weapons rattling in the back of the Cadillac.

———

AT LAS PALMAS, Thompson found Churchill beside himself with excitement—he'd found a short-wave radio in the library and had dialed the BBC, which was transmitting the news of the violent revolution in Havana.

"I must go see it, Thompson, it will be the crowning touch to my reportage!"

"It's not safe there, sir," countered Thompson.

"Safe? Safe? Destiny has other plans for me than to die in in a tropical scuffle."

"And the weapons in the car, sir? What shall we do with them?"

"Bring them! They might be of use yet!"

CHAPTER TEN

ON THE WAY back to Havana, Thompson and Churchill witnessed more of the awful spectacle of revenge and destruction in every small town they passed. The Guardia and Porra barricades had been torn down, and the bodies of uniformed Machado henchmen were a sight as common as the rotten fallen fruit from the myriad trees. Thompson and Churchill checked back into the Nacional, where, to their surprise, all the Army's officers and even the US ambassador had taken refuge.

Once the mobs satiated their thirst for blood, the mad initial destruction of the uprising ebbed, and over the next few weeks Batista's army imposed a semblance of order. After Churchill delivered Lena's weapons to Batista, the two leaders became fast friends, with Churchill giving Batista advice, over many a cigar and cafecito, on how to respond to his political adversaries, even how to handle the troublesome issue of land reform and other controversies.

Thompson thought that for Churchill being in Cuba was like playing with lead soldiers at Blenheim again, a game where you move the pieces and create scenarios advancing your side, only for real. But in every game, as in life, the enemy must be disposed of, which means blood must eventually be spilled. For Batista that meant disposing of the former Army officers who had holed up at the Hotel Nacional, refusing to recognize him as the country's strongman. After trying repeatedly to parley with them, Batista sent a thousand soldiers to surround the hotel and demanded their surrender.

A group from the ABC arrived at the scene, gathering in the hotel's tennis courts. Thompson, coming down from his room, spotted Lena among them. It was the first time in weeks he had seen her—since their stay at Las Palmas. She had been appointed women's rights representative in the brief administration of Carbó and his allies but had resigned when a new government took office. Thompson walked over to the group, which was singing L'Internationale, interspersed with Communist slogans.

"Still in the fight, I see," Thompson said to her. She had lost weight, Gibson girl turned rangy revolutionist. She hugged him with wild abandon.

"We're building a new Cuba, Walter, and those sons of bitches are our last remaining obstacle. Winston still advising Batista?"

"Afraid so."

"At this rate you'll both be aplatanados pretty soon," she laughed.

"Begging your pardon, what is that?"

"When a foreigner stays in Cuba for so long that he becomes like a native, like our plátanos, he grows roots here. Look, why not settle down here? There's so much we can offer you—peace, tranquility, social justice," she said, sarcastically.

"I'll think about it," said Thompson, grinning.

"Okay, but don't wait too long, 'cause here comes trouble," she said, pointing at an armored car rumbling down the

Malecón and stopping in front of the hotel. The tank's turret wheeled about; the cannon pointed straight at the building. A black Cadillac soon approached and stopped, out of which exited Batista, in civilian clothes. Behind him came Churchill, looking not too comfortable to be in that position.

Churchill spoke quickly to Batista, which surprised Thompson, as either Churchill had learned Spanish in a hurry or Batista was a faster learner than Thompson thought. Batista nodded; Churchill dashed into the building.

"I have to go," said Thompson to Lena and hurried after Churchill. He found him in the hotel lobby, discussing with a general the terms of the officers' surrender.

"Mr. Churchill," said the old man, stooped, rail thin, with a florid mustache that covered half his face, "I am a graduate of West Point, the equivalent of your Sandhurst."

"I know it well; Sandhurst is my alma mater," said Churchill.

"In that case, you will understand that I have only this to say to these rebels."

"What is that, sir?"

"I have not yet begun to fight!"

As if in response, a fusillade broke at that instant from the upper floor of the hotel. The blare of an Army machine gun outside replied in kind with a blast of sustained gunfire.

"Tell your officers to stand down, General, this is your last chance!" shouted Churchill.

"Never!" said the old man, crouching as he made his way to a window and, shouldering a rifle, began shooting back.

A blast from the tank shattered the front windows of the lobby, blasting everything inside, scattering broken masonry, jars, flowers in its wake. A giant shard of glass whistled past Thompson, who jumped on Winston to protect him. Machine-gun fire raked the lobby next, bullets whizzing right above their heads like angry hornets. Winston pushed Thompson off and they crawled to behind one of the main columns.

"Thus a useless doomed effort begins, with desperate men in desperate means," whispered Churchill to himself. He looked at Thompson, shook his head. "What news, my friend?"

"Sir, Lena is outside."

Churchill paled, and the attraction he had felt for Lena surfaced again in an urgent cry for protection. "What? Where? Get her out of here, she's bound to get hurt!"

Thompson turned and, crawling to the front of building, he looked through a window, Churchill right behind him. To their horror, they saw Lena, who had taken a step forward to crouch behind a low garden wall, drop to the ground—gunned down. Thompson moved to run to her, but Churchill grabbed him, pushed him down.

"Wait! You won't make it through this firefight. Her people are taking her away, see?"

Churchill pointed to a group of ABC fighters, who had picked up Lena and were hurrying away with her. As if in reply, Batista's army hurled a blizzard of artillery shells that pockmarked the hotel's concrete façade, picking off the old general shooting from the window, who fell back with the top of his head blown off.

After the officers finally surrendered, Thompson questioned the ABC fighters, who told him they had taken Lena to the Hospital Municipal of Havana, but when Thompson went there to inquire, the nurse in charge told him she had died en route.

Churchill was shaken by the news, his features crimped in remorse; tears dropped from his eyes.

"She died a patriot's death, fighting for her country, Thompson," he said, drawing a deep sigh. "Perhaps then it's time for us to go. We've been gone from Britain for too long. These quarrels are no longer our own."

Two days later they boarded the SS Mauritania for their return to London. On the steamer's way out of Havana, as they passed Morro Castle, Thompson leaned on the railing, staring at the speckled houses of Havana receding from view, remembering the end of his affair with Fabiana . . .

————

AFTER THEIR INITIAL TRYST, Fabiana had turned cold and dismissive for no apparent reason. One afternoon, when he knocked at her door, a handsome young man in soldier's garb had answered. He spoke only Spanish.

"¿Fabiana aquí?" said Thompson, already fearing the worst.

She appeared moments later, in her negligée. "Mr. Thompson, meet my husband, René García," she said, draping an arm around the man's shoulders.

She turned to the man and spoke in Spanish—he brightened at that and ushered Thompson in, saying, "Mr. Churchill! ¡Amigo! ¡Entre, entre!"

Thompson declined, but the man grabbed his hand, pumping it effusively, still speaking.

"He says it's an honor to meet the man who saved Winston Churchill's life," said Fabiana.

"Yes, he would think that," said Thompson. Then, to Fabiana: "I never knew."

"You never asked."

Thompson pulled his hand away, shook his head no. García looked at Fabiana and his expression changed. He understood. She shrugged.

"Sorry, Mr. Thompson," said Fabiana. "Easy come, easy go. It's the Cuban way."

"I see. Then, adios," said Thompson, and walked away.

The door shut behind Thompson and he heard García angrily yelling inside the house, then a slap and Fabiana's crystalline laughter in response, as if she'd heard a tremendous joke . . .

———

CHURCHILL CAME ALONG, stood next to Thompson by the ship's railing, silently watching the flat sun light up the receding Havana skyline.

"Strange interlude, wasn't it?" said Churchill at last.

"Yes, sir, a bit painful, too."

"So are all memorable experiences, Thompson. It's part of the price we pay to have them. But England awaits us. Who knows what else Fate has in store for us?"

"Something good, I hope," said Thompson.

CHAPTER ELEVEN

1940
London, England

A DREADFUL SEPTEMBER NIGHT, the worst since the Blitz had begun. Two hundred Nazi bombers had attacked London, three hundred people killed just that evening. At the time, London was the largest metropolis in the world, with a population of close to nine million people crowded on a landmass of six hundred and seven miles, and none of it and none of them was immune. Every night Nazi bombers, preceded by Luftwaffe fighters, dropped tons of explosives. Not only ordnance, but firebombs that would consume a building within minutes. Right away the local fire brigade would set out, and anti-aircraft guns would strafe the bombers but to little effect, as the waves of airplanes kept coming like Wagnerian harpies until they emptied their bowels and flew back to their Teutonic Hades.

That one September night, after the bombers wrought their havoc, Thompson and Churchill drove out of 10 Downing

Street to inspect the damage. Churchill sat up front, with Thompson. Churchill would have driven, save for the fact that he was the worst driver Thompson had ever seen, and Thompson never relinquished the wheel.

"Head out by Buckingham Palace. I saw some bombs falling out there. I don't want their majesties to lose any more of their resolve."

"Not to worry, sir," answered Thompson, "you still have the people."

"Yes, until I don't," he answered, morosely.

Few outside the top political strata were aware that King George and especially the Queen were not the most stalwart supporters of Churchill's leadership. The King had even called Winston and his political allies—Anthony Eden, Lord Hoare, Lord Beaverbrook—gangsters.

The name had greatly amused Churchill, who told Thompson, "Sometimes it takes gangsters to defeat other gangsters," referring to Hitler and his crew. It was right afterward that Churchill made a point of being photographed firing a machine gun, as if he were in some Chicago back alley—or, in his case, the war-torn streets of Europe.

On this night the mayhem had been horrendous, buildings blasted to bits, people walking around in a daze, covered in dust and ashes like ghosts. Fire brigades fought fiercely to contain spreading blazes, while rescue teams dug through hills of debris to rescue those trapped in the rubble; everywhere, the awful smell of explosives, plaster, and blood.

By Buckingham Palace Thompson and Churchill noted the bombs had not struck the royal residence, although one had landed in the gardens, leaving a gaping crater while shattering windows. Days later their majesties would proclaim themselves grateful for the near miss, for whereas before the palace had been spared the bombing, now, as the Queen said, they could show their face to the East End, which had been so frightfully hit.

Thompson was driving by Embassy Row, near Kensington Gardens, when Churchill ordered him to stop the vehicle. He got out and immediately was surrounded by people who, recognizing him, declared they were more determined than ever to keep fighting, to never ever ever surrender, as Churchill had recently declared.

Churchill was in tears at seeing the destruction. "Look, he's crying," someone said. "He cares!"

"Give it to 'em, Winnie," said a woman. "Are we going to hit back?"

"You leave that to me!" cried Churchill, righteously agitated.

The neighborhood they had stopped at hosted the embassies of small countries like Romania, Thailand, and Paraguay. Most had been damaged, but one had been totally smashed to bits, as the explosives had fallen directly on it. Home Guard crews were pulling out of the rubble a boy, about six or seven years of age, bleeding, unconscious. Churchill walked over.

"What building is this?" he asked one of the rescuers.

"The Cuban Embassy, sir—or was. Took a direct hit."

"Any other survivors?" said Churchill, coming close to the boy on the stretcher.

"None, sir. We found the boy by chance. His hand was sticking out of the rubble, otherwise we would not have noticed him."

Suddenly Churchill's features hardened into surprise, as he stood by the bleeding child.

"Bring your torch here," he commanded.

When the Home Guard came close, the yellow light revealed a slim, fair-skinned boy, with such regular features you would have taken him for an English or Welsh child. Something about him stirred deep in Churchill, who stared wordlessly at the young victim.

"Sir?" said Thompson, finally. "Anything wrong?"

Churchill snapped out of whatever reverie he might have had—and then, like a doctor, leaned over and pried open one of the boy's eyelids, revealing a light blue orb. Churchill stepped back, as if jolted by an electric current. He turned to Thompson.

"Let's return, Thompson, I have orders to give," he said.

Thompson nodded. Although it was after midnight, it was Churchill's habit to stay up until three or four in the morning, working through the many responsibilities of his charge.

They were walking back to the car when in the crowd Thompson spotted a familiar face, one he thought he'd never see again: Riley, the man Thompson knew as Patrick Whitsett, the man who'd tried to assassinate Churchill in Havana, staring back at him.

Stunned, Thompson halted and looked again, to make certain, but Riley realized he had been recognized and took off at a run.

"Keep an eye on the prime minister!" Thompson shouted out to the constable accompanying them, and ran after Riley.

Thompson broke through the crowd, but the effort of dodging a pregnant mother and a woman with a perambulator made him lose some ground. He sighted Riley at the far edge of the crowd, looking back at him then racing away again. Thompson had finally eased his way through when yet another mob ran into the crossroads, as a four-story building impacted by the bombs collapsed in a cloud of dust and masonry with a great boom. The fallen debris blocked the way forward, and Thompson could see the fleeting figure of Riley rounding a corner, losing himself in the dark, blitzed streets of wartime London.

Uncertain at that point if the man he had seen was indeed Riley, or whether he'd even be able to catch him, Thompson thought it best not to leave Churchill alone any longer and returned to the car.

"Anything wrong, Thompson? Who were you chasing?" said Churchill.

Thompson paused to think for a moment. He was no longer certain the man he'd seen was Whitsett—he couldn't believe Fate would deliver such a strange coincidence. But if he was wrong, why did the man run?

"Sorry, I thought it was someone I knew."

"All right, then. Now, Thompson, I wish for you to find out about that Cuban boy. I want to contact President Batista and offer my condolences on the tragic loss of the embassy and its people."

"Will do, sir."

"Now heave to, man, I have work to do!"

CHAPTER TWELVE

MARCUS RILEY KNEW he had been seen—and he cursed his luck, that the one time he had ventured out from the East End, the old hellhound Thompson had caught his smell.

Jesus, Mary, and Joseph, how was that possible, he thought. It was only the equally implausible collapse of an old Tudor from the delayed effect of the bombing that had given him cover to escape that night, mingling with the horrified crowd fleeing the catastrophe. He had deliberately zigzagged down darkened streets, alleys, and backways, dashing, and running, then stopping to backtrack until, a half hour later, confident he had eluded all pursuit, he returned to his hiding place in Bow, staying inside for days.

But all that was behind him. On this night he had to concentrate on the job at hand, a meeting that would culminate in his most fervent desire—the elimination, and if possible, the slow painful death of Winston Churchill.

Riley made his careful way to the wharves of Wapping, where he was to meet his contact, as per his IRA commandant. He walked along the shoreline, past the jetties where stevedores were at work late into the night unloading cargo ships from the West Indies, past the warehouses where constables guarded the bins of rationed supplies, down to the pubs which stayed open after hours with a wink and a nod from the authorities in time of war.

He arrived at one such drinking establishment, the Brazen Head, right about the time that the proprietor, a blowsy woman wearing Wellingtons and a stained print dress, was turning out the lights.

"Closing time," said the woman, gruffly, then, as an afterthought, "Sorry," not meaning a single syllable.

"I was looking for McCarthy from Cork," said Riley, relaying the information he'd been sent in a postcard from Wales.

The woman shook her head, her greasy ringlets flopping about. "Ye micks will be the death of me. The stairs, to the right."

She jerked her head at a narrow side door leading to the second floor of the pub, behind stacks of wooden boxes full of empty gin, whisky, and rum bottles. Riley traipsed up the rickety, damp-smelling stairwell, to a landing with a scuffed door bearing a sign hanging askew, "McCarthy & Sons, Import/Export." Riley righted the sign, knocked. A man's deep voice answered from inside:

"Come in, you're late."

Riley swung open the door, causing the sign to again tilt up rightward. Riley ignored it. He walked into a dimly lit room with a round table and chairs. On the center of the table, a bottle of Bushmills and two water glasses next to a lone thick taper supplying the only meager light.

"Close the door, will you?" said the voice.

Riley did as asked. Out of the shadows stepped a little man, a Negro dwarf with a hunch, black clothes on coal-black skin.

He smiled, showing the whitest teeth Riley had ever seen, shining even in the penumbra of the dingy room.

"You be liking my choppers?" said the little man. He spoke with a pronounced Galway accent, as disconcerting to Riley as if King George was speaking German and Riley could understand him.

"They're shiny indeed," said Riley. "Come natural?"

"Nah, bloody Brits beat the real ones off me in jail. Once out, I procured the best set I could afford. Have a seat, take a drink."

Riley poured himself a shot of the whisky, gratified for the warmth spilling down his gullet. He proffered the bottle.

"You?" asked Riley.

"Don't touch the stuff. Makes a man lose control of himself, and in this business, one canna have it."

Riley nodded. His eyes beginning to adjust to the gloom, he noticed a door slightly ajar at the back end of the room.

"Well, I can handle it," said Riley, swigging another shot.

"We know you can. A regular barkeep in New York, weren't you? From brew master in Cuba to publican in America."

Riley felt the hairs in his neck standing up—this was not what he had been expecting. How could this gnome know anything about his life?

"Maybe," he drawled, more warily this time. "But I'm not here to discuss my affairs. Since you mention Cuba, perhaps you can tell me when the last time was it snowed in Havana."

The little man smiled so widely Riley thought his dentures would fall off.

"Ah, the password, yes. Now, lad, that's a trick question. The answer you're expecting is 1857, are you not?"

Riley nodded, beginning to wonder who the little man was

and why the long delay in telling him just how they were going to kill Churchill.

"For your elucidation, that answer is wrong. It has never snowed in Havana. But on the said date it did snow in Cárdenas, a town about seventy miles away. But let's get down to brass tacks, shall we?"

The little man drew closer, sat on a chair opposite Riley, leaning in so close Riley could smell his violet gum–scented breath.

"We know about your attempt in Cuba on . . . that man. This time we want to make certain you succeed."

"We being who?"

"The same blokes brought you here from America, lad. You think the IRA doesn't have enough people here already to bother with the expense of bringing you over? You have been chosen and we have big plans for you."

"I see, Mr. . . . . what is your name?"

"No names here, lad. Call me Cypher."

"Well, then, Mr. Cypher, and what if I don't like your plans and I refuse?"

"Come off it, man, we know how much you want revenge, how *he* authorized the killers who murdered your kin. Let's not play pretend games. But I shall answer all the same. Should you refuse our offer—and by the way, we will cover your living expenses while here with a nice recompense at the end—we'll have to send you back. I'm not sure where, though, if it be Havana where you're wanted for attempted murder, or Belfast, for the murder of that Captain of the Royal Guards. What will it be, my lad?"

Riley nodded, grinning. "You have me there. I'll go along with your plan, whatever that is."

"Oh, but it's a splendid plan. In a few days we are expecting a certain party from a foreign land across the

Channel to arrive with a new and wonderful weapon. It will be your privilege to use it to our good purpose."

"You mean there's a Nazi coming with a secret weapon for . . . the mission?"

"Aye, and we've been told a wonderful piece of work it is."

"What might that be?"

"That's for you to find out in good time. You are still staying at the parish?"

"Yah. My cousin may be a priest, but he carries Ireland in his heart."

"That's good. Stay there, but be careful, let no one see you. We'll provide the men to assist you. We'll call upon you when it's time."

"Fine."

"And now, to celebrate our friendship, I think I will make an exception and allow myself a wee drink."

The little man grabbed the bottle of Bushmills, poured a dram in Riley's glass then filled his own to the brim.

"To Ireland!" he said.

"To Ireland!" said Riley, downing his shot and watching in amazement as the little man drank his glass of whisky in two gulps as if water.

"Ah, but it's been a while! Well, off you go, my lad. We'll speak again soon."

Moments after Riley left, the back door in the darkness opened. A tall, cadaverously thin man in a double-breasted suit walked in, left arm dangling with an artificial hand.

"Was that to your satisfaction, my lord?" said the little man.

The man in the suit nodded, tossed an envelope with pound notes on the table.

"Most grateful, my lord," said the little man, rapidly opening the envelope and counting the notes.

"There will be more to come at each step of the way. I expect discretion," said the tall man.

"You shall have it, my lord."

The tall man looked down disdainfully at the little man, took out a gold briquet, and lit a cigarette, which he held with his artificial hand.

"And stay off the whisky," he said.

"I shall, my lord," said the little man, who eased back into his chair, hugging the envelope with the pound notes against his chest. Closing his eyes, he fell into an alcohol-induced sleep.

The tall man chuckled, sat to smoke his cigarette and give himself time to leave the premises unobserved, then he departed. He failed to notice Riley hiding in the shadow of a phone booth, who followed him all the way from the pub to a parking lot behind a nearby warehouse, where an idling Rolls Royce sedan awaited.

The tall man nodded at the driver and got in. The sedan rolled away, but not before Riley wrote down the letters of the license plate—unnecessarily, because he had already identified the man from his pictures in the newspapers as onetime heir apparent to the prime minister's post, John Philip Edward Burton, Lord Chadwick, Marquess du Bellay, commonly referred to as the Right Honorable Earl of Fairfax, now foreign minister in Churchill's War Cabinet.

CHAPTER THIRTEEN

"I'M NOT SURPRISED, if you did see him," Chief Inspector Angus Henderson at Scotland Yard said. "We've had reports of IRA operatives sneaking back into the country. Let's have a look at the latest."

Walter Thompson nodded, trying his best to hide his disappointment—and concern.

Scotland Yard had been the height of police work worldwide when Thompson was hired as constable. He had been pleased to no end on finally joining the force, as in his eyes there was something so very English about it. Even the Gothic architecture of Scotland Yard's headquarters reflected the spirit of the nation: dependable, thorough, fair minded, the qualities that made Britain admired around the world.

Yet, over the years, as Thompson worked his way up, he was forced to modify his opinion of the Yard, especially about the people who served there. A rigid insistence on rules, regulations, and procedure structured their very lives, as if even a smoke and teatime had to be regulated, accounted for, and duly noted on some unseen ledger.

Chief Inspector Henderson was one of those unfortunate bureaucrats. His office, with its portraits of the king, the queen mother, and Prince Edward seemed a repository of ancient beliefs and standards. The man even wore a morning suit to work, as if he were a Whitehall pencil pusher instead of a high-ranking investigator.

"I see here this Whitsett character was detected by one of our confidential agents in New York," said Henderson, scanning the file. "Not certain if Whitsett is his real name. We believe it's Riley, although he's also used the surname Jerome, as well as Rooney and McEvoy."

"In New York? What in heavens was this Riley character doing there?" said Thompson.

"Not exactly clear. Some sort of menial job, the kind the Irish tend to do, what? The point is, Thompson, he was associating with known IRA members. He may have traveled to Boston as well."

Henderson hummed to himself, as if reading a piece of music that struck his fancy.

"This is interesting. It seems he became close to one of our female informants. I quote, 'in a drunken stupor claimed to be one Kevin Marcus O'Riley, whose brother was killed by the Blacks and Tans, and he has sworn revenge on WC.'"

Henderson smirked at Thompson. "That's Winston Churchill, it's safe to presume, and not the loo."

"Quite," replied Thompson, dryly. "Mind if I take a look at that?"

"So sorry, confidential."

"But I am the prime minister's bodyguard!"

"That may be, but those are the rules. You may take it up with MI5 if you wish. You'll have to submit a formal request in writing, but under the current circumstances, the war and all, it might take some time before you receive a response."

"How long?"

"Hard to say. Months, I'm afraid."

Henderson smiled with cold glee. Another high muckety-muck appeaser who wants to cut a deal with Hitler, thought Thompson. I wager he wouldn't shed a tear if Churchill was killed.

"Of course, you may take it up with the prime minister and have him issue an order obviating all the regular channels," Henderson went on. "I understand he's prone to do things like that."

"I wouldn't want to bother the PM in the midst of the current crisis."

"You haven't told him about your observation?"

"Not yet."

"Well, then, there's not much to do, is there? You'll just have to keep your eyes and ears open. Contact us if you spot this fellow again. Better yet, detain him if you can. We'd love to have a friendly chat with him."

Thompson nodded, outwardly calm. He was livid that the Yard would cross its arms and refuse to conduct a proper investigation, but kept it to himself.

"Anything else, Thompson?"

"Yes, one thing. What happened to the old man who ran the brewery where this character worked? I met him when we visited Havana during the revolution years ago. I understand he was arrested."

"Let's see."

Henderson quickly scanned the pages of the file, raised his eyebrows.

"Didn't notice this before. A back-page footnote. That person, a certain Brandon O'Connor, was taken into custody after the incident, but was released after the Cuban government seized the brewery and sold it off. O'Connor died a few

months later, possibly from the aftereffects of his imprison-
ment. It says he was related to your man, Whitsett, Riley, whatever, who is believed to be connected to a Catholic priest, a
Father Alonzo O'Riley, parish priest at Our Lady and Saint
Katherine of Siena in Bow. His cousin, reportedly."

Henderson looked up, shook his head in dismay.

"It says here they have a sizable congregation. Didn't know
that. Always thought Bow was Church of England territory.
Oh well, there are Papists everywhere, like Jews, I suppose.
Anything else, Thompson?"

———

WHEN THOMPSON RETURNED to 10 Downing Street,
the prime minister was in an uproar. The appeasers, people in
and out of government who wanted an immediate truce with
Germany, were at it again. This time they were circulating a
letter in Commons asking for a vote of no confidence. There
were still enough followers of former Prime Minister Neville
Chamberlain among Tory backbenchers to provoke a crisis that
could tumble Churchill's unity government of Conservatives,
Labour, and Liberals. The plotters had thought they could slip
the petition around without attracting suspicion, failing to
realize Churchill had hidden followers among the appeasers
who forwarded him a copy.

"This I will not put up with!" he roared, waving the letter
in Thompson's face.

"Begging your pardon, sir, but what of it? You still have
your majority support in the House."

This appeased Churchill somewhat, and he bellowed about
the ingratitude of mankind, how he'd even included Chamberlain in his War Cabinet precisely to avoid sedition such as this.

Churchill was dressed in his usual gaudy Chinese silk robe,

reclining in bed, surrounded by newspapers, the red box with official documents, and a tray with the remains of his breakfast and his whisky and soda. Seeing as his aide de chambre was not around, Thompson moved to take the tray off his bed lest in his fury Churchill break something and injure himself. Churchill stopped him, and with his usual lightning change of mood, moved to another topic.

"Leave that! Any word on the Cuban boy? I telephoned President Batista last night to give him my condolences. He took it very well, all considered. About twenty people worked at the embassy, he said. All gone. I naturally told him we'd rebuild the structure—in due time, after we win the war. Do you know what that scamp said? So soon? he said. Ah, I always liked that half breed. Brilliant man. Could not get him to declare war on Germany, though. Please obtain that boy's identity, will you? I had a dream last night about him and Cuba that . . ."

Churchill's features softened, the tropical interlude nagging at his memory. Thompson joined him in the sentiment for the briefest moment. "Understood, sir. I'll head to Wanstead Hospital right away."

"Good. Have Eden come here, will you? Tell Anthony to phone Beaverbrook, I need more numbers from that bloody aircraft factory!"

"Yes, Prime Minister."

"And get me the new girl, what's her name?"

"Mary, sir. Miss Layton."

"Right. Have her come here as well. I must write another telegram to Franklin—we need those American ships. Well, go on, man, what for are you waiting?"

After summoning Anthony Eden from the library—him looking like a fashion plate even in the middle of the war—Thompson swung by the typists' room. Mary Layton was already at her desk, redoing some previous missives, her face pale and drawn, bags swelling under her wide brown eyes. She stopped the moment she saw Thompson, issued a wan smile.

"Late night?" he said.

"Till four this time. Frankly, I don't know how he does it. And the drinking!"

"Yes, I know, but he can handle it. The drinking, that is. Do you know the anecdote about Abraham Lincoln and his top general, Grant, during the American Civil War?"

"I'm sorry, the only civil war I know is our own Glorious 1688, Cromwell, all that," she said, relaxing a bit.

Thompson had liked the girl since she came in for her tryout. Now he moved in closer, breathing in her Pecksniff talcum powder, her Evening in Paris perfume.

"Right. Well, some people complained to Lincoln about Grant, who at the time was blazing his way through the South, defeating all the rebel forces. They asked Lincoln how he could possibly have that man in command, he's a drunk! To which Lincoln said, 'Please tell me the brand of whiskey that Grant drinks. I'd like to send a barrel of it to my other generals.'"

Mary laughed. "Wouldn't have thought you cared much for history."

"Gives me something to occupy me when I'm on my cot down in the basement. Now go in, he's asking for you."

"Once more unto the breach!" she said, grabbing Thompson's hand. "See, I know some history too!" and exited in a flurry of woolen skirts and Thompson's rising hopes.

Old boy, stick to your last, Thompson told himself, and headed out to see the Cuban child.

CHAPTER FOURTEEN

THE LOBBY at Wanstead Hospital thronged with the injured from the previous night's bombing, attended by exhausted doctors and nurses working practically twenty-four-hour shifts. The head physician, a Dr. Patel, a very dark fellow from Madras, spoke with the crispest Oxford accent Thompson ever heard.

"Terribly sorry about the crowds, can't be helped, you know," he said, leading him through the corridors. "We've had a ton of transfers from the other hospitals. Queen Charlotte is no longer safe and Great Ormond caught on fire. I understand the prime minister's office called previously, seeking information about the victim?"

"Yes," said Thompson. "We don't want this tragedy to become a diplomatic issue."

"That's what I thought," he said.

They stopped at a long ward with dozens of beds crowded together like cribs in a nursery, all filled with wounded children, with bloody bandages and splints. Dr. Patel pulled the chart off one of the bedsteads, read it. The boy, bruised and gashed but clean, slept on.

"Severe concussion, broken tibia and ribs—we expect him to recover."

"Any word on the identity, Doctor?"

He took a quick look at the paperwork. "Says here they found the child's passport in his pocket, along with an airplane ticket to Spain. Apparently, he was on his way to Madrid when the bombs struck."

"Name?"

"Hm. Say-ess. Zay-ess. Mother is listed with the same last name, first name Magdalena."

"Zayas, you mean, sir?"

"Yes, that's it. Never was much good with these Spanish names. They don't have the proper pronunciation, don't you think?"

The doctor went on, talking about how he had taken German at university and done some studies in Heidelberg, but Thompson really couldn't quite concentrate, his mind reeling from the news. Now he understood why Churchill was so keen on the boy.

"And the father?"

"Don't know. It was left blank in the passport. Say, is he the child of some prominent family?"

Thompson chose not to answer and, thanking the doctor, left the hospital in a hurry, for if his suspicions were correct, the boy could very well turn out to be Churchill's son.

———

LENA LIVED and bore my child, thought Churchill, only to die in a German hecatomb. Such is the way of all flesh.

Perhaps. Perhaps not.

But if the boy is not mine, then how to account for the incontrovertible evidence? The dates match, and he is a living copy of my resemblance when at Blenheim. How is that possible otherwise?

Churchill stared at Thompson, sitting across the desk in the study at Chequers, the prime minister's country residence. Thompson's long lean face was creased with concern as he awaited Churchill's response. Faithful and wise steward, whom the lord will set over his household, thought Churchill, remembering Sunday services at Harrow.

"Well, have you questioned the child? He may be able to tell us who his mother was, if that passport is true. It might not be. I am sure there must be others with that name. It's not that unusual. Most importantly, who is his father, does he know him?"

"I'm afraid that won't be possible at the moment, sir," answered Thompson. "The boy is still unconscious."

"Any word when he will come to?"

"Doctors are not certain. He suffered a massive concussion, and what with all the victims from the bombings, well, I'm afraid they are not able to devote much attention to him. Already the attending physician was asking if he's from a prominent family," said Thompson.

"No, that won't do. Here's what. If anyone asks, just tell them he's a . . ." Churchill hesitated a moment.

"A what, sir?" said Thompson.

A bastard, thought Churchill. We are not royalty, still, should those wretches from the *Mirror* find out, no, better not.

"Say that he is the son of an old friend of mine and you're concerned about his welfare. When and if the boy wakes, let me know. That will be all."

From the window Churchill watched Thompson making his rounds around the perimeter of the country estate, notwithstanding the dozen or so guards posted throughout the grounds. With his long legs, saturnine expression, and ramrod bearing, Churchill couldn't help but compare him to the bloodhounds of his youth, always sniffing round for the elusive prey. If ever there was a man whose visage so perfectly matched his profession, it is he. Be careful there, he told himself, go look at yourself in the mirror.

Moving a few feet to stare at his reflection in the medieval roundel in the bookcase, he wondered if in fact he resembled the famous English bulldog some in the press were comparing him to lately. Hmm, the jowls, yes, the strong jaw, the compact body. I wonder, he thought, does our profession shape our bodies or are we drawn to our professions and rise to our aspirations because of the shapes of our bodies?

Look at de Gaulle, a giant who wants to embody the greatness of France—and see where that's taken him—nowhere, not even able to get support in the African colonies. No, it's best to simply be human, with all our faults—one of which is my dillydallying over matters of literature when I should be concentrating on supplies, armaments, planes, planes! Where is that bloody Beaverbrook?

And with that last thought, Churchill turned to the latest figures from the factories at Midlands and Coventry and the precise number of aircraft that would help him face up to the nightly German deluge of death.

CHAPTER FIFTEEN

SIX HUNDRED MILES AWAY, the man who deliberately conflated his person with the fate of his people was having a very un-Germanic but symptomatic fit of rage. Adolf Hitler was indulging in yet another of his infamous tantrums over the conduct of the war. He had just given a speech at the Sportpalast, threatening to make the British pay for their recalcitrance to surrender, and he was demanding results. Quickly. Or else . . .

As always, his top lieutenants listened quietly, while trembling discreetly, lest he turn his explosion of fury upon them.

"How is it possible that after all these bombings and attacks we have not received a single offer of peace from England?" he sputtered, stomping his fist on his desk in the Reichshauptstadt.

"How can they withstand it?" he fumed, waving a sheet of official numbers in the air. "I have here that our air force has made over a thousand sorties a day over the last month. Churchill himself admits that more than a thousand civilians have been killed in our raids, and still they won't come to the table. Why? Why?"

"It's been much more than that, Mein Führer," said Field Marshal Göring, nervously thrusting forward yet another packet of documents. "They are lying about the number of casualties. But we'll soon be unleashing the full ire of the Luftwaffe on them, as you asked, and that they won't be able to deny. We are going to demolish entire cities. Coventry, Liverpool, Birmingham, we will blast them all to bits as an example to show them they have no recourse but to submit to your grand designs, Mein Führer. They will come on their knees to us."

"Those cities are not enough, we must have more!" snapped Hitler, partially mollified by the prospect of massive destruction. "We are in preparation for Operation Sea Lion, and until our forces are ready for the invasion of England, we must destroy their air force. If they will not seek terms of surrender, the skies must be ours!"

"They will be, Mein Führer, forever!"

We'll see about that, thought propaganda minister Joseph Goebbels, sitting quietly next to Göring. He knew better than to object or interrupt Hitler when he indulged in one of his tirades. The best way to deal with the führer was to let him exhaust himself, then once the fireworks were shot, calmly steer him to a more rational decision. But still Goebbels listened, took notes for his next radio broadcast, and nodded enthusiastically at Hitler's harangue.

Goebbels didn't think that the Götterdämmerung Göring was promising over England, or even the complete destruction of London, if it came to that, would alter the will of the British people. He felt there was another way to assure the triumph of Hitler's will, as Leni Riefenstahl would have said, but he couldn't quite put his finger on it.

It finally came to him that night when Heide, the youngest of his eight children, the führer's godchild, and Goebbels's favorite, came down with the croup after a nasty cold. His wife

Magda and the children's caretaker were aflutter, panicking when the little girl began to have labored breathing—a hoarse sound, like a broken bellow, was all that issued from her little lungs.

Goebbels remembered what his own mother had done with his brother, so he took little Heide from her bed in the children's wing of his mansion in Schwanenwerder, which he had recently taken over from an exiled Jewish family. Down the wide marble staircase he went with the child in his arms, reminding himself to remove the tiny Stars of David inlaid on the landing pavers, and walked out the back terrace facing the broad, clean waters of the Wannsee.

September had ushered in with unusual chilliness and fog in Berlin, and he knew that the cold, moist air would open the child's lungs. He carried her tenderly in his arms, crooning a lullaby, watching the tendrils of fog reach out to shore from the far corners of the broad lake, until she fell asleep, and her breathing became regular and normal.

When he returned to the house, he placed Heide in bed, propped her head up with two pillows, and admonished the governess to keep the window open. It's too stuffy in here, no more old wives' tales about night air. And that's when he realized what his plan should be.

He walked back down to the library on the first floor, going over the details in his head. It was brilliant, but also daring—not the sort of thing the führer would approve of, yet if he could pull it off, he'd earn his eternal gratitude, and finally put that lard gasbag Göring in his place.

The plan was quite simple but, as in all schemes of utter simplicity, it was the execution that could prove difficult. One thing was certain: as long as Churchill was prime minister, Britain would not be defeated. But he couldn't simply be murdered; that would only make him a martyr and his successor would be constrained to follow his policy of no surrender. Churchill must be disposed of, leaving him alive but powerless.

Goebbels picked up the phone and called his trusted contact in the Foreign Chancellery—it was time to activate their most valuable asset in the heart of the ruling circle of England itself.

Late that same night, the phone rang in the master bedroom of an aristocratic townhouse in London's stately neighborhood of Belgravia. A gray-haired hand reached over the body of a young boy, lying naked in the bed next to the man answering the call.

"Yes?"

The man listened intently to the voice on the other end, which was curt and to the point. The plan was outlined, the date to be set soon.

"I understand," said the man as sole reply.

When the call concluded, he put down the receiver and, still feeling the aftereffects of the night's champagne, snuggled next to the handsome young man sharing his bed.

CHAPTER SIXTEEN

MORNINGS IN MADRID made the Duke of Windsor nostalgic for London. In the high plains of Spain, September could be the most harrowing month, with fever-high temperatures and a dry brutish wind that seemed to carry the dust of dead conquistadors and foreign wars.

But in London, (ah, in London!) September was the last day of the wondrous, tremulous spring called an English summer, dawn opening with a welcoming mist that gave way to a splendid morning once the sun broke through, droplets of dew clinging to the gleaming roses in one's own garden.

These thoughts and many more like them crossed the duke's mind as he strolled with his pug on the gravel-strewn orchard behind his Madrid townhouse. Not a day went by that he didn't think about the land and the throne he'd left behind, not for the power and the glory he'd forsaken but for the little things that made him feel that he belonged, that he was someone with a proper job to do, for the inchoate feeling that he was mystically attached to a larger destiny, a larger cause, to his people—instead of being outcast by his own brother for daring to love his own way.

But all those deficiencies would soon be remedied, he hoped, perhaps this very morning after the visit from Herr Stumpf. Great things could perhaps still come from Germany after all—like the Windsors themselves . . .

The pug having finished his business in the shade of a scraggly orange tree, the duke started up the pebbled path to the stately mansion his friend, the Marqués de Pozos Dulces, had kindly lent him for his stay.

At the back steps to the loggia waited Josefina, the stern-faced ama de llaves who had taken the place of the duke's ever-faithful mademoiselle, who'd gone back to occupied France to retrieve Madame's belongings.

"*El señor . . .*" began Josefina.

"*Français, s'il vous plait,*" replied the duke.

"*Ah, sí,*" she said, proceeding to murder the soft sounds of Montaigne with the blunt edges of Cervantes.

"*L'homme est arrivé, l'Allemand, Seigneur.*"

"*Merci, je l'attends au salon. Et Madame?*"

"*Encore dans sa chambre, avec sa belle amie.*"

"*Bon, merci.*"

The duke handed the pug to Josefina, the animal growling at the housekeeper, who pinched it to keep it quiet. The animal yelped and turned hopeful eyes at the duke for salvation, but the former king of England was already walking briskly to meet the representative from Berlin.

During a visit to Germany with his wife, the duke had reached a secret gentleman's agreement with Herr Hitler, that is, if a house painter like the führer could ever be called a true gentleman. Both understood that England and Germany had many bonds in common, and that an Anglo-Saxon/Teutonic alliance would allow Britain to keep its colonies and independence, while granting Germany the freedom to obtain its much-needed lebensraum in continental Europe. Recalling how he and Wallis had been cheered by the throngs in Berlin, he thought most people seemed very happy under Herr Hitler anyway.

And the Jews? A passing fury. Don't they always say, "Next year, Jerusalem"? When the duke regained the throne, he would be very happy to help make that return a permanent reality.

The duke glanced at his reflection in one of the ornate mirrors that his host hung on practically every wall. The duke straightened his tie, flicked an imaginary mote of dust off his jacket sleeve, and strode into the vast Salón de Recepciones.

A very tall, very blond, very fair man with Nordic features stood at attention the moment the duke entered the room. He was dressed in a fine gray woolen suit and bespoke shoes—details the duke never overlooked. The visitor's expression was a mixture of surprise, anticipation, and regret.

"Your Highness," he said in accented English, bowed his head. The duke graced him with a wan smile, shook his hand.

"Herr Stumpf?" he said, surprised by the appearance of his guest. Most Germans he had met in Hiler's entourage were short and dark, as if their Aryan convictions were more of an ideal than a reality.

"No, Your Highness, I regret I cannot say that I am he. I am Axel Lundgren, President of Electroventus Industries of Sweden."

"Oh!" said the duke, realizing that Josefina, seeing the Teutonic appearance of the man, had mistaken the identity. "I am sorry, sir, but I am not receiving today any ..."

"If I may, Your Highness, I am here on behalf of my country's embassy, who wish to convey discreetly the desire of the

German Chancellery—of Foreign Minister Ribbentrop and the führer himself."

"Oh!" said the duke again. He wished his aide, Fruity Metcalfe, would be there to handle details like this—but then, this was supposed to be confidential. Still, how could that be so if this Swede was involved?

"And Herr Stumpf?"

"I understand he is indisposed, Your Highness, which is why I have been chosen to relay this message of the greatest importance. I know this might appear puzzling, so permit me to present to you this letter of introduction," said Lundgren, extracting a sealed envelope from his Moroccan leather briefcase.

The duke tore open the envelope, stepped a few feet away to inspect the missive. He took out a heavy linen and rag sheet, embossed with a familiar coat of arms, bearing a note written in the intimate yet stilted mode of address of the few who breathed the rarefied air of British royalty.

"Dearest Edward,

"I have taken the liberty of transmitting via this envoy some information that I believe will be of the highest interest to you, and all those who hope and trust in your rightful return.

"Your Faithful Friend and Devoted Servant,

"JP"

There was no mistaking it—the signed letter came from John Paul Burton, Lord Fairfax—the duke's childhood playmate and trusted adult companion on many a visit to France's best *bordels*. The duke folded the letter, placed it back in its envelope, thrust it into the inside pocket of his red-silk-lined jacket. He turned to the giant Swede and waved at a damask fauteuil under a giant crucifix on the wall.

"All right then, have a seat, sir. Let us hear this message."

It took Lundgren a good half hour to explain all the intricacies of the scheme hatched by the duke's followers—the complications ensuing from recruiting the fiercest enemies of the state in an effort to regain the crown for the duke. The enemy of my enemy is my friend, thought the duke at the end. Witness what just transpired between Germany and Soviet Russia. One minute they're sworn enemies, the next they're welcome allies.

It was all a game of power and supremacy—didn't his own brother renege on him, selfishly pouncing on the throne instead of supporting him in what was a simple request, to let him marry the woman he loved? What sort of family was his, that would deny him a basic right? Had not the Church of England been born out of a king's desire to marry? And was the king not the head of the church?

The hypocrisy of it all, the duke often reflected. The archbishop with his tonsured boys and Baldwin with his countless mistresses preaching morality at him, only because Wallis was a divorcée. Keep her as the royal whore, that's what they urged him, not as the queen. And his own brother Albert, who refused to grant her the title of Royal Highness, driving the duke and her to France and now to Spain? Bastard.

All these feelings swelled in the duke's chest, after the details of the plan were laid out—a plan that, although farfetched, was ingenious enough to succeed. He had listened quietly, smoking several cigarettes, neither giving nor denying consent, until Lundgren finished his presentation.

The duke flicked the ashes of his final smoke into the crystal tray on the marquetry table before him and stared thoughtfully at the El Greco portrait of one of his host's ancestors, the Duke of Alba, whose schemes had kept Spain as the greatest power in Europe longer than anyone could have foreseen.

There was just one little detail to clean up.

"And the prime minister?"

Lundgren cleared his throat, blushed—an unexpected sight in someone so tall, so strong, so blond.

"He will be disposed of, Your Highness."

The duke was about to inquire precisely what that meant but thought better of it and simply nodded. It was best not to look too deeply into such matters. If at some future date some investigations were to be conducted, or some pesky historian or wretched scrivener scratched beneath the surface, it would be convenient to plead ignorance of the details and pretend the plan did not scream bloody murder to one's royal countenance.

Still, it would be a shame about Winston. He'd been the only man of rank to support the duke, advising him to hold his ground and refuse the awful deal the archbishop and Prime Minister Baldwin insisted he accept.

Winston, poor Winston. Oh well, I'm certain this is just what Henry VIII felt when ordering Lord Cromwell's beheading. It's a nasty business, the throne.

The duke stamped out his last cigarette.

"Please tell our friends that we would be pleased to aid in their plans as necessary. Communism is our greatest threat, not Germany. Inform them of the fact, and that we will support retaking Ireland and declaring peace in the continent."

He stood, audience over. Lundgren also stood, bowed again, his face now flushed with gratitude. I wonder what he's getting out of this, thought the Duke, watching the tall Nordic stride like a Viking down the marble halls of the townhouse. Man's cupidity is always surprising.

Just then the duke heard the bright laughter of Wallis. He found her at the gallery above the staircase leading to the apartments, saying goodbye to the gorgeous Countess Benavente, who had spent the night.

The countess nodded at him and curtsied before quickly

exiting. The duke felt a throbbing in his groin as Wallis stared down at him from the top of the stairs.

"Come here, bad boy. I think you need correction," said Wallis.

"Yes, mommy," said the duke, ascending the stairs.

CHAPTER SEVENTEEN

"COUGH, YOUR MAJESTY."

The royal physician, Sir Hugh Northrop, dutifully bent down and examined the white and yellow sputum King George VI expectorated onto the white gauze.

"How bad is it?" said the king. "Is it, a new, new, pneumonia?" he stuttered.

"Hmm," said Northrop, placing his stethoscope on the monarch's back. "Breathe deeply, sir."

The king took a large breath, the air echoing in his lungs with a slight wheeze.

"Again."

The king obeyed; Northrop wrapped up his stethoscope. "You may get dressed, Your Majesty."

"Well, what is it?"

The king slipped into his white shirt forcefully, the odor of nervous perspiration filling the room—the monarch disdained deodorants, colognes, and all kinds of men's perfumes, affectations he left to his older brother, the Duke of Windsor.

Northrop sat on a stool by the bed in the infirmary of Buckingham Palace, where he was treating the king.

"You have a common cold, plus a slight irritation of the lungs, provoked no doubt by your smoking. May I inquire, sir, just how many cigarettes a day do you consume?"

"Oh, I don't know, thirty, forty, I suppose."

"Well, sir, if you could manage to cut that down by half, I expect you should recover nicely. I recommend you get as much bed rest as possible, under the circumstances."

"Yes, that's the thing, isn't it? Under the se, see, circumstances. How am I going to do that with that bloody bli, bli, bombing going on all night?" said the monarch, fiddling with the upper button of his shirt. Northrop smiled, helped the king with his button and the tie he invariably wore, even to breakfast.

"Perhaps Your Majesty might spend a few days in Balmoral, away from here . . ."

"Not a chance, Hugh, I'm nee, ne, needed here, I'm in, in, in, irreplaceable."

"Undoubtedly, but a few days will not lead to the end of England, Sire, and it will aid enormously in your recovery. You are only human, after all."

"Ha! Tell that to We, We, Winston!"

"Churchill much of a bother, sir?"

"Bother? Bother? Only if you call a boil in one's ass a bother —he's a pa, pa, pain!"

"A royal pain, Your Majesty?"

The king laughed and for once his perpetual expression of sad acceptance of life's inequities vanished.

"Yes, you might say that. War, war, war is all he talks about and doesn't give a fi, fi, damn about the thousands of lives we're losing every day. What with all this German invasion nonsense . . ."

"You don't believe they will invade?"

"Not at all. Any military man can tell you they would be an, an, anhi, destroyed if they try it. But we must stop this bomb, bomb, bombing somehow. No reason why we can't have a tre, treaty . . ."

The king suddenly grew quiet. He slipped on his tweed jacket, cleared his throat.

"I may have spoken out of tu, tu, turn. I, I, I trust . . ."

"No need, Your Majesty. I understand. Discretion."

"Hm, that's goo, goo, good. By the by, speaking of the Devil, have you time in your appointment book for We, We, Winston?"

"Pardon, does he not have his own physician?"

"Muir just died, one of the bo, bo, bombs, poor old man. Burned to death. Now, I may disagree with We, We, Winston— gangster that he is—but I need him alive. He's the only one holding this thing together. And the only one who can end it. Someday. I hope. Soon. If I can co, co, convince him. Any chance you can fit him in your she, she, schedule?"

"It will be my pleasure, Sire. What ails him, do you know?"

"Oh, you know, the usual. Overweight, overworked, overtalked. His throat is going out on him, ra, ra, raspy. Please take good care of him. Like him or not, we're stuck with him for the due, due, duration."

"As you wish, Your Highness."

The doctor bowed to the monarch, who strutted out of the infirmary—then Northrop dared a small, self-congratulatory smile on realizing how well the plan was developing.

Northrop had thought the plan was too bold, fearing that even in a bombed-out city, killing a high-society physician just so they could get closer to Churchill was a bridge too far, a scheme too lunatic to succeed—even if the suggestion for his appointment were to come from deep inside the palace.

When he'd received his instructions during a well-placed walk in the Whitehall Gardens, he'd been tempted to refuse the assignment, but he silently agreed, believing it had scant chance for success. But the maleficent genius of the German volk was again showing—with no one realizing how they were all, the king included, pawns in a deadly game called by the master gambler, Adolf Hitler.

The doctor gathered his things, threw on his mac for the drizzle, and stepped out of the royal palace to his waiting car. Passing through Buckingham Gate to Victoria Street, it occurred to him that there was still one large and obvious obstacle to the plan—Churchill's damned bodyguard, Thompson.

The man had a preternaturally acute nose for detecting and defusing threats against the prime minister. So, if Northrop were to finally pull off his part of the plan, he'd have to do the work he had to do quickly, so the invasion and the other pieces would fall into place. But how?

The answer came to Northrop that afternoon, as he was treating Lady Rothman for her canker, having to smile throughout her incessant gabbing about a forthcoming dinner with Beaverbrook and the prime minister.

"Of course," he muttered to himself, "it's perfect."

"Perfect? Naturally it will be a perfect dinner. What else can it be with the PM and my husband?"

"Yes, Milady," he said, congratulating himself on his perspicacity. "Perfect indeed."

———

AT THAT VERY MOMENT THE man who stood as the main obstacle to the doctor's and Goebbels's scheme was trying desperately to come up with a face-saving answer to an innocent question.

"What was that, Mary?" said Walter Thompson over the tumult of the pub, even though he had heard her perfectly well.

"I said, why haven't you remarried?" said Mary Layton, taking a sip of her pint, then bending over closer, making sure he heard her clearly. Thompson breathed in the intoxicating scent of her perfume.

"It's been years, hasn't it? No one ever caught your fancy?"

"Well," drawled Thompson, embarassed. "I . . . what is it to you?"

The answer miffed Mary, who looked away, shook her head.

"Curious, that's all," she said, glancing longingly at a nearby couple—both in uniform, nuzzling urgently in a corner booth.

Thompson was annoyed with himself. It's a perfectly proper question, he thought, answer the girl, you fool! It was obvious that she was interested in him, although to what end was not yet clear to Thompson. She had asked him out for a pint after a long day and he had accepted, more out of curiosity than anything else, not quite believing his attraction to her would amount to anything.

Yet here she was, asking personal questions as if indeed there was a chance of a future for them, as if there wasn't a twenty-year gap between them, as if she really felt something more than camaraderie, something closer to—what? Friendship? Lust? I should be so lucky, he had thought at the time.

Her question had put him on the spot with the unerring emotional accuracy of women. A lifetime of professional evasion and suspicion, plus an innate reluctance to reveal himself, had bred in Thompson a careful carapace of apparent stoicism, even if beneath the mask his feelings were as stormy as those of any silver-screen romantic hero. Even now, anguish, anger, and fear mixed in a dreadful cocktail of impatience and desire.

Where to start? Well, with the truth, that's always best. He leaned over, took her hand.

"I'm sorry, Mary, I didn't mean to be curt. I . . . I find it hard to talk about myself. A lifetime of police work breeds that in one."

Mary's soft, rounded features relaxed into a sympathetic smile. She squeezed his hand, leaned forward again.

"My apologies if I was out of turn. I know it's difficult to disclose oneself to strangers . . ."

"I would not call you a stranger either," he countered.

"But I am! We are! We know so little about each other! It's, at work, Miss Layton, the PM wants all this typed straight away. Or, Miss Layton, good morning, miss, please correct that mistake, and how would you like your tea, Miss Layton, and watch out for the old man, he's in a drunken mood today! Sorry, I didn't mean to say that—I was repeating what Alice in the typing pool says sometimes. You won't report me, will you?"

"You secret is safe with me," he said, charmed by the effort-less grace of the girl—and again let himself be momentarily beguiled by thoughts of a different future, of . . . she's twenty years younger, you old fool, whatever are you thinking?

He let go of her hand, leaned back in his chair. "Well, Miss Layton, if you must know . . ."

"I don't."

". . . I will tell you anyhow. Yes, I was attracted to someone, but it didn't last. My wife and I were already separated and that was the last nail in that coffin, I'm afraid."

Mary Layton grinned. "Well, then, I shall call you Lazarus! For you have come back from the dead! You have, haven't you?"

"Emotionally, you mean?"

"Yes!"

Her round brown eyes sparkled—and Thompson realized he wasn't mistaken after all, that for whatever reason, to Mary their age difference was no longer a breach but a mere crack in time, to be vaulted over with intention and desire.

"I suppose I have," was all he dared to say. "One must love, after all."

"Yes, one must," she answered—just as the wailing siren of an incoming air raid sliced through the wall of noise and talk in the pub.

Damn it to hell, said someone. Bloody buggers, said another. Down we go! exclaimed a third. That Hitler! If I get me hands on him, I'll cut him to ribbons and hang him from my window, said a woman laughingly as the crowd moved to the shelter in the pub's basement.

Mary and Thompson followed the crowd for a few feet, then Thompson whispered in her ear, "You know, if we go down, we might be caught here all night."

She looked up brightly, eyes sparkling with glee, then shook her head, regretfully.

"No, I can't . . . you're right, Mother is expecting me. But, oh! Do you dare?"

"Dare what?"

"Come with me? I'll try to walk home. It's only two miles away, our flat's in Bow. Do you feel like chancing it?"

"Is she not going to a shelter herself?"

"Not Mother—she says she'd rather die in her flat than spend the night in a filthy basement with strangers."

"Well, if you're going to go, it's the right thing to go with you, I suppose."

"Thank you, you're a peach!"

She turned and impulsively gave him a peck on the cheek.

Thompson felt the skin burning from the touch as if her lips were a red-hot poker.

"Let's go, then," he said, taking her hand, and moving against the swelling crowd, they stepped out into the night.

CHAPTER EIGHTEEN

THE SKY OPENED before them in its wartime awfulness, great bars of light crisscrossing the starless blackness barely illuminated by a lambent moon, the howling of sirens and the rat-tat-tat of antiaircraft guns echoing like warring sentinels down the narrow streets.

Thompson and Mary dashed across the alleyway fronting the pub, hand in hand, giddily laughing like school children running in the middle of recess. They weren't the only ones taking a chance on the raid—a handful of people were strolling very deliberately in front of the shuttered storefronts, some even in the middle of the deserted road, as if daring Nazi bombers to drop one on them, to blast them out of their native imperturbability.

But those were few. Most Londoners were moving quickly into the shelters every few blocks, trying to get out of harm's way before the blight they knew would rain down them.

"You should come in here, you two," said an old woman in a line as Thompson and Mary hurried past, still laughing.

"No, thank you," said Mary, "we must be home or Mum will go barmy!"

"Good luck to you then, blessings!" said the old woman, who pushed forward with the small crowd entering what used to be a Presbyterian chapter house.

"You know, she's correct, it might be dangerous if there's a hit nearby," said Thompson, sizing up the old brick and mortar buildings lined up like so many little toy Tudors in a row. For some almost miraculous reason, that side of Lindon had been spared by the bombers, and the half shadows created by the moon made the narrow, deserted avenue seem a stage set for some romantic movie.

"I thought so too," countered Mary, "but this is the fastest way home—we'll be there soon!"

The sounds of anti-aircraft guns shooting far away, in the East End, rang louder the father they moved from The City, the streets becoming progressively emptier the closer to Mary's home.

"What I don't understand," said Mary quickly, almost panting as they hurried, "is why can't we see them? Or hear them?"

"We'll see them soon enough. Hear them, actually," Thompson said. "It's a whistle at first and then it's all hell exploding before you. I've seen quite a few the last few nights with the PM. Old man likes to stand on the roof of 10 Downing Street and smoke his cigar as if watching a picture show— growls and curses at the bombers."

Mary stopped for a moment to shake a pebble out of her shoe, leaned on Thompson's arm.

"How come you're not with him tonight?" she said.

"He's up in Chequers with the American envoy, Harry Hopkins. The PM asked me to go, but given there would be plenty of protection, this one time I said I had a previous engagement."

"Oh, and with whom, if I may ask?" said Mary, teasingly.

"Well, given that I had accepted your kind invitation, I felt it would be the height of discourtesy to leave you standing."

"Really now, what a gentleman! You are a man of many . . ."

All at once the air broke before them—a sharp whistle pierced the moonstruck shadows and a great thud followed that rocked the ground, as two bombs rammed into the street a few hundred yards ahead of them. A sheet of flames rose before them, crackling like a wall of fire from a dark inferno, mud and debris sucked up into the void like a satanic whirlwind of destruction.

Immediately Thompson covered Mary, who sheltered behind him. He wrestled her down, flinging the two of them behind a low garden wall, right before the second blast, which pounded their ears like a pulsating piledriver, shattering the façade of the houses fronting the alley.

The shock knocked them out for a few seconds. Thompson came to first and lay completely still for moments that felt like an eternity, the shock wave still ringing in his ears. Mary came to, opened her eyes.

"All right?" he asked. She nodded yes.

They got up slowly, their face and clothes covered with plaster bits, mud, debris.

"Anything broken?" said Thompson.

Mary opened her arms, looked them up and down as if seeing them for the first time, and began to laugh uncontrollably.

"What? What?" asked Thompson, but then he too caught the virus and broke into laughter, a deep, full-bodied laughter as if he'd never laughed before, unaccountable, life affirming, defiant.

"We've been bombed!" cried Mary. "We've been bombed!"

"Yes, we have, we have!" said Thompson, laughing, and they hugged, happy to have survived, and in the excitement of their escape from death, their cheeks touched. Mary stopped, looked into Thompson's eyes, and kissed him, hard, eagerly. He kissed her back, his tongue sinking into her willing open mouth, thrilled to be still alive, in one piece, in her arms . . .

"Yo! Are you two all right?"

Thompson and Mary turned to see the tin-hatted neighborhood Home Guard, accompanied by a crew of volunteers already smothering the incendiary with dirt and chemical foam, the dying sparks of the bomb breaking into embers that tinkled like breaking glass as they were doused.

"We are fine, thank you," said Thompson. "We'll be on our way."

"We've been bombed," said Mary, brightly. "Did you know that?"

"Yes, miss," said the Home Guard. "And lucky you are to be here still. Now go on home or a shelter, will you? Jerry's bound to have another go at it tonight."

"Yes, home, Walter, home!" said Mary to Thompson. "I must tell Mother we've been bombed! Bombed!"

CHAPTER NINETEEN

THE RAID that for a few feet of distance would have taken Thompson's and Mary's life changed Marcus Riley's plans for the assassination of Winston Churchill.

Up to the time that he met with the dwarf, Cypher, Riley had dutifully followed what he thought were the instructions of an IRA commandant. He had been a good soldier, assuming his superiors had the same objective and desires as he, to unify Ireland and throw the British out forever—and in the process, stamp out poisonous vermin like Churchill. But seeing Fairfax was behind the plot threw Riley off the well-oiled track of his convictions.

The evening of his discovery, he had walked slowly back to Bow and the refuge of the rectory at Our Lady and Saint Katherine of Siena, a thousand questions besieging his mind. How far up did this plan go? Who in the IRA chain of command was aware that the plot was all part of a British, most likely an MI5, scheme?

For days he pondered on this, waiting for Cypher to

contact him. Yet the more he thought about it, the more convinced he became his was a rogue operation. Not IRA, not MI5, but a cabal of people within the establishment who wanted to get rid of Churchill. Which was fine by Riley; nothing would give him more pleasure that executing that stuck-up little pig. It was the way Riley had been recruited that told him his job was even more treacherous than it looked.

Someone of Fairfax's money and stature would never associate with people like Cypher unless the operation was privately funded—and had no official sanction. If the job was a government plan, he would have been arrested a long time ago, as Cypher knew where he was hiding, and Scotland Yard had no tolerance of IRA commandos. Moreover, it was Cypher who was going to put him in touch with the German and his secret weapon. Yes, Riley was certain it was all a cabal operating outside official purview. And the moment the operation was finished, he would be equally finished.

Permanently.

He thought back to New York, how Matt Doyle, the mayor's aide who often came to the pub on MacDougal Street where Riley worked, asked if he was interested in returning to England to finish the job. Riley had been surprised. He had stayed away from his IRA contacts, knowing the FBI was always keeping an eye on them, and without papers and with his dubious background he would be an easy case for deportation. In any case, he had believed his usefulness to the cause was blown after Cuba, so when Doyle made the proposal, he immediately assumed it was the IRA using Doyle as a cut-out. But as his cohorts always used to warn him, assumption is the mother of all fuckups. And this was a bloody fuckup.

His stomach churned thinking back to chubby little Matt, with his beady little eyes and slovenly manners, how he had taken Riley for a ride. Doyle had intimated it was IRA money, had supplied the fake passport, the money, even knew about his cousin Father O'Riley, made all the arrangements for his trip. If Riley ever returned to New York, he'd settle accounts with that fat Dublin rat.

Riley felt betrayed. By everyone. He realized he was a pawn in a higher game. But he reasoned that a pawn who knows he is one such is a dangerous piece, for if he manages to reach the opposite side, he becomes the most powerful player in the game. So then, who was behind Fairfax? How far did their reach go? Did his cousin know—or suspect—what he was there for?

One night Riley could no longer stand to stare at the print of Pius XII, at the carved crucifix, at the calendar from Finney's Grocery on the wall without getting an answer. He eased out of the service closet his cousin had converted into his cramped bedroom and headed up the stairs of the rectory.

At the landing he nodded hello at Father Cunningham, who thought Riley was another poor kinfolk of Father O'Riley who needed temporary shelter in London. So did the nuns who dutifully cleaned the rectory, cooked the food, and washed the soiled priestly laundry.

Nice getup they have here, thought Riley, I should have joined the seminary. But what about the cailíns? He smiled remembering his last affair, a honey-haired sheila from Dublin with a penchant for fellatio, then put away all thought of female attentions, lasciviousness, and occasions prone to sin, and knocked on his cousin's bedroom door. He briefly heard the strumming of a guitar inside the room, then the music stopped and Father Thomas O'Riley opened the door.

Tall, stocky, red cheeked, Riley's cousin bore all the earmarks of a County Mayo alderman, or of a prosperous wheat grower, both of which he'd been before one day announcing he'd had a vision of Jesus asking him to preach to the lonely Catholic faithful in England. Leaving behind a stunned fiancée and an even more stunned political and agnostic family, he'd taken orders and joined the Congregation of Christian Brothers, which assigned him to Latin America, serving in Chile and Brazil before finally being allowed to follow his vision and preach to a small congregation in London. Now he smiled as if still looking for votes in the town square.

"Good evening, Marcus. I'd given you up for lost. Haven't seen you the last few days, not even at morning Mass."

Riley nodded, glanced inside the room. A tawny-skinned novice sat on the edge of his cousin's bed, a guitar on her lap.

"I'm sorry, I didn't want to disturb," said Riley.

"Think nothing of it. Margarita was only teaching me a few chords of one of her country's songs. A samba. Perhaps you're familiar with it?"

"I go now, Father," said the novice in a soft, whispery voice. She got up, picked up her guitar.

"*Obrigado*," said the priest, quickly muttering phrases in rapid Portuguese, which Riley, who had studied Castilian in Cuba, could not understand. The novice smiled sweetly and headed down the stairs.

"Well, then, man, come in," said the priest, ushering Riley into the cramped bedroom. A tall boy stood against the far wall, next to a small desk and chair; on the opposite side, by the narrow window, the single bed on which the novice had lain, the impression of her body still on the slightly disheveled sheets.

"How can I help you, cousin?"

Riley sat on the bed, the faint scent of the novice's jasmine scent lingering in the room. The priest grabbed the lone chair, turned it around, and sat with the chair's back facing Riley, as if a protective shield from anything that might transpire.

Riley sighed heavily, shook his head in apparent pain. "Well, cousin, do you remember old man O'Toole, when he was selling his farm in Kilkenny?"

"Most certainly. We were barely lads, your folks come to stay with us as your pa had to recover."

"Aye, we were young. Well, then, you may recall how the old man wanted to sell his ten acres, but he had a deadly quarrel with his neighbor, Mr. Murphy, who'd offered to buy the farm, but O'Toole said over his dead body?"

The priest's features hardened, his smile dropped, his jaw set firmly. He nodded grimly. Riley saw his cousin had grasped his intent, but he continued the tale, wanting to make sure there was no misunderstanding.

"And how one day this lass with her deaf and dumb brother showed up, a widow with some money from insurance, and O'Toole took pity on her and sold it to her at a discount."

"I recall," broke in the priest. "She turned around and sold it to Murphy the very next day, took her profit, and sailed to America without the so-called brother, who she'd borrowed from the asylum to pluck the old man's heartstrings. Your pa made a great deal of it to my pa, them laughing at the gullibility of people."

"Well, cousin, I find myself in a similar situation as old man O'Toole. I've been deceived. And I believe you know all about it."

The priest glared silently at Riley for a long while, then shook his head and, whistling, walked to the tall boy, opened the top drawer, and pulled out from underneath a mound of snowy white undergarments a bottle of a clear liquid.

"Well, boyo, whilst I was in Brazil, I grew very fond of this particular beverage—a rum called cachaça. Might I interest you in trying some?"

"Gladly, cousin," said Riley.

The priest produced two shot glasses from the drawer as well—one smudged from recent use—and poured out two measures. The cousins clinked, raised their glasses high.

"To free Eire!" said the priest.

They swallowed, the biting sharpness of the raw rum burning all the way down Riley's gullet. The priest repositioned his chair, sat facing Riley.

"You would like to know why you were chosen?"

"It has piqued my curiosity," said Riley.

"Indeed. Well, I do not know all the details, but I do know this. Your mission is of the utmost importance and has been approved by the highest levels of government."

"Lord Fairfax?" said Riley. The priest gave him the smile of the teacher happy to see his ward advancing.

"He is of the faith. His family has been Catholic for centuries, never wavered under Henry VIII. During confession he personally asked for my blessing, and I was glad to give it. He stands to become the next prime minister after you complete your work. He has promised us the return of Northern Ireland if you succeed. Imagine that, Marcus, our country whole, united at last. How could I say no?"

"And the fact that there will be a man killed?"

"It's a war, Marcus. A war against godless Communism. We are defending our people and our land. It's a just cause, the Holy Father has said so."

"He has blessed an assassination?"

"I would not call it that. It's an execution. And forgive me, but why all the trepidation? Did you not attempt such a thing earlier in Cuba?"

Riley nodded. "Aye, but I'm a changed man. My conscience weighs heavily on me."

"Is that what troubles you?" said the priest, standing up.

"On your knees, my boy."

Reluctantly Riley kneeled on the ratty carpet, as the priest began his peroration in Latin.

"*Ego te absolvo . . .*" he said, then stopped. He looked down at Riley, shook his head. "I better bring out the oils, make it official, won't we?"

He walked back to the tall boy, opened a small drawer from the bottom of the reredos, and extracted a wooden box with aromatic balms. He turned to see Riley on his feet now, with a gun pointing at him.

"Marcus, what are you doing?"

"As I said, I'm a changed man—and my conscience is telling me to trust no one—be they family, priest, or both."

"What are you talking about?"

"The way I see it, cousin, the moment my job is completed is the moment I will be disposed of—and I appreciate my life. I like living it. I don't want to lose it, even if I do still want to do the job. I have to make sure as few people know who I am or where to find me as possible. You, cousin, are unfortunately one of those. I am terribly sorry, but the job demands it. As you said, or should have said, mine is a sacred mission, for which I'm sure I'll find redemption . . ."

Riley did not complete his sentence, for at that moment a sharp whistle pierced the air as the same German squadron that had almost killed Walter Thompson and Mary Layton a mile away dropped a bomb smack on the rectory's roof.

As in a slow motion movie, Riley saw the walls of the room crumble, the bed flying up in the air, the bottle of Brazilian rum spinning crazed and spilling its contents in one long liquid flow and the priest knocked across the room as if flying with seraphs and Riley felt his own legs give out under him and the mattress of the bed fell on him as he tumbled down to the ground unconscious.

Riley came to a few minutes later, waking to the cries of rescue workers already going through the remains of the building, scratching through the smoking rubble. He moved his head, not quite remembering his location, dazed as if waking up from a dreamless sleep, then he remembered the blast and the mattress that luckily had covered him, protecting him from serious harm. He pushed out from under the mattress, staggered to his feet.

The far wall of the bedroom had fallen away from the bones of the building, the debris creating a hillock of destruction leading down to the street. Now he heard cries and moans from all over, desperate calls for help in the wreckage. A smell of plaster and sulfur filled his nostrils as he moved his limbs to make sure nothing was broken, then he got on his knees and searched the rubble for his gun. Finding it a few feet away, he saw it had been damaged by the explosion, the cylinder stuck, the barrel bent, the ejector rod broken. He threw it away and, under the wan light of the pitiless moon, moved around the remains of the building looking for his cousin.

Riley found the priest under the bricks of the nearest wall, his face on the reredos, still as a corpse. He was about to go when he heard his cousin move, muttering something in Latin, and his whimpered cry for help. Riley knelt beside him.

"You're still alive, cousin?" he asked, solicitously. The priest, jaw cracked from the explosion, a deep gash on his forehead, nodded yes.

"That's too bad, cousin. You remember that night you buggered me in the hayloft? I never forgot," he whispered in the priest's ear.

Riley grasped the priest by his hair and smashed his head

on the ground, knocking him unconscious again, then, grabbing his neck, twisted it until he heard it snap.

"Now go to hell!" he spat out.

Riley got up and walked away, stumbling down the mountain of rubble to the street, avoiding the searchers with their torches, and quickly lost himself in the darkness of the bombed-out London night.

CHAPTER TWENTY

THE BEATERS MOVED ON AHEAD of the shooting party, the dog handlers barely able to restrain their charges, which barked fiercely at the prospect of red grouse. A cold, sunny morning in the hills of Yorkshire, perfect for the hunt, yet Lord Fairfax, despite carrying his well-oiled Purdey for a shoot he'd anticipated for months, was distracted by his conversation with the Earl of Rosewood, known to intimates as Rosey, his guest at the Fairfax country estate.

The talk had begun innocuously enough, with idle chatter about the crisp weather, a wonderful charge from the unusual hot spell London was experiencing. It drifted to the Blitz and the near misses of the St. James Club, Buckingham Palace, and the House of Commons, all of which had been the latest targets of the German raids.

"I do hope you've stashed away enough of the 1921 Haut Brion," said Rosewood. "I just ran out of mine. Now that France has fallen, heaven knows when we'll get another shipment."

"The moment Churchill became PM, I had my people put away four cases. We'll have some for dinner tonight."

"Splendid!" said Rosewood, his eyes set on the line of beaters trying to roust the birds from their hiding places.

"By the by, how are you getting along with Winston?" added Rosewood, the two friends trudging through the coarse brambles grown over after the last burn-off. Fairfax frowned, his usual dark features growing even gloomier at the mere mention of his political enemy.

"Winston Churchill is a man who hasn't grown up. To him life is a series of swashbuckling adventures, *The Boy's Own Book* kind of tale. Lloyd George was right, you know. Winston has Negro blood in him. And like all the inferior races, he thinks only of his own aggrandizement, no matter how many people die as a result of his love for danger. He must go."

"I see you two are still in love," said Rosewood, with the bright grin that had drawn Fairfax to him ever since meeting at Eaton.

"Hardly," said Fairfax, finally cracking a smile at his friend's teasing.

Charles David Benedict Tyndall, first Baron of Courtenay, Duke of Marymont, and Earl of Rosewood upon the death of his childless uncle, was heir to a landed family dating back to William the Conqueror. Tall, hefty, and fair as his Norman ancestors, as a boy he already towered over all but one in his class. Only Fairfax equaled his height and his titles, but whereas Rosewood was of a sunny temperament, and with the musculature of a warrior, Fairfax was rail thin and swarthy, with sad eyes that rarely brightened, perhaps due to the congenital defect that had him born with a withered stump for a left hand.

Rosewood was the only boy who had not made fun of Fairfax's defect, protecting him from many a taunt and challenge to a fight. The two of them were also the only Catholics in their grade, both with deep connections to France—in Fairfax's case, his maternal grandmother, the Marchioness du Bellay, whose family chose to stay in England after fleeing the Jacobins.

Throughout the years Fairfax and Rosewood found their personalities complemented each other, for whereas Fairfax was deliberate and calculating, Rosewood was impulsive and prone to the usual vices of his class—gambling, horses, women. Rosewood had strayed from the church, but Fairfax remained devout, attending Mass every morning at seven, even if he occasionally fell into the willing arms of a particular demimondaine in Paris—the separation from her being yet another burning log in the fire of his hatred for Churchill and all he stood for.

Rosewood did not quite harbor the same contempt for Churchill as Fairfax, and at times found his friend's derision of the prime minister excessive. Aware of this, Fairfax had not brought him into the circle of plotters aiming to depose Churchill—but still gave him enough information to keep him abreast in case they would need his help, which he was certain Rosewood would gladly provide.

"Hallo!" shouted one of the beaters.

A pair of grouse skittered then flew like arrows out of the underbrush, zigzagging this way and that, daring the hunters to halt their frantic flight. Rosewood spun around and fired his twelve gauge but missed. Fairfax lifted his Purdey and in one swift, elegant motion, the stump of his left hand holding still the barrel of the gun, he raised his trusted over and under above his head until it was perpendicular to the ground. Quickly sighting the prey, he fired, bringing down in quick success the two birds.

"Go boys, go for 'em," said the handler, who released his two Airedales, which raced to retrieve the downed grouse.

"That is what I wish we could do with that impostor, that

clown, that perversion," said Fairfax, moving ahead after the dogs.

"You know, there are rumors that perhaps you might be progressing from words to action," said Rosewood out of the corner of his mouth, keeping his eyes on the beaters moving forward, should another flight of grouse suddenly appear.

"I cannot say with certainty, Rosey, but there are certain parties who have been engaged to remedy the current situation," said Fairfax coldly.

"I see. Permanently?" asked Rosewood.

"We certainly hope so. It is expedient that one man should die for the people and not that the whole nation should perish," said Fairfax.

"Hmm, as I recall, that did not turn out so well for the Sanhedrin," said Rosewood.

"Those were Jews. We know better. For the sake of England and our people dying in those raids, we must be rid of this madman. We're losing thousands every day, all for his dreams of childish glory."

"And the king?"

"Edward's behind us. Look!"

The forward beaters flashed a band of grouse, which took off in a pinwheel of feathers and fear into the cold morning air. Rosewood lifted his gun and, with two quick shots, downed one of the birds.

"Finally got him," said Rosewood.

"My sentiments exactly," replied Fairfax.

CHAPTER TWENTY-ONE

THE OBJECT of Fairfax's fierce hatred at that moment was preparing for his future meeting with the leader of the most powerful political force in Great Britain, the 1922 Committee.

As Churchill was aware, the power of the Committee wasn't to be taken lightly. Churchill himself had only become PM after his predecessor, Neville Chamberlain, was forced to resign following a no-confidence vote called by the Committee, even though Chamberlain's opponents had not garnered a majority but only a plurality of the votes.

Now, a year later, following the disaster of the bloody retreat from Dunkirk and the nightly bombing raids on London, a large segment of the Tory membership was demanding a vote to oust Churchill in turn. The letter campaign against him had been launched by a disgusted member of Parliament whose twin Pomeranians had died in a Nazi bomb blast. Fairfax had taken the ball and run with it, leaning on likeminded colleagues over vinous lunches and leisurely conversations in private clubs to send in the secret letters. Being the great behind-the-scenes manipulator,

Fairfax had left the job of leading the no-confidence vote campaign to a lesser man, Robert Erskine, a member of Parliament from Scotland, and that's where Churchill saw his chance.

While Churchill had many secret allies among the appeasers, he had no regular means of digging up what Americans would call the inside scoop, the nitty-gritty behind a politician's persona, the skeletons in the closet that can destroy marriages and, most importantly, political careers. So he had drafted Thompson to sound Erskine out.

Thompson did not relish the thankless task of being the secret agent of 10 Downing Street. Unlike the fellows over at MI5, such as the young naval commander Ian Fleming, Thompson had no designs to write about his wartime experiences or much less pen some cheap spy novel about his adventures. Yet he had to recognize that doing some investigation, especially if it involved the future of Churchill's government, could be construed as within his purview to protect the body and health of the prime minister, so he had agreed to make some discreet inquiries of colleagues in and out of Scotland Yard.

Still, Thompson grumbled to Mary, who had become his lover after their near-death experience on the way to Bow. "He's just like the kings of old. His every wish must be taken as a command," he confided after a lovemaking session at her mother's flat—the old woman having been persuaded to move to the safe hills of the family farm in Cornwall.

"It's what he always wished for, it seems to me," she said. "Probably regrets not being born royal. Doesn't everyone?"

"Not me," said Thompson, easing back into bed, delighting in the smell of her sheets, her hair, their lovemaking, clinging to them like a perfumed veil. "I am perfectly happy being a plain voting citizen."

"Oh, but you are much more than that to me," said Mary, grabbing him. "Come here, my prince."

———

"WELL, Thompson, cat got your tongue? Speak up, man, my water's getting cold," said Churchill, sitting plump and pink in his second bath of the day. "Tell me what you dug up about the Committee chair, Erskine. What have we got on him?"

Thompson had had enough. "Prime Minister," he began, but Churchill cut him off.

"You're not going to start with me again about boundaries and courtesies, now, are you, Walter? We've been together for far too long," said Churchill, swabbing his belly with a sponge. Thompson ignored him, went on.

"Exactly, sir. After all this time, I must demand mutual respect. No more sending me off to pick up clean laundry when aboard ship, no more snapping of fingers, expecting me to leap at the slightest order. If that attitude persists, I'll have to consider . . ."

"Oh, bloody hell. Yes, yes, yes, once again, my apologies. I was only asking for the latest result of your investigations. You are the best man Scotland Yard has ever had and I need you. You do know I am under some pressure here, what? And could you please fetch me that towel? See, I can be polite as well."

Thompson had to smile as the portly politician rose from the water, pink and fragrant of Castille soap.

"Rubber duckies," said Thompson.

"What?"

"I said, rubber duckies. If you're going to waddle about in the tub like a child, you might as well enjoy it and play with rubber duckies."

Churchill chortled. "Splendid idea! Make sure and get

me . . ." He stopped on seeing Thompson's frown. "Never mind, I shall get them myself. Harrod's might still have some . . ."

"Doubtful," said Thompson, handing Churchill the towel, "with the requisitioning of rubber, Malay taken over by the Japs, and . . ."

"Right, right," said Churchill, "I need not be reminded of our shortcomings." He wrapped himself in the towel like a toga, leaving him looking like an obese Roman senator.

"Let us get on with this. What have you learned?" said Churchill, stepping out of the tub to light his fifth Cuban H. Upmann cigar of the day.

"Not much, I'm afraid. Major Erskine is apparently fault-less. Unionist, represents a district near Glasgow. His father was . . ."

"Never mind his family, Thompson, little good they will do us in this instance. As I recall, his pater was a jurist, met him back in '03 during my first run. He too was an MP, Unionist through and through. Even met Constance, his wife, a harridan with a dry bark for a laugh. Teetotalers. One time at some celebration I had to suffer their national dish, boiled lamb's stomach crammed with oatmeal, and not a drop of liquor, not even cheap champagne, to wash down the awful concoction! But that was the old man. I need to know about his son, that consummate fool Fairfax has under his thumb. What Erskine really is like when out of public view, indulging in his vices. Tell me, regale me with all the sordid details."

Thompson was astonished by Churchill's prodigious polit-ical memory, able to recall a bad luncheon and a brief acquain-tance of almost fifty years before as if it had happened the week previous. Thompson was equally astonished by the man's contempt for anyone who did not share his devotion to the pleasures of the flesh. I wonder what he thinks of me, thought Thompson. I must seem like the starchiest of shirts.

"Frankly, there is nothing objectionable about his life. He's quite the war hero, awarded a Distinguished Service Order while in Flanders. Rents a flat in Mayfair when he's in town. Two boys, twins, about to take exams at Oxford. The family estate is well managed. Wife is Presbyterian, he's Anglican, but not particularly devout. Not a whiff of scandal, I'm afraid."

"Gambling?"

"No."

"Horses?"

"No."

"Drinks to excess?"

"Afraid not, as far as I can tell. I made some discreet inquiries at his club. He's not inherited the abstemiousness of his father that you indicate. He enjoys his regular drink, but nothing excessive. Only . . ."

Thompson stopped, not certain if the last bit of information he had garnered from friends at Scotland Yard made any difference. Reluctant to mention what he thought was an insignificant detail, he gave it up, thinking that his lack of usefulness might get him discharged from this skulkery.

"What?"

"He has a collection of African art—masks, spears, the like."

"That is unusual. Was he posted to the colonies? Was he in the Foreign Service?" said Churchill, pouring himself a dram of Scotch while still in his bath-towel toga.

"No, but he did command a troop of Cameroon soldiers while he was serving in France during the Great War."

"Ah! I've got it! He's one of those lovers of the lower races, a philoafrican. I wager he voted for the India Bill while I was out in the political wilderness . . ."

"Well, in fact, he did, sir. He gave a speech in Glasgow

comparing granting the right of self-determination to India to the rights guaranteed to Scotland by England."

"Balderdash! When have Indians taken up the sword to defend English rights?"

"Well, we do have the Punjabis and the Sikhs, and they fought valiantly in the World War."

"You are missing the point, Thompson. Indians are a beastly people with a beastly religion who breed like rabbits. They've tried to kill me before; I wouldn't be surprised if they were to try again."

"Sir, I find it objectionable that you would compare Africans to Indians as equally lesser. I have a wonderful colleague, Detective Kumar. He's as stalwart and dedicated a chap as any Englishman, even if his skin is dark."

"Bah, it's no less than they deserve. Anyway, Erskine is our man. He goes to Paris frequently, does he not?"

"Yes, three or four times a year to amass pieces for his collection."

"Nonsense! It's a woman."

"Pardon?"

"*Cherchez la femme, mon vieux!* He's one of those who have been hooked by the passion that the darker races bring out in the white race. I'm certain he's got a black filly in France who's birthed him a brood of half breeds."

"Really, Prime Minister! I have no information of the like, and furthermore . . ."

"I never took you for a liberal, Thompson," smiled Churchill. "I'm sorry if my views on race offend you. But that is not the point here. Politics is a blood sport, man, and I will not allow anyone to force me out when England needs me the most. If not for me, everyone would have already offered their backside to Hitler, Goering, and their gang. I must control the Committee, and everyone has secrets they don't want revealed.

That's how I've controlled Chamberlain and Fairfax so far; they'd rather not have their dirty linen out in full view. But enough of that. Find out from your contacts who Erskine sees in Paris—and bring me the proof. This revolt must be nipped in the proverbial bud. Now, go, man, go!"

Thompson nodded, then realized that for once he was about to have the last word.

"I shall. Incidentally, there's something I've been meaning to tell you, Prime Minister."

"What?"

"The Cuban boy, Zayas"—Thompson wanted to add, your bastard son—"he's come to."

"Is he awake?"

"And talking. French and Spanish, but talking."

Churchill shook his head pensively, as if wanting to toss some unwanted thought out of his head, then, in a calculated theatrical move, dropped his towel toga on the floor and walked naked over to his wardrobe.

"I have nothing to hide. I'll go see him soon," he said, easing into one of his colorful silk Chinese robes.

CHAPTER TWENTY-TWO

LONG BEFORE HE became an adopted Irishman, before joining the IRA, before his capture by the British and becoming their informant, the black man known as Cypher was called Malcolm Boyd. Born in Bluefields, Nicaragua, he'd grown up in British Honduras, the son of an alcoholic shrimp fisherman who decided that his brilliant, if physically handicapped, child would attend school, although he himself could barely write out his own name.

The nuns at St. Martin's in Belize City took a liking to the small boy, who demonstrated an almost photographic memory and a moving aptitude for the intricacies of the Roman Catholic catechism. During the hurricane of 1915, which devastated the colony, his father died in a mudslide that swallowed up their lean-to. Little Malcolm, now an orphan, was taken up by the nuns as their charge, and when the order closed its doors and the sisters returned to Ireland, Malcolm went along with them, the adoptive child of the only real family he'd ever known.

Once Malcolm reached puberty, he left the care of the

nuns—women and drink held stronger attraction than the
sisters who, like Caliban, taught him to read and write only to
better rage at the injustice of his fate: a smart, black hunchback
in a land of tall, benighted white people. Yet he quickly found
that the things that made him different, as is often the case,
were also his greatest strengths. Because of his physical condition, he was the last person the British occupiers suspected of
belonging to the insurrectionists. Soon, for the considerable
sum of a pound a week, a wily IRA recruiter hired little
Malcolm to become a highly effective planter of bombs and
deliverer of news, money, and weapons, as most people could
not believe a black dwarf would be involved in events of such
great consequence.

At least that was the story British intelligence drew up
about Cypher. The fact that most of the information could not
be corroborated and was supplied by Boyd himself after his
arrest made some in MI5 feel it was suspect, but they adopted
the story in the end, feeling there must be some element of
truth to it since it held together so perfectly.

Boyd was captured during a failed attempt to bomb the
local branch of Lloyd's in Londonderry. When he refused to
disclose any details about his IRA cohorts, an irate judge
sentenced him to a twenty-year sentence at Crumlin Road
Gaol, the worst prison in the entire United Kingdom, reserved
for murderers, child abusers, and the criminally deranged.
After a week's stay at the facility—during which time inmates
took to throwing Boyd around like a rugby ball, breaking his
front teeth with a sharp kick— he reached out to the British,
offering to become their eyes and ears on the IRA.

At first the newly appointed Special Branch officers
laughed, asking what full-blooded Irishman would trust a black
dwarf. But they changed their mind when he gave them the
names of all his contacts and proposed opening an import-

export company for the British West Indies that would serve as a cover for delivery of weapons to the IRA and passage of its members abroad, yet all the time being tracked and, if need be, intercepted by authorities. British intelligence agreed on one condition—he'd still have that twenty-year sentence hanging over his head, so that if at any time he failed to do their bidding, he'd be thrown back in Crumlin Road.

Malcolm Boyd then became Cypher, the little man who held the keys to information that could bring the mighty British empire to its knees. At least, that's what Boyd felt when making the rounds of his favorite whorehouses, where his more than adequate member, large even for a normal-sized man, always drew sighs of lust and admiration from the sex workers.

It was at one such house of ill repute, not too far from the docks where he'd set up his office, that Cypher stood late one night, chatting at the door with the red-haired madam.

A light-skinned black woman from Trinidad, her business catered to West Indian laborers and pasty white Brits in search of chocolate thrills. Now, in the chill hours before the dawn, she adjusted the fedora on Cypher's massive head.

"Best be careful, Malcolm, the Huns might still return with their awful bombs," she said, fondly remembering the hours she had spent with him in the shelter, where his insatiable lust had satisfied her and her six girls.

"I am ready for them, my dear," said Cypher, still half tipsy from his bottle of Old Elgin whisky. "In fact, I have an appointment with them, at Nelson's statue, where I shall defend the honor of England and swipe them all down!"

"Go on, man," she laughed, "go on home."

Cypher gave her a half salute, then spun on his heels and, wobbling slightly, headed down St. Katherine's Way, past the still-smoldering remains of the warehouses bombed overnight. The moment he knew he was out of sight of the whorehouse, he renewed his normal gait and walked as straight as any steve-dore coming home from a hard night's work.

Cypher had learned to dissemble at an early age, pretending to be that which people thought he should be: a devoted acolyte, a fervent Irish patriot, a heartless turncoat, a dissolute dwarf with an alcohol addiction. In truth, he was all these things and none of them—that is, he could portray them, play them, act them out, all the while retaining a stone sober eye on his surroundings.

He prided himself on his chameleon identities, yet failed to consider that he was not alone in such traits, and that excessive trust in one's own faculties can led to terminal failure. Which was why when Riley came up to him out of the shadows by his door and put a knife to his throat, Cypher was, for once, genuinely surprised.

"I have no money, chum," he said, not recognizing the man behind the blade.

"That's not what I saw Fairfax give you," said Riley.

Cypher immediately recognized the voice and stood still.

"I thought you were dead. The bomb destroyed the rectory and half the church," said Cypher, careful not to move lest the very sharp edge of the blade slip and slice his jugular.

"Aye, and it's a good thing everyone thinks that, too. I need money and shelter and you're about to give it to me. Now, go on, open the door."

Cypher slipped out the key, showed it to Riley, slid the key in, then slid it out and reinserted it, turning first counter-clockwise then clockwise, deactivating the detonator of the jerry-rigged explosive he'd set up to permanently deter thieves and burglars. That's when he realized perhaps Riley was not as dumb as his stolid Irish peasant face seemed to imply.

"Thank you, didn't quite want to get blown up to St. Peter's for the pleasure of your company," said Riley, shoving Cypher inside the flat, his blade nicking the little man's neck.

"Ow, you bastard, you done cut me!" yelled Cypher.

"Sssh, you want to awaken Mrs. Grayson upstairs? She might be hard of hearing, but that's a mite too loud even for her."

Riley grabbed a multicolored scarf draped on a wall lamp and threw it at Cypher, who applied the silky fabric to his neck to stanch the bleeding.

Cypher's flat was a small one-bedroom, with a living room full of overstuffed furniture and odd tropical touches—a painted wooden parrot, a steamship Caribbean poster, a fisherman's net. A narrow kitchen, the sink brimming with dirty dishes, was to the side, an even narrower loo next to that, and at the far end, a spotless bedroom, the bed sporting a chenille bedspread with the letters L-O-V-E stitched in red yarn.

"What is there to talk about?" said Cypher, sitting at an easy chair so large he seemed even smaller than his usual diminutive self. "Your usefulness is over."

Cypher eyed a lamp table that he had strapped a handgun underneath, just for occasions like this. If he could reach it while Riley was unaware, he could shoot him claiming he was a robber and that he didn't know him, the cut on the neck proof of that. His work for the Special Branch would take care of the following investigation about his possession and use of the gun.

Riley smiled, grabbed a rickety bamboo chair, straddled it with its back facing Cypher.

"Not at all. Who would be a better killer than one that's supposed to be dead? That's what you're going to tell Fairfax. But you're still going to put me in touch with the German and his weapon. Just because I'm dead doesn't mean I don't want the job, hey? I'll be the avenging ghost, you might say."

"You want to proceed with the . . . elimination?"

"That's a funny one. Elimination, yes, that's one piece of shite we have to dispose of. My brother and many others died because of him, so of course I will carry out the job. Now tell me all about it."

"All right, but first satisfy my curiosity."

"I don't have to."

"Then kill me right now and be done with it. But you'll never know the who, the where, or the when about the German and his weapon, now, will you?"

Cypher stared coldly at Riley, a cobra and mongoose staring contest, then they both smiled simultaneously, as if accepting they would have to work together.

"Sorry about the cut," said Riley.

"No, you're not," said Cypher. "How long have you been keeping an eye on me?"

"Since we met, you little fuck. Did you really think it was going to be that easy?"

Cypher shrugged. "You're Irish. Your people are not exactly known for their smarts."

Riley slid off his chair, walked over to Cypher, and slapped him so hard he fell to the ground—just as Cypher wanted—an arm's length from the revolver strapped to the underside of the table. As soon as Riley turned to go back, he'd jump for it.

"You little monkey bastard, you ever insult my people again, I'll slit your throat," spat out Riley.

"Fine, fine, my apologies," said Cypher, readying to leap for the table—but instead of returning to his chair, Riley stepped back, still facing him, towering above him.

"Talk to me like a man, if you ever learned how to do that."

"I might," said Cypher, refusing to get up from the floor, "not that you can give me any lessons on it, you Irish poof."

Cypher was hoping Riley would strike him again, pushing him closer to the table, and in that moment, he'd be able to get ahold of the gun. But Riley smiled. He crouched next to Cypher, his breath smelling of Guinness.

"You're trying to get me all worked up, aren't you? It won't work, mate. Now, let's pretend we're gentlemen like Fairfax and disclose our intentions, shall we?"

"Fine," said Cypher, rubbing his face, the blood from his cut staining his shirt. He slid away, edging closer to the table with the gun. "What do you want to know?"

"How did it all start?"

"How do things begin? Someone I know said there was a high-class fellow had a special job, needed a go-between. I put the two of them together. You know how that goes. They picked you from New York, brought you over. It's a conspiracy, and you're the muscle, chum."

"What about the Germans?"

"My job puts me in touch with all sorts of people."

"Nazi spies?"

Cypher shrugged. "Who else? Spaghetti lovers are no use to us anymore. Berlin's sending this chum over to help set up the secret weapon."

"Where's the weapon right now?"

"In the docks. It arrived yesterday. It was sent via Honduras. My part of the bargain, I'm supposed to get it out."

"When is the German agent coming?"

"In three days."

"Where?"

"He's to come to my office in the P.M. Get it?"

"Clever."

"There's another thing."

"What?"

"They're sending a second man to also help with the weapon. I'm supposed to meet him at Waterloo Station."

"When is that?"

"Day after tomorrow."

"Name?"

"Goes by Mueller."

"Password?"

"The weather in Sula."

"The Roman general?"

"We do have an education, don't we? San Pedro Sula, main port of Honduras."

"The answer?"

"Twenty-eight centigrade."

"Good. What does he look like?"

"Don't know. He's supposed to wear a white rose, stand under the clock. Damn Jerries read too many spy novels."

"Fine. You shall be there to meet him. The plan will go on as is. Fairfax will have his perfect alibi. Tell me, how much is he paying you?"

"Four thousand quid."

Riley whistled. That was a working man's yearly salary. "I'm going to need me some of that to leave England after the job's completed." Riley got up, turned his back to go into the kitchen. "Now, I'm hungry. Been out in the cold for days without a solid meal. What have you got?"

Cypher leapt to the lamp table, overturning it, and reached for the gun strapped to the underside. Gone, the remaining piece of tape dangling like a broken rosary string beneath the table.

"You're looking for this?" said Riley, taking out the Luger from his waistband. Cypher turned around, shaking uncontrollably as Riley calmly walked back to him, gun pointing straight at Cypher's head.

"You prepare the front door but neglect the bathroom window—what is wrong with you, man? It was so kind of Mrs. Grayson, your landlady, to tell me all about that window, how it never shuts down completely, when I came to investigate the gas leak. Shame I had to put her down, I liked her. Some things can't be helped, can they?"

"No," said Cypher, "I suppose they can't. Look, I, I have more money, I have . . ."

"I'm not interested in your money. This is a war, remember? And you are my enemy, even the Church says so."

In one swift move Riley dropped the gun, flipped open his knife, and sliced through Cypher's neck. The severed jugular spouted blood like a fountain, spraying the walls a crimson shade. Driven by Riley's strength, the blade cut through the neck muscles and spinal cord of the little man. Cypher's head tumbled to the ground.

Riley picked up the head, whispered at it. "Now, if you don't mind, I must go visit Mrs. Grayson and stay there a while. Her death was not half as messy as yours," and tossed the head down.

CHAPTER TWENTY-THREE

LADY CLEMENTINE CHURCHILL was dreaming about sex, dreaming about it in a way that she never allowed herself to think about during her waking hours. In fact, even in her dream she was carrying over some of the same restraints and inhibitions she suffered under when awake.

She would not let the handsome young hussar in his shining armor touch her sex, even after he had rescued her from the sightless monster in the crystal greenhouse with the wild profusion of orchids. She only allowed him to caress her budding breasts under her nightgown—for in her dream she had become fourteen again.

Although time and again the hussar ran his hands down her thighs, which quivered with pent-up lust, time and again she pushed them away. Yet he would not give up, his hands wandering to her crotch, and each time she'd push them aside with less enthusiasm, feeling her whole body swept up in a pulsating fever of desire, until finally she let him touch her and he drew out his long shiny sword from his scabbard.

She trembled on seeing how long it was, and then he

stabbed her with the sword, plunging it deep into her entrails, and she writhed in painful pleasure and gasped as the hilt bumped into her while bombs boomed in the far distance and the glass panels of the greenhouse shattered and . . .

Lady Churchill awoke to find herself in her bed at Chequers. She groped the pillow next to her, hoping to find her pug sleeping soundly, but then remembered Winston was in London for a meeting—and that she still had not forgiven him.

Née Hozier, Lady Clementine had been born of a noble but impoverished family. Before her marriage she had suffered the indignity—for a woman of her class—of having to teach French part time to put food on the table. Her horror of penury now was heightened by her husband's aristocratic disregard for the cost of living. As he always reminded her, he was like Oscar Wilde, easily satisfied with the very best.

Winston seemed to accumulate charges as he did extra pounds with the sheer extravagance of his daily living. Silk underwear because he had a "delicate cuticle," custom-made shoes because he had trouble walking, bespoke shirts and suits to properly dress as a politician, an unending forest of cigars, a flood of liquor and champagne. And to make matters worse, his gambling!

You would think that with the war and all, the creditors trying to collect his debts at the casinos of Montecarlo and Biarritz would have had the decency of staying their collection efforts until the war ended, she thought. But as she reminded herself, money has a life of its own and cares nothing about men's armed conflicts.

The casinos had sold their debt to a Swiss banker—probably backed by the Nazis—who was pressing the case in Chancery Court. Twenty thousand pounds, now where was one to obtain such a fortune! True, Winston's books were selling, but the sheer expense of keeping Chequers running, as well as Chartwell and the flat in the city and the host of servants, and the children, Randolph, Mary, Diana, always with their hand out, was more than any woman could bear.

The enormous amounts Churchill owed rose before Clementine like creatures in the night, and she earnestly wished for some magic potion, some lamp she could rub, some knight in shining armor like the hussar she vaguely recollected she had been dreaming of. It then came to her.

A loan.

A loan until the war was over and Winston had the time to write his way out of his troubles again. Yes, most certainly, that was the answer. Lord Beaverbrook, with his *Daily Express* and his Canadian paper mills. Or the American financier, Bernard Baruch, or any of his wealthy friends. If Winston would not do so, then she would approach them.

They can afford it and will be too embarassed to say no. And with that comforting thought, a plan already gestating in her troubled mind, Lady Churchill turned back around in her bed, closed her eyes, and forced herself to fall back asleep.

———

BACK IN LONDON, her equally troubled husband could not sleep so easily either. Not only was the onerous weight of the war effort trying on him, but also all the maneuvers that he had to employ to prod the sluggish bureaucracy to produce more armaments, deliver more food, prepare the population for the lonesome struggle against Hitler's nightly bombardments.

Now, to add to the number of calamities he faced every day, the appeasers had achieved the magical fifteen-percent threshold to show him the door and had sent their letters of no confidence to the 1922 Committee. A vote would soon be taken of the Conservative rank and file as to whether he was fit to stay at 10 Downing Street. And this right in the middle of the bloody blitz.

Already former Prime Minister Lloyd George was spreading word that he would be able to make peace with Hitler on the most favorable terms for Britain. And the Cunning Fox, as Churchill called Fairfax, was running around contacting the Italians to act as intermediaries for a peace treaty, chatting up the appeasers, even getting the king himself to join in his cockeyed plan. As if Hitler would respect whatever piece of paper he signed, thought Churchill. Peace with that madman would last only a couple of years, if not months, until he subdued the Russians and moved to swallow England and her empire.

Churchill had heard rumors bruited about that there was no bottom to the depths Fairfax would go to oust him, but Churchill refused to believe a man of his class would indulge in such base acts. He briefly remembered the warning Thompson had given him after seeing in London the mad Irishman who tried to kill him in Cuba. Bah, thought Churchill. Even if he has come over, there is no evidence the man is involved in anything here. The episode in Havana now seemed to Churchill as if in another lifetime, replete with song, dance, peril, and romance, like a fanciful novel by Conrad or Maugham.

But there was still the boy, he told himself, a remembrance of sins past.

He wondered if there was some sort of cosmic law of retribution, what the Indian fakirs called karma, that for every violation of the universal order there was a consequence, a price to be paid. But then again, he smiled, there is always what Oscar Wilde said, no good deed goes unpunished.

At that point Churchill stopped his free association of ideas, which he indulged in when he couldn't sleep. Ordinarily those thoughts would eventually turn into softened images that opened the door to blissful if brief sleep. But tonight all they brought was more tension from decisions to be made.

He got out of his cramped bed in the basement of 10 Downing Street and moved to a nearby bar cart, pouring himself a dram of Johnny Walker, just enough to still the nerves that came upon him when he thought about the Cuban boy.

His silk Chinese robe rustled softly as he carried the tumbler to his easy chair and automatically reached for a cigar. He stopped when about to light it, looked at the band, chortled. "To Prime Minister Churchill, defender of liberty, from his Cuban friends." The puro was one of a batch that Batista had sent him on taking office. MI5 had insisted on testing them for poison, and it had only been in the last few days that they'd released them.

Cuba. For a moment he thought back to when he first visited the island in 1895, learning about siestas, rum cocktails, and cigars, the Cuban rebels fighting the Spanish as fiercely as the English the Germans now. Only the Cubans were fighting for their own country, in their own land. Let us hope that parallel does not come to pass, he thought, lighting the extra-long cigar named in his honor.

Think man, think! About the vote. Thompson must have found out about Erskine's French filly, like I asked him to. I'll ask for his report. Neville knows that I know about him and that affair; I will lean on him to support me. The Committee vote . . . I will ask for an immediate vote. I'm scheduled to show the American, Hopkins, our naval forces at Scapa Flow this week, but that can be delayed whilst I handle this.

What about the boy?

Well, he certainly looks like you, Winston. That night when you had him out of the rubble, it was as unsettling as watching your own reflection from sixty years past, transported to present time. Is he a symbol, I wonder. That all the hopes and strengths and mad resolve of my childhood that were covered over by the crumbling apparatus of civilization, which almost took my life, have now been uncovered? Or is he the fighting spirit of England, which lives on, despite the carnage and willful destruction of this attempted German Götter-dämmerung?

Or perhaps he is troubling you simply because he is, he might be, your son. I suppose I should have a blood test done, like Chaplin after his affair with that soubrette.

That won't do. If word were to get out, the scandal would be the end of my government—and mayhap my marriage as well. No, I don't think it would end my marriage. Clemmie the pussy kitten is, no matter what, devoted to me. Although it would be a very cold hell for a very long time. But I fear the public, not to mention the Cunning Fox and his band, would clamor for my head. Oh, the hypocrisy of it all, as if Neville and Fairfax and the rest had not sired their own little out-of-wedlock bunches.

All right then, if the boy is mine, I do have a moral obliga-tion to take care of the little bastard. The little orphan bastard. I should contact his great-uncle, President Zayas. No, no, he died a few years ago, I recall the notice. Then it would be his cousins. But who knows what tender care, if any, they would give the poor child.

No, I must do the right thing and ask that the blood test be done. But are you sure, Winston? It was only a few-weeks-long affair . . . it only takes one successful insertion for the magic of Nature to occur. Your own father had one such, did he not? Not certain. And Clemmie herself, who was her real pater? Yes, yes, many of noble birth have done the thing. But the greatest—Marlborough, Nelson—acknowledged their failings and accepted the consequences.

Well, perhaps if done discreetly, Thompson can manage it? I'll have Thompson look into it. But I should go talk to the child myself first and question him now that he's up and about. And talking. Yes, that's the answer. We'll speak French. That's what we shall do. I'll schedule a visit.

And with that resolution Winston Churchill, the besieged leader of the equally besieged last hope for freedom in Europe, put out his cigar, downed his Scotch, and slipped back into bed. He was sound asleep and snoring within minutes.

CHAPTER TWENTY-FOUR

"WELL, WHAT DO YOU THINK, THOMPSON?"

Churchill's bodyguard put down the secret report, took a deep breath, looked out the window of the office in Wormwood Scrubs at the small park across the way.

Calla lilies are in bloom. I wonder how ours are doing in Manchester, he thought, remembering the small garden he had so carefully planted before Cuba and the end of his marriage. At least now I have Mary. It's true, the love of one good woman is enough to make life worth living.

"I think I would like to speak to him," said Thompson, turning his head to look at the florid face of Sir Humbert Hopkins, the MI5 director of espionage cases. The faint smell of porter and gin already wafted from Hopkins at ten in the morning, an archipelago of broken capillaries on his wide, pink nose a testament to a lifetime love of Bacchus.

"You shall, of course. I must say it was quite a surprise, stumbling onto this chap. Coming in from Ireland on the train, just like any other commuter on the Brighton Express, what? Not quite proper," Hopkins sniffed.

"You mean the forged papers?"

"That. You'd think Jerry would be able to print better pass-ports—and send someone without a blasted accent. If that's the sum of their talent, I do believe we stand a chance."

"Tell that to the lads come home from Dunkirk with their tails between their legs—or to the bombers every night."

"Yes, well, I'm only talking about our people; we are a cut above them. As I said, if not for the PM's request, we might have let him go and then tailed him, like we've done with everyone else. You are aware that we know everyone from there who's here, don't you? Every single damned spy of theirs, we know who they are and what they're up to."

"With all due respect, Sir Humbert, that's an awfully cocky thing to say."

"Well, it's the truth, and as they say, and the truth . . ."

"Shall set you free, of course, yes. Now, may I see this man?

"Yes, but one thing. We want to be certain this will not be used in a disinformation campaign to influence certain, ahem, political issues now pending in Parliament."

Thompson swiveled his head so forcefully he felt a kink in his neck. "Just what exactly is it you mean?"

"Well, we have become aware of certain discreet inquiries you made regarding Major Robert Erskine, and we were wondering whether his personal life might affect an upcoming vote of the 1922 Committee. As might this case."

Thompson stood up. "Sir Humbert, you can rest assured that wherever inquiries I made were authorized by the prime minister, and in any case, again, with all due respect, sir, none of that is of your concern."

Hopkins graced Thompson with a condescending smile. "You're wrong there, Thompson. At MI5, everything in England is of our concern. Always was, always is, always shall be."

He stretched over his desk, retrieved the report from Thompson's hand. "We are granting your request to interview this man, but I advise you, this better be for security reasons and not political objectives. This office is not partisan. We do not conduct political investigations or autos-da-fé. We are devoted solely to the safety of the kingdom."

Hopkins rang a small silver bell on his desk. In seconds, a young, plain-faced woman appeared.

"Miss Thimble, please escort Inspector Thompson to the interrogation room."

"Yes, sir."

The girl led Thompson down a set of stairs to a maze of narrow windowless corridors and closed doors, the whole smelling of fresh oil paint, turpentine, tobacco. She knocked at one door. A burly bald man in a siren suit opened the door, blocking the entrance with his massive body.

"Inspector Thompson to see the detainee," said the girl.

The man nodded, extended a callused, bruised hand. "Papers, please."

"Really!" said Thompson, annoyed, as he handed over his identification.

"Regulations, sir, no one's exempt. If King George were to show up, I'd still 'ave to ask him for it."

"What about her?" said Thompson, nodding at the girl.

The man cracked a wide smile, as menacing as the dark pits of his beady eyes. "We know Miss Thimble quite well, now don't we? She's quite welcome anytime." He looked over Thompson's papers quickly, gave them back.

"You may come in."

Thompson entered a small, windowless cell, in the middle of which stood a long rectangular table and several chairs. A single yellow light illuminated the room, the bricks of the back wall gleaming with condensed moisture. At a chair by the table sat a small, dark-haired man, wearing rimless eyeglasses and a ratty mustache. Dressed in a wool suit with a regiment tie, he looked disheveled and used up, the folds of his shirt collar showing dirt and dried perspiration. His frightened blue eyes darted immediately to the door and Thompson.

"I am free to go?" he said, with a marked German accent.

"I don't think so," said Thompson.

"I have cooperated, I have been made a promise, I want to obtain that which I have been promised," said the man, fear piercing each of his words.

The girl snapped back at the man in a torrent of German, the bite of her reply stinging even to Thompson's monolingual ears. She looked at Thompson.

"I was the translator for the questioning of this man. I can assist you, if you wish."

The cold eyes of the girl reminded Thompson of a female jail warden he'd once met—stout and blowsy, whereas this girl was thin and shrewish—but both with such venom in their eyes they could cause the most hardened prisoners to tremble.

"Thank you, but I'd rather speak to him alone, if you don't mind."

"Oy, we can't do that!" the guard began to say, but the girl whipped around, and her withering glance quieted the man. She looked again at Thompson.

"Of course. I'll be right outside, should you need me," she said.

"Me too!" said the guard, who looked at the girl and lowered his head. "I just said me too," he whispered, almost but not quite apologetic.

They closed the door behind them and locked it, the click resounding loudly in the cold, damp room. Thompson glanced around, spotted a ventilation grill. I wager they're recording this, he thought, then sat at the table, across from the man.

"My name is Walter Thompson. I am in charge of security for Prime Minister Churchill. I understand there's something you'd like to tell us."

"Ja," said the man, sweat beading his forehead. "My name is Hans Mueller. I was sent by the Abwehr to help with a plot."

"What is the plot?"

"To kill Prime Minister Churchill."

Thompson took in the man's fear-laden eyes, seeing his obvious desire to please mingled with the premonition that no matter what he said, death was the only door waiting open for him. Thompson nodded, willing his features to remain calm and noncommittal, even as he felt his hearty racing. If true, this was even bigger than the last attempt on Churchill in Cuba. That had been just one man. This could be wider, deeper. Deadlier.

Thompson reached into a pocket, took out a pack of Woodbines. "Cigarette?"

"Ja, please."

Thompson offered the pack, but the man lifted his hands halfway, showing he was cuffed and chained to his metal chair. Thompson got up, knocked at the door. The guard opened, the girl standing some distance away, leaning on the wall and smoking. The faint outline of lipstick smeared the guard's mouth.

"Please remove the restraints from this man."

"Can't do that, governor, it's . . ."

"Go ahead, Miles," said the girl, a look of cold mischief on her face. "Mr. Churchill's bodyguard has our full cooperation."

"If you say so, Miss Thimble," said the guard, looking not too happy about the order. He entered the room, removed a large key chain from his belt, took off the handcuffs, then turned to Thompson.

"It's on you, governor, he's all yours," snapped the guard.

"Thank you," said Thompson, closing the door after the

guard. The detainee rubbed his wrists, his face relaxing into wary gratitude.

"The cigarette, please?" he said.

Thompson shook one out, gave it to the man, who put it to his lips with trembling hands. Thompson took one for himself, lit both, let the man inhale a couple of puffs to calm himself down, then Thompson took out the small leather-bound notebook he always carried along with his Waterman pen.

"I shall be taking notes to make certain I have all the details right. Hope you don't mind," he said, being deliberately polite to gauge the man's reaction.

In Thompson's experience, if a suspect objected to the notes, that meant his story was not well thought out, which meant it was either false or incomplete. If the suspect agreed and praised the notetaking, it meant the story was either a complete fabrication that had been carefully rehearsed, or a rhetorical weapon to be used later against an undisclosed enemy. But if the story was completely true, the interviewee would pay no attention and just launch breathlessly into his narrative, saying every so often, make sure you write that too.

Mueller did none of those things. He only nodded nervously, taking a deep drag of his cigarette, his eyes shining with understandable concern.

"Good," said Thompson, "let's make ourselves comfortable, shall we?"

Thompson got up and took off his jacket, revealing his shoulder holster with his Webley .38 revolver, so Mueller would see he was no ordinary Whitehall pencil pusher.

"Now," said Thompson, sitting down again, taking up his Waterman. "Let's start with some personal information. What is your name?"

"Hans Mueller."

"You are a German national, are you not?"

"I am."

"When and where were you born?" asked Thompson, leading him to a series of questions revealing the man had been born in Cologne, was in his mid-40s, a member of the Nazi party although not a very fervent believer, with a wife—Helga —and two small children, Dieter and little Hans. They chatted for a while and Mueller began to relax, telling Thompson about the economy under Hitler, how different it all was from before 1933 when people were starving and there were no jobs to be had. Now everyone who wanted a job had one, there was plenty to eat, and Germany was winning the war.

"So, when you were asked to come here, I assume you couldn't say no."

"That is correct."

"I understand. And what you were asked to do was to help with this plot to assassinate our prime minister."

"Ja."

"And you were sent from Berlin to aid in this plot."

"That is correct."

"What was your part going to be?"

"I was to help put the murder weapon together."

"Weapon? What sort of weapon?"

"That I do not know. But I am a trained mechanical engineer from the Berlin Mechanical and Metallurgy Institute of Higher Studies. I have expertise in many fields related to war machinery. The Abwehr thought I should come help if there are mechanical problems."

"I see. Who were you going to help?"

"A man named Cypher."

"Cypher is the killer, or are you?"

"Nein, nein, nein. I am no killer. I am engineer. I draw plans, I prepare tools, I repair. Killer I am not."

"But Cypher is?"

"I do not know. I was informed only Cypher, the man, he would put me in touch with the killer, who will use the weapon we are using for the mission."

"The mission being . . ."

"The killing of Prime Minister Winston Churchill, naturlich."

"I see. All right, then, suppose we start from the beginning once more and you tell me . . . no, first, one thing. When is this assassination going to take place?"

"Soon."

"How soon?"

"This week, next, no more. Before Operation Sea Lion."

"Before the invasion of England by your Nazis?"

"Ja. Soon."

"And why are you telling us now?"

"Why? Why?"

Mueller removed his glasses, his blue-gray eyes shining with desperation.

"Because I want to live! I did not choose this assignment, it was chosen for me. I renounce the National Socialist Party! I renounce Adolf Hitler! I renounce mein Deutschland! I want to live, that is the why! I am glad you have found me because I want to live!"

"Get ahold of yourself, Mueller. No need to shout. We are civilized people here. Now, as I said, let's begin from the beginning."

Mueller spoke for four hours straight, spinning a different story that began with his poverty-stricken childhood in Cologne and ended with the guns of the Abwehr pressed against his back and putting him on board a cargo ship from Hamburg to Dublin. He decried Nazism as a cancer, a growth that everyone in Germany at first thought benign, perhaps even beneficial for the health and wealth of the nation, but that by the late 1930s had become a sickness that afflicted everyone.

Thompson paid no mind to Mueller's disclaimer of anti-Nazi sentiment, nor how he had helped Jewish colleagues to hold on to their jobs when the SS cleansed the steel factory he worked at of non-Aryans. Neither did Thompson believe Mueller's declaration of love for his two young children back in Frankfurt, who waited for their papa to come home from his assignment. Typical German sentimentality. None of that was even of tangential interest, but he had to suffer through all of it before Mueller finally arrived at the details of the plot.

As Mueller was told, the plan was concocted at the highest level of government, perhaps even by Hitler himself. Nazi sympathizers, IRA members, had been alerted in Ireland to welcome him. They hid him in a stash house and then put him on the train where he was found—as Thompson knew from the report, courtesy of an anonymous tip and a vigilant train conductor.

Cypher, the go-between, was to meet Mueller at Waterloo Station at six o'clock on September eighteenth. If no contact was made that day, he was to continue trying at the same time on each successive day at the same time until the twentieth. If still no contact by then, he was to head back to Dublin and enter the German Embassy.

At the end of the interview, having smoked the full pack of Woodbines and drunk a tepid tea Miss Thimble had brought down, Thompson was convinced the man was a fake, a diversion, to what purpose he did not know but a fake all the same, perhaps to throw MI5 off the trail of a real plot.

Thompson slapped close his notebook.

"Well, I have given the cooperation to you. Will you the promise keep?" said Mueller.

"I don't know. What was the promise?"

"I am allowed to stay here. New identity, new papers, ja?"

"What about your children and your wife, Hans?"

Mueller shrugged. "Bah. She is a whore and loves the Nazis. The little ones, they are not even mine, she had them before me."

"What about everything you said before, how much you loved them?"

"They are better off without me. I will miss them, not she, but they I will miss. But I am here, and they are there. Zo, I have the promise, then?"

Thompson got up, slipped on his coat, sat down again. "I cannot say. It's out of my hands. But what I can say is that you are not being truthful."

"I have told you the truth! All the truth!" shouted Mueller.

"I don't believe you, sorry."

"What will happen to me?"

"You'll be detained, tried as a spy. If lucky, you'll be exchanged for others. If not, it's the hangman for you," said Thompson.

"That cannot be! I cannot go back, it will be the death of me! I was promised freedom with cooperation!"

"Then tell the truth!"

"I have, mein Gott, I have!"

"Sorry, I don't believe you."

Thompson's words finally got through to Mueller. The man's eyes went round with fear, his body shaking in an uncontrollable tremor. "I will be tried and hanged?"

"Most likely."

"Then I die my way," he said.

In a swift motion, Mueller moved his hand to his mouth, removing a capped molar, from which he extracted a small glass vial that he immediately crushed with his front teeth.

Thompson vaulted across the table to extract the remains of

the vial from Meuller's mouth, but it was too late, as the powerful poison took immediate effect and Mueller, frothing at the mouth, went into convulsions, fell to the ground.

Thompson bent over him, shouting: "Who sent you? Who's your real contact?"

Mueller grinned, in a rictus of pain, whispered "Heil Hitler!" and died with a final shudder.

CHAPTER TWENTY-FIVE

THE ROYAL PHYSICIAN, Sir Hugh Northrop, looked in the mirror and asked himself, not for the first time, if it was all worth it. The answer not forthcoming, he turned his eyes on his latest lover, the young Marquis of Hartshorne, sleeping off another night of drunkenness and revelry in the clubs and boites of London.

How long can I wait? Northrop asked himself. How long can anyone wait?

The only child of a well-off family of German origin, where Haut Deutsch was still spoken at the dinner table, the doctor was originally a trained psychologist. He'd studied with Alfred Adler and was imbued with the Austrian's theory of the will to power in humanity's constant struggle for supremacy. It was no surprise then that upon meeting a certain magnetic speaker in the home of a wealthy Viennese patient, Northrop was drawn to the life force that flowed unimpeded from that small man.

When the orator later turned his creative genius to political organizing, fashioning his party's flag with the ancient Eastern symbol of power while constructing his political platform on the objectification of Adler's ideology, the doctor became a faithful acolyte. He offered his services to the leader, wanting to spread the news of his doctrine among the people of his native England, but the farsighted leader had other plans for him.

Adolf Hitler told Northrop to abide, to wait for the moment when his sword would strike the final decisive blow. The Führer quoted the famous passage of that other great revolutionary who commanded his followers to go forth as sheep but with the cunning of the fox when preparing the way for the New Order. The doctor, brought up in the strictures of the High Anglican Church, with its emphasis on duty, loyalty, and obedience, agreed and abided.

As Hitler counseled, Northrop forswore psychology and became instead a general practitioner, the physician of choice to the top ranks of British society to which his money, breeding, and good looks gave him unimpeded access. His sexuality gave him entry to another subset of English life, the aristos who developed a taste for sodomy in the student halls of Eaton and Oxford. All the while Northrop waited, trying his best not to lose the faith, his hope that a rejuvenating government would smite the corruption and weakness of contemporary Great Britain and turn it into the virile, powerful society he had known in his childhood before Communists and foreigners corrupted it.

During all these years he'd only received one message from Der Führer after his accession to power in Berlin: stay away from Oswald Mosley and his social set. The doctor did as he was told, and after the war broke, he was grateful for Hitler's order, as Oswald and his Black Shirt followers were either in jail or in constant surveillance under new policies set up by Churchill.

When Northrop received that first phone call in the middle

of the night, and later learned of the brilliant plot devised by the leader himself, he was thrilled to finally join in the struggle. But in the lonely hours of the early morning, when the protective veil of alcohol vanished, the machinations of medicine were stilled, and life appeared with its naked face, he wondered if it was enough, if his part of the plan would be sufficient to bring forth the New Day.

He walked into his study, poured himself another Scotch, and once more reviewed the plan. He had to admit it was brilliant. If it succeeded England would no longer have to put up with the constant bleating and warmongering of that popinjay, that would-be Napoleon, that imitation Disraeli leading all to ruin and devastation. The doctor had his part, and he would carry it out, as ordered. In the meantime, it was all a matter of waiting, the time drawing very near indeed.

He heard the patter of feet on the polished wood floor. The young marquis, slender and graceful, walked into the study, naked.

"Something wrong?" asked the young man.

"Nothing really, thinking about work, that's all."

"Oh, you mean all the hypochondriac old biddies and beggars you tend to?" said the marquis, easing closer, his long uncircumcised penis swinging freely.

"Hardly beggars, old boy. If they were, they couldn't afford me," said Northrop, feeling his excitement rising again.

"Well, if you ask me," said the marquis, teasingly kneeling in front of the doctor, "they are all beggars, because they are always begging you for something."

"And you never beg?" said Northrop.

"Oh, no, dear. I take, like this," said the marquis, sinking his head into Northrop's crotch as the doctor sighed with immense relief.

———————

THE SIGHT of the long line of hospital beds made Churchill quiver, even after all his years witnessing war and slaughter from the Sudan to the Somme.

One would think that one would grow accustomed to the grotesqueries of armed conflict, he thought, the death and mutilation that follow the great clashes of civilizations. Yet perhaps it is a good thing that one's soul is not hardened to the plight of human existence—for if so, what kind of man is one? A bloody beast, like these Germans bombing innocent civilians just for being British, that's what, concluded Churchill as he walked briskly down the halls of Wanstead Hospital, stopping here and there to exchange a quick word with the wounded.

"Give 'em back some of what we got, Winnie!" shouted an elderly woman, both of her legs gone from a bomb, her face a map of cuts and bruises. Churchill tried to contain himself but felt the familiar flow of tears falling from his eyes, pent-up rage vibrating like a tuning fork in his body at seeing so many of his people injured and maimed.

"Leave it to me!" he shouted, as always, "leave it to me!"

Moved continually to tears, he shook hands and patted shoulders and gave words of encouragement for a half hour, then Dr. Patel guided him to a smaller ward where the most pitiable victims, children injured by bombs, were treated. On seeing him, older children cheered, while younger ones, and a few not so young, laughed and asked him for sweets. He promised they would be getting sweets as a prize for their bravery, then ordered Jock Colville, his aide, to make sure they would all indeed be gifted with, if not chocolate bonbons, at least Cadbury candies.

"I'll handle that, sir," offered Thompson, who, as was his custom, walked a few steps behind Churchill, his experienced eye constantly inspecting the surroundings, ever on the alert for any sign of danger.

When Thompson had informed Churchill of the plot against him, the prime minister had shrugged off the threat, again affirming that his time was not due yet. But he authorized Thompson to investigate further and not leave it all in the hands of the appeasers in the Security Service, who probably wouldn't mind him getting a one-way ticket to Valhalla.

Dr. Patel nervously steered Churchill, Colville, and Thompson down a narrow corridor to a small room off the children's ward.

"The subject is quite talkative," said Patel. "Do you speak Spanish, Prime Minister?"

"My French is good enough for that," harrumphed Churchill.

"Yes, sir. Sorry to say, I do not speak it. I speak German. But our staff, our nurses, some of whom speak Spanish, they say he also speaks some French and has recovered quite nicely. Almost completely, in fact," prattled Patel. "He asks for his mother, apparently."

Patel opened the door to the room. A white-garbed nurse by a cart was retrieving a bedpan with its contents. She blushed, nodded. "Prime Minister," she said, in a half curtsy to hide her excitement.

"Nurse Goodall, sir, our best. Educated in France. She can be your translator, if you wish," said Patel.

"The morning's bowel movement?" said Churchill, nodding at the pan, scrunching his nose.

"Oh yes, sir," said the nurse. "He devours everything set in front of him. He's quite healthy."

"Evidently," said Churchill. "Where is he?"

"Oh!" said the nurse. "He was just here . . ."

Churchill scanned the room. A nightstand next to an

unmade bed, an opened Tintin book in French on the sheets, a wrinkled pillow. He detected a rustling of the set of long curtains by a far window.

"Come out, come out, wherever you are!" said Churchill, remembering his own youthful escapades. *"Sortez, sortez, de là où vous êtes!"*

He dashed to the curtains and threw them open. Before him stood a boy of rosy cheeks, blue eyes, and reddish hair, beaming a mischievous smile. Churchill felt a shudder go through him, as if he were looking at himself almost sixty years before.

"Vous m'avez trouvé!" cried the boy.

"Certainement," said Churchill. *"Touché!"*

The boy giggled, stepped away from the curtains, and looked around at the newly arrived assembly—Churchill, Thompson, Colville, the doctor, and the nurse, all smiling at him. The boy's expression changed to wary puzzlement, and he addressed Churchill:

"Qui êtes-vous?"

"Je suis . . ." Churchill began to say, when he heard a commotion outside the room door, and a familiar woman's voice that cried out, "Where is he? Where is he?"

"Ma'am, you cannot go in there!" ordered another woman. The sound of footsteps rushing to the room. Churchill turned to see, as Thompson slid his gun out of his holster, ready to point and fire.

Through the door, followed by two agitated nurses, stepped Lena Zayas, née Magdalena Zayas Guzmán y Almejeira, niece of a Cuban president, former minister of culture in Cuba, and once Churchill's lover.

"¡Mami!" cried the boy, rushing to Lena.

She hugged her son, as Churchill quietly observed her. She was dressed in a white linen dress that heightened her reddish-brown tan and her wide green eyes; her auburn hair fell grace-fully on her shoulders, and for a moment Churchill wished things had turned out differently for them.

Thompson put his gun back in the holster. "Miss Zayas, good to see you again."

"Same here, Walter. You too, Prime Minister."

Churchill nodded, staring mutely at the beautiful Cuban aristocrat.

"Ma'am, you must leave at once!" barked one of the two nurses, grabbing Lena by the arm.

"No need for that, nurse," said Churchill. "Miss Zayas and I are well acquainted. Besides, she's the boy's mother, and who among us would have the heart to separate mother from child?"

"Of course, Prime Minister," said the nurse, "we only thought . . ."

Thompson came to the rescue, as the two former lovers stared at each other, smiling, each uncertain of what to do or say next. "That will be all, nurse. Prime Minister, would you like some privacy with Miss Zayas?"

"Yes. Yes, I would."

"Well, then everyone, if you will please follow me and exit the room. I'm certain Miss Zayas means no physical harm to the prime minister. I'll be outside in the hall if you need me, sir."

"Thank you, Walter."

"¡Mami, mami!" said the boy urgently after everyone had left, the Spanish words coming in a breathless rush, where have you been all this time, what had happened, I thought you were dead. Yes, yes, replied Lena absentmindedly, still staring at Churchill, let me talk to this gentleman. I'll tell you everything later. This quieted the boy, who, sensing something odd, glanced back and forth at Lena and Churchill. With a stern expression he addressed his mother, who laughed.

"If I may ask the source of the merriment?"

"My son says if we're going to stare at each other, we should sit down, that we look like two old statues in a museum."

"Well!" chuckled Churchill. "He's right about one of us. But you, my dear, are as lovely as ever."

They sat on the edge of the bed. Lena again urged the boy to be quiet for a little while, that she would tell him all about her adventures when she finished talking to the gentleman. The boy nodded, said a few words in Spanish to Churchill, and returned to his book of Tintin in the Congo.

"What did he say now?"

"He says that you're fat and you better be nice to me," said Lena, with a warm smile.

"Tell him not to worry, that I appreciate his candor and that I wouldn't dream of harming a hair of his mother."

"I will tell him. Later."

"But first the facts, Lena. We all thought you were dead after the shootout at the Nacional."

"I was briefly wounded, but I pulled through. They gave you the wrong information. Things were very hectic then."

"Evidently. I believed you were gone, so I left."

"I know. I've followed your career ever since."

"And not a word to let me know you were still alive?"

"Oh, Winston! Our affair had reached its conclusion. There was nothing left to say."

"What about the boy?"

"What about him?"

"Well," said Churchill, blushing, "he does mightily resemble me at his age, and I must say he has the same kind of precocity I had back then. I was the one who found him in the rubble of your embassy, you know, and when I did all the calculations, I thought . . ."

"That he was yours?"

Churchill nodded. Lena laughed, her liquid laughter as adorable as Churchill remembered.

"Men! You are so full of yourselves! No, Julien's father is Marcel Rignaud, a French diplomat. We met at the hospital in Cuba shortly after your departure. He was visiting a French tourist who'd been wounded in the revolt. One thing led to another and, well, here we are!"

"Julien is his name?" said Churchill, with a French accent.

"Yes, that is my name, sir, how may I assist you?" said the boy in French, looking up from his book. Lena and Churchill both laughed, and Lena told the boy to be quiet for a while longer.

"Fine, I accept your word. But where have you been? Everyone but your son died in the bombing."

"I was in France, helping people, Jewish artists and others, cross into Spain over the Pyrenees. It's a tragedy what's going on over there, Winston. The Nazis are rounding up the Jews, sending them to prison camps if not killing them outright. You have to do something!"

"The one thing we can do for them is win this war. We are alone now, Lena, and we must hold. They might even try to invade England, but our people are showing their spirit, and we will fight to the last man, the last woman, the last child, I am certain. Your husband, is he with us?"

"Yes, he's with the Free French—De Gaulle."

"*Ah, le grand Charles! Quel tourment!* But thankfully, he's with us. Didn't surrender like the rest of his countrymen."

With a sigh, Churchill stood up. "Well, it's been a nice chat, dear. Please call my office and ask for Colville, my assistant. We are setting up a new kind of overseas service, to fight the Germans in France and elsewhere. I think you'd be a good candidate, if it interests you."

"I believe it would. I will call him."

"Good," said Churchill. He glanced at the boy.

"And now, young man," he told the boy in French, "take care of your mother. She is a precious jewel."

"*Oui, monsieur premier ministre,*" answered the boy in French, saluting. Churchill nodded, wondered just how much of the conversation the boy had understood, remembering his own youth when he used to pretend not to hear in order to obtain information.

A knock at the door, a worried man's voice. "*Lena? Tu es là?*"

"*Ici,*" said Lena. In came a tall, rangy man, dressed in khaki uniform, with reddish-brown hair, fair complexion, and large blue eyes of the same hue as Churchill's—and the boy's.

"Prime Minister, my husband."

The man, recognizing Churchill, flushed, and snapped to attention.

"Sir, Lieutenant Colonel Marcel Rignaud, with the Free French Force," he said.

"At ease, Lieutenant. I have just been enjoying a brief conversation with your wife. We met while I was in the political wilderness back in Cuba."

"Yes, sir, she's told me all about it."

"Has she, now? Well, then, there's no more to be said. We should all return to our posts. There's a war waiting for us."

Rignaud moved to the bed to greet his son, who jumped up and down excitedly until his father calmed him down with some candies he took out of his uniform jacket pocket. Churchill glanced at the happy scene and again, for a moment, longed for what could have been.

Lena stood up, moved to kiss Churchill on the cheek, but he stepped back, offered his hand.

"We shall see each other again, I am certain."

"I would like that," said Lena.

Churchill waved at the boy. *"Adieu, mon petit ami."*

"Goodbye, Prime Minister," said the boy in English. Churchill smiled, seeing Lena hug her husband and her son. Rapscallion understood everything, he thought. Like father, like son. He is mine after all.

Out in the corridor, Churchill approached Colville. "Miss Zayas, or rather, Madame Rignaud, shall be calling you in the next few days for a post in Special Operations. Take care of it, won't you?"

"Yes, Prime Minister."

He turned to Thompson. "Did you bring one of my cigars, Thompson?"

"Sir," began Thompson annoyed, "I must remind you . . ."

"Yes, yes, of course, my apologies, you're not my manservant."

Churchill began walking down the corridor, head down, deep in thought, when he looked at Thompson, right behind him.

"By the way, is today the day?"

"Yes, it is, Prime Minister."

"Well, then, off to it, man. Good luck."

"Thank you. I will tend to that business as soon as we get you back to safety at 10 Downing Street, sir."

"Don't you ever rest, Thompson?"

"Occasionally, sir. But duty first."

"Yes, yes, the great Nelson said it, it's what England expects."

"That she does, sir."

CHAPTER TWENTY-SIX

SIX O'CLOCK IN the evening and the crowds kept surging out of the platforms at Waterloo Station—soldiers and sailors out for a night on the town despite the blackouts and the Blitz, families reuniting or sending their children to safer places in the countryside, office workers thankfully heading for home in the suburbs. A great mass of humanity that regardless of the nightly German bombing insisted on carrying on as if life were still normal, as if the prospect of losing life, limb, and home were natural consequences to be expected from life in London.

Thompson stood under the big clock at the station, wearing the white rose in his lapel that would identify him to the man he knew only as Cypher. In his bowler hat, pinstripe suit, and umbrella, he felt like an impostor, a man dashing to a costume ball. This was the uniform of Whitehall and The City, of bankers, civil servants, and commerce, folks who had an image to keep. MI5 had insisted he don the getup to make himself as unobtrusive as possible. But now, standing under the massive clock overhead marking 6:02, and observing the crowds,

Thompson thought a soldier's khaki would have made him blend even easier in the crowd.

Every two minutes he heard the rumbling of electric trains pulling into the station, interspersed with the hiss of hundreds of steam engines reaching their urban terminus after long trips from the furthest reaches of Britain. From the loudspeaker came a clipped voice announcing in monotonous tones:

"The train 34 leaving for Kimberly and Redding will leave from Platform 2, calling at Richmond, Twickenham, Witham . . ."

Thompson looked up discreetly at the catwalks above the platforms. About a dozen agents were in place watching him with binoculars, ready to spring to action whenever the man known as Cypher appeared. A half-dozen others were stationed around, standing by the florists and the newsstands, keeping an eye on the surroundings. In the distance, a mail train rumbled to a halt, attendants hurling sack after sack of unsent correspondence upon the platform.

6:03 p.m.

Still no sign of anyone approaching, thought Thompson. Where is this man? Is he even coming or is this just one huge ruse?

Thompson often had to turn and move aside to avoid blocking the people walking by all in a hurry, going to and fro, none of them giving him even a second glance. The loud-speaker broke in again:

"Special Announcement. Will Mrs. Perry, who's lost her son, Arnold, please go to the station master's office, which is opposite Platform 16? Calling Mrs. Perry, please go to pick up your son at the station master's office, opposite Platform 16 . . ."

Thompson looked around with rising anxiety, taking in the News Theatre across the way, its lights flashing for the evening's feature—*Tugboat Mickey*—which would show until the banshee sirens of the night alerted everyone to head to shelters before the bombing began anew.

He felt for his gun in his shoulder holster, an involuntary movement of frustration, which to a trained observer could signal he was carrying a weapon. He corrected it by patting his vest and taking out a pocket watch attached to a golden chain, as if a fastidious businessman double-checking the accuracy of his timepiece. He glanced up at the giant globe hanging above his head.

6:05 p.m.

A hand on his shoulder. Thompson whipped around. A smallish man in grimy shirt and jacket, tie askew, showed badly stained teeth in imitation of a smile.

"Sorry, guv'nor, didn't mean to startle you," said the man.

"Cypher?" blurted out Thompson, about to give the cue that would set the capture plan in motion.

"Begging your pardon, only wanted to know which way to the board. I'm checking the arrival time of the Windham local, you see," added the man. The loud creak of a mail train picking up the dropped-off bags of correspondence at the far end drowned out the man's words.

"What? What did you say?" asked Thompson.

"The board, guv'nor, for trains arriving and departing."

"It's over there," said Thompson, pointing to the other side of the station.

"Much obliged, guv'nor," said the man, walking briskly away.

Thompson shook his head discreetly, to signal it was the wrong man. A loud racket of the electric carts with the mail going by, a railroad employee at the head of the long, snakelike line blocking half the length of the station. A second man on a cart in the middle of the convoy looked all around, jumped off, and walked up to Thompson, who'd turned his back.

"I'm sorry," said Thompson, turning around and seeing the man approach, "I'll be out of your way . . ."

Thompson's bowler had slipped down over his forehead. When he adjusted it and glanced up, he took in at first the station worker's uniform, which he noted was an ill fit for the massive fellow before him, the sleeves were too short and the pants too loose. He looked up at the man's face—his surprise echoed in the other man's features.

"Riley!" said Thompson, immediately reaching for his gun.

Riley shoved him with all his strength and Thompson fell back, almost losing his balance. Riley spun around and ran off. Reaching the baggage train, he jumped on it, leaping from cart to cart. Once at the front cart, he pushed the driver to the ground and took the wheel of the convoy, accelerating to the maximum while swerving the carts to and fro, the mounds of mail and packages spilling out, striking people as they fell.

Thompson gave the signal and the half-dozen agents posted around the station ran after the convoy. Riley took out a handgun and fired into the air. The sound of gunfire and the rushing of the convoy and the spilling of packages strewn in the walkaways spread panic, people crying and shrieking, running in all directions, blocking the agents from reaching Riley.

Thompson ran alongside the convoy and, with a great leap, climbed onto one of the last wagons. Riley kept the convoy zigzagging throughout the station, knocking over people and bags. Thompson, barely able to stand, took a shot at Riley and missed—his firing only adding to the confusion, the screams of terror and panic.

Riley drove the head cart to a service entrance, crashing the convoy against the tiled wall, then, with a giant leap, dashed through the door. Oh, no, not this time, you shan't get away, thought Thompson, rushing after Riley.

Crossing the threshold, Thompson found himself in a small

chamber, with several station employees standing against the wall, arms raised. In the middle, a service elevator rushing down the shaft. Thompson glanced down the shaft and a bullet singed his bowler hat, which flew off his head. He stepped back, fired three shots at the elevator. Riley fired back, the echo a terrifying sound. Thompson turned to the employees, still standing with their arms raised.

"Scotland Yard," he said. "Where does this elevator go to?"

The oldest of the group, an overweight bald man in overalls, stepped forward. "Down to the tunnels, sir, they connect all the way under the station."

"Do they lead out to the street?"

"Yes, the loading dock at Nepham and the dock at Belvedere—one's for mail, the other's for . . ."

"Never mind that, is there another way down?"

"Those stairs over there," said the man, pointing to an iron door.

"Will the elevator stop anywhere else?"

"No, sir, she's a straightway drop, she is—no stopping till the end."

"Thank you," said Thompson, dashing for the heavy door, which he swung open, racing down a narrow stone staircase.

"Thank you, sir," shouted the man behind him, "we were all frightened and, God save the King! Gilbert, get . . ."

The man's voice was cut off as the door slammed behind Thompson, who frantically ran down the brightly illuminated stairs, taking the steps two and three at a time. He cursed the moment he'd agreed with MI5 to be the contact, since he'd been the last man to talk to the German spy. You'll be the perfect decoy, Hopkins had told Thompson. Besides, you have experience catching and disarming these fellows. They won't escape your grip, will they?

Now, while hurtling down the steps, he wondered if

perhaps this had all been planned, if he had been set up so the meet would fail . . . That makes absolutely no sense, he told himself, and put the thought out of his mind as he finally arrived at the last landing, only to find the sliding door of the service elevator raised, the cab empty. A short tunnel, lit by yellowish, dusty bulbs, opened before him. He could hear the slapping of shoes on the concrete ahead of him, running away.

He ran out to a high-ceilinged, wide chamber with two tiled arrows pointing in opposite directions—one to Nepham, the other to Belvedere. Thompson hesitated—which way?

A shot reverberated, bullet whizzing past him, ricocheting off the tiled wall. He glanced at the tunnel to his left—to Belvedere—and took off at a run, the echoing sound of Riley's footsteps not too far from him.

Another bullet, the sound of breaking glass, and his section of the tunnel went dark. He's aiming at the light fixtures over-head, Thompson realized. He glanced back and saw the fifty yards or so he'd run were all pitch black, and so was the stretch in front of him, light only shining about a hundred feet ahead.

Thompson raced on. He's got one more bullet left if it's a regular revolver, two if it's a Luger, he thought, running as if in a nightmare, where you're moving without getting anywhere.

Thompson felt his legs burning from the effort but willed himself to keep running as fast as he could. He glanced back and spotted a lone light heading toward him. Can't be him, he thought, when, as if in answer, he heard a shot and a scream up ahead. Thompson forced himself to run even faster. That's his last bullet, he thought. I hope.

The tunnel coursed into a dimly lit bend, with two different openings leading in opposite directions. In the middle of this crossway, a station employee on the ground, bleeding but still alive. Thompson ran up to him.

"Scotland Yard. Are you all right?"

The man nodded. "Bastard shot me in the shoulder, took my luggage cart."

"Which way?"

The main pointed at the tunnel to his left. "York," he said.

One of the workers from above ran in, wearing a headlamp, an ax handle in his hands.

"Gilbert Bundy, sir. There's more lads on the way, your men."

"Good. I will need that lamp," said Thompson. "And the ax handle, please."

Bundy gave the items to Thompson, who quickly slipped on the headlamp, grabbed the handle.

"Take care of this man. Any communications with up above?"

"There's a phone around the bend, sir."

"Call them up and have men meet me at the York exit immediately!"

"Will do, sir."

Thompson took off running again, hearing the slight rumble of the fleeing cart ahead of him, the lights all smashed by Riley as he drove by—the tunnel a long, dark nothingness, illuminated only by the faint beam of his headlamp.

The rumble of the cart ahead stopped. Thompson picked up the pace, thinking either the cart had run into an obstacle or Riley was ditching it altogether. He ran around another bend and up ahead found the cart, smashed into a wall. Up above, a faint light from an opening somewhere overhead—a fixed ladder on the wall leading up, Riley hanging from its last rung, waiting for him.

A shot.

The bullet struck Thompson's headlamp, glass shattering, the projectile bouncing off the metal, but the force of the impact threw Thompson to the ground. Wincing, he took out his gun with his right hand, holding the ax handle with his left, barely conscious. He fired the rest of his bullets, their report echoing mockingly in the empty tunnel.

"Damn you!" shouted Riley, as one of the bullets struck him in the ankle and he scrambled up the stairs. Thompson struggled to get up, then slipped and fell, striking the back of his head on the concrete floor, and blacked out, ax handle still in hand.

CHAPTER TWENTY-SEVEN

MARY LAYTON KNEW EXACTLY how Thompson liked his tea—tepid, with a slice of lemon, no sugar. She smiled as she prepared it and poured it into the Thermos container, thinking this was what he must have become used to during his days as a constable walking the beat. For her part, she liked her tea very hot and very sweet, with milk. That was probably why the two of them got along so well, she decided, they complemented each other—youth and maturity, sweetness and tart.

She screwed on the top to the container, cleaned up quickly in the kitchen, and dashed down to the basement of 10 Downing Street, where most of the government had moved as a precaution following the last nightly bombing. She passed several officials hustling by, strangely cheerful under the circumstances, considering how awful the war was coming along, with every day more news of further destruction and the constant fear of a German invasion.

They must know something I don't, she thought, even if all the documents and letters she typed up for the prime minister had nothing but urgent messages urging more production, more armaments, more assistance from the Americans.

She found Thompson still in his cot in the small chamber next to the map room where Churchill seemed to spend most of the daylight hours.

"Well, hello there, bright eyes," said Thompson as she entered. He still looked awful to her, bandages around his head from the impact of the bullet and the pieces of metal from the headlamp removed from his forehead during surgery.

Thompson put aside his copy of Gibbon's fifth volume, sat up.

"Hello yourself," she said, handing him the Thermos. "Here's your tea. Are you certain you're capable?"

"I expect so—the doctor has given me the go-ahead to resume duties."

"And the concussion?"

"A headache or two for the next few days but nothing to worry about. Only to call him if I see double again."

"You haven't?"

"It's all gone. See, I could even pick up my reading, right where I left it off, at the private life of Mahomet. Did you know that he had seventeen wives, and lived off dates and milk?"

She shook her head, grinned. "Oh you! As if we gave a fig for the Arabs! What could they ever do for us?"

She leaned over, gave him a quick buss on the cheek. "Now you be good and go slow, no use rushing back to work right away."

A knock at the door. Churchill pushed his pink face in. "Good morning. How's my favorite inspector?"

Mary jumped to her feet, blushing. "Prime Minister! Good morning." She turned to Thompson. "Well, I must be off, Mr. Thompson. I hope you enjoy your tea."

"Much obliged, Miss Layton," said Thompson, sitting up

straight in his cot, watching Mary bow her head to Churchill and scoot out of the small room.

"Thompson, have you gotten the news?"

"Yes, sir, I've been declared fit for duty again!"

"Oh, that. Well, congratulations, the benefit of being hard-headed. I meant about Erskine, the head of the 1922 Committee. Remember?"

Thompson frowned, nodded. That particular bit of sleuthing still nagged at him. He'd hated digging into a man's private affairs, but excused it, seeing how it would influence if not completely halt the war effort.

"I had a very interesting breakfast with him yesterday. Erskine was most reluctant to have the knowledge of his black mistress made public, much less the two mulatto children she's given him. He pledged to make every effort to convince the appeasers to withdraw their petition."

"That doesn't sound very cricket."

"Damn it all, Thompson, it's war, and all is fair. Incidentally, Bletchley Park is getting some encouraging news. Operation Sea Lion might be off."

"The Germans are calling off the invasion, sir? That's wonderful!"

"Not clear yet, but all the indications are they've changed their plans. It seems the house painter is after something called Barbarossa. One hellish toil after another. The devil never sleeps. We're keeping this confidential, of course. Can't let our guard down just yet. But we're grateful for anything we get, are we not?"

"Of course."

"Any word on the fellow that shot you, that Irishman?"

"No, sir. He was wounded, I know. Hopefully, fatally."

"Hmm, one can hope. That was wonderful work you did."

"Thank you, sir."

Churchill walked back to the door, looked behind him. "By the way, we're having a small get-together at Chequers with friends this weekend. Do you think you'd be up for that?"

"I've been cleared for duty, sir, I told you."

"I did not mean that. I want you there as my guest, Thompson, not as a worker. You deserve some time off. Get Jenkins to replace you. And bring Miss Layton with you, she's always cheerful company."

Churchill walked out of Thompson's chamber and headed to the adjoining map room to check up on the latest advance of the war, leaving Thompson grinning at Churchill's invitation— no use pretending in front of the master dissembler.

CHAPTER TWENTY-EIGHT

A FEW MILES AWAY, in a small brick building at Wapping that had survived yet another night of German bombs, Marcus Riley dragged his wounded foot inside Cypher's office. Thompson's bullet had gone through the fleshy part of his ankle, causing him pain but only a minor disability. After the encounter at Waterloo Station, he'd wrapped a bandage around his left ankle and hobbled back to the flat, just another wounded man in the war-afflicted city.

The fact that he had been discovered did not concern Riley to any great degree. No one had any idea where he was, and in a city of nine million people, with the confusion created by the bombing, it was highly unlikely that Scotland Yard would have enough men to track him down. The only man he thought would be stubborn in his pursuit would be Thompson, and Riley was confident that his wounds would keep the bodyguard out of commission a while.

For limp or not, Riley had no intention of walking away from his mission. He had come much too far to let some minor wound alter his plans. To him the assassination of Winston

Churchill wasn't just a revenge killing, it had become the central axis of his existence, the only thing he cared about. He would be doing all of humanity a favor by getting rid of the one man who was the only impediment to peace, a man who deserved to be killed for all the suffering and deaths he had caused the Irish people, Riley's family, and Riley himself. All Riley had to do was stay focused, and he would succeed. First thing was getting his hands on the secret weapon that the Nazis had sent Cypher.

Upon going through Cypher's papers, Riley was surprised at finding the bill of lading for the cargo with the weapon resting in the top drawer of the man's desk. It was if Cypher never expected to have anyone come after him or search his papers. Or as if he thought his cooperation with Special Services gave him all the protection he would ever need.

When he went to pick up the crate with the weapon, Riley encountered not a wisp of suspicion—the customs man only stamped the bill and asked for the ten pounds tariff. Riley hired a dray cart and, with the help of a layabout in the nearby dock, brought the crate back to Cypher's office.

Opening the crate, he was puzzled by its cargo—a collection of handcrafted tropical goods. Painted coconuts, colorful shells, wooden birds and frogs, fishing nets, coarse fiber mats, and the like stacked on what seemed nothing more than a collection of interlocking tubes, alongside a long reticle sight. He took the scope to the window, looked at the Thames through the lens.

Structures on the opposite shore jumped into view, seemingly as close as if just an arm's length away. He put down the scope and scanned the horizon, trying to gauge exactly where, in plain sight, was the bombed-out building with the Marshall's Biscuits mural on its half-standing wall that he'd spotted. He could not find it.

Riley scanned the horizon again with the scope, which had a rotating mechanism to pinpoint the focus. It gave him such a wide horizon of sight, he had to slowly adjust it a millimeter at a time to locate the building with the mural. Finding it, he slowly lowered the sight down to street level. He saw pedestrians walking around mounds of rubble from what he assumed had been the biscuit factory, again as if they were just across the street. Slowly moving the scope sideways, he spied a street sign—Gordon Road and Brayards Road.

He hobbled back to the desk, rummaged through the small bookshelf, found a map book of London. Opening the volume, he spread out the chart, searching for the intersection he'd just noted. Finding it, he measured the distance.

Five miles away.

Riley was stunned. To his knowledge, no one had ever made a telescope with a sight field longer than a mile. Which also meant that whatever the weapon was, it allowed its user to fire from an extraordinary distance. Long-range cannons could do that, but not any kind of handheld weapon.

He returned to the box and took out the pieces he'd assumed were tubes. Laying them side by side on the floor, he realized they had matched grooves and lands. When he assembled them, they interlocked into a long barrel, one of the pieces having notches to fit the scope. He mounted the scope on the back piece of the long barrel and, placing the tube on his shoulder, returned to the window, and pointed toward the city. He could easily sight St. Paul's, Big Ben, even the Houses of Parliament. Clicking the mechanism of the scope to its maximum allowance, he saw faces and could almost read the writing on the newspapers people carried on the streets of London.

Extraordinary, he thought. But what about the rest of the weapon? What is the use of such an incredible magnifying scope on a barrel without an action, a receiver, a trigger? And what sort of bullets will it take? And most importantly, how am I supposed to get the ammo? Did they send it as well?

Riley returned to the crate and took out more of the gimcracks, inspecting them closely. Four pairs of maracas rattled in a way that even to Riley's untrained ears sounded wrong. They were oblong in shape, with a long handle, the bulbs covered with a sheath of shells that made a grating sound for what was supposed to pass as a musical instrument. The maracas were also far heavier than any he'd ever handled.

He took off the sheath around the bulb of one the maracas, scraped at its black paint. German lettering was printed on the surface: Achtung! These are not maracas, these are grenades! On a hunch, he took the stripped maraca and inserted it into the back of the tube. The ersatz maraca went in easily, staying in place.

"Sweet music you will make, won't you, girls?" he said to the maracas.

He returned to the cargo. The fisherman's net, he realized, could be used as cover or camouflage, a wire effigy of some supposed African deity could be disassembled and made into a workable breech, while the trigger and the rest of the action were also disguised as curios for tourists.

Riley attempted to put the pieces together, but each time he did so, he found that he could not assemble them the way of ordinary weapons. There seemed to be some catch that impeded the total assembly—the sight was on the wrong side, the trigger and the barrel fashioned in such a way that the projectile would shoot backward. He tried all day to put it together, then finally gave up as night fell and the lights of London, which had earlier flared to life, began to be doused in expectation of the German bombers.

Riley took one last look through the scope, still fascinated by the sheer potency of the thing. To his surprise, he saw that the dimming light did not offset the view through the sight. This can't be, he thought, how can one see just as clearly in the dark? He turned the scope this way and that and found he had accidentally slid a hidden button that turned the sight into night-vision mode.

Damn Jerries, he thought, with weapons like this the bastards are sure to win.

He went to the small office kitchen to eat the last of the bangers Cypher had left in the icebox and returned to the window to wait for night. When the skies turned black and only a glimmer of moonlight broke through the low clouds, he glanced once more through the scope. Again he discerned shapes and people moving in distant streets. Then he heard the screeching sirens blaring the arrival of the German air squadron nearing London.

Riley pointed the scope at the sky. While nothing could be seen by the naked eye, through the scope he could clearly view masses of aircraft miles away and even each individual Iron Cross and identifying numbers on their fuselage. Grinning at his discovery, he was preparing to go down to the basement to spend the night in the shelter when there came a hurried knock at the door.

"Cypher? Open up, we haven't much time!" said a man with a plummy patrician voice.

Riley hesitated for a moment, debating whether to open or not, then, taking a chance, slipped Cypher's Luger in the back of his waistband and hobbled to the door. There stood Lord Fairfax, all six feet six inches of him, in evening attire, looking like a harried undertaker with a body to prepare. He carried a leather satchel in his good hand, the other hanging uselessly by his side.

Fairfax gave a start on seeing Riley, stepped back.

"Cypher's not here, my lord. How may I help you?"

Fairfax gave a quick nervous nod, his somber features quickly brightening into a smile of complicit recognition.

"You're the man," he said, without hesitation.

"So it appears."

"Is our business still on?"

"Most definitely."

"Have you received the merchandise?"

"I was just inspecting it."

"Good. Take this. It will assist you in your duties. It has instructions," said Fairfax, proffering the satchel. "The subject is hosting a dinner at his country residence this weekend in honor of an American visitor. Do it then. I'm enclosing the remaining half of the payment as a show of good faith. Cypher knows how to contact me once it's all done."

"That won't be necessary. Once the job is completed, I shall be traveling to warmer climates."

"Excellent. Good hunting, then," said Fairfax, who spun around and dashed down the rickety stairs. He bumped into an overweight man in a mechanic's suit trudging up.

"Hey!" said the man.

"Sorry," muttered Fairfax, who hustled out of the building. Riley had just closed the door when there came a second knock. What the hell, thought Riley, don't these chaps know there's a war going on?

Riley opened the door in a rage, faced a confused-looking, burly man in overalls. "What the bloody hell is it, mate?"

The man looked around, whispered in German: "Herr Cypher? I am der Mechaniker . . ."

"Hush, man! Step in, quick, we're about to get bombed!"

CHAPTER TWENTY-NINE

"THIS IS MY EMPIRE," said Beaverbrook, pointing proudly at the enormous press spewing miles of newsprint for that evening's edition of the *Daily Express*. "While England and Winston worry and fret about their possessions, I tend to mine, the world of news, politics, and ideas."

Lady Clementine smiled primly, at a loss for words to express her feelings.

Beaverbrook had already showed her his newsroom, the vast cavern with dozens of men at their typewriters and telephones, preparing articles for that evening's edition. He'd given her an extensive tour of the building, with its enormous library of clippings, reference works and research material, its Old Masters on the walls, its efficient cafeteria for the paper's workers and the luxurious dining room for the executives, and throughout it all, Lady Churchill had been torn by conflicting emotions.

She felt sincere admiration for what he'd accomplished, knowing of Beaverbrook's humble origins in the Canadian outback, of how through skill, guile, and ruthlessness he'd amassed first a fortune in Canada then jumped over the pond and become the most powerful press lord on Great Britain, and how now, with the war at its most incandescent point, he had become minister of aircraft production, the man whose efforts could well decide the fate of the empire.

But she also found herself puzzled why a man of such wealth and power would think so highly of something as trivial as newsprint, which, once read, as the phrase went, was fit only for wrapping fish. On a more personal note, she also wondered why it was that powerful self-made men tended to be so plain, so physically nondescript—and so short. Beaverbrook barely reached her shoulders, and she was hardly the tallest woman in her set.

Well, look at Winston, she thought, almost my height when we married but now has shrunk a good two or three inches. The fierce pugnaciousness of the height-impaired has changed the world, she concluded, then admonished herself to pay attention to the rest of Beaverbrook's impassioned speech.

"And I'll wager that my empire of words will outlast the physical empire of Britain," said Beaverbrook.

"Really," said Lady Churchill, skeptically. "But doesn't one depend on the other, or rather, don't you need the physical empire to sustain your business?"

Beaverbrook waved at the entire panoply of work before them, his eyes glinting with the sparkling confidence of the self-made.

"My lady, do not misunderstand me. I would gladly give up all these things to save Great Britain. My love of country is second to none, and I shall do my utmost to defeat the Nazi horde. I believe that is why Winston has placed his faith on me. But I am referring to the future, for I am sure we shall win this war, but what then?"

"Ah, yes, the future," said Lady Churchill, seizing her

opening, "the future is precisely what I wanted to discuss with you."

"Strangely enough, Lady, that is my exact desire as well. If you would be so kind," said Beaverbrook, escorting her to a sitting room a few steps away from the picture window facing the printing press.

The room was plush, discreetly lit, and quiet, as if the library in some distant manor where medieval manuscripts and Walter Scott novels were the only object of contemplation, instead of the logistical needs of a nation fighting for its survival. They sat at small Regency table on padded Louis XV chairs, and after a few pleasantries, Lady Churchill barreled straight to the point.

"The thing is, Maxwell, this war has cost us all, in lives, possessions, dreams even. I can hardly keep my eyes shut at night worrying about the latest bombing. Even at Chartwell I can hear the German planes overhead."

"Yes, this is certainly a costly war. I don't know how much Winston has told you, but our gold reserves are almost gone. We might have to declare bankruptcy if something is not done —and quickly," said Beaverbrook.

"Well, that is also our personal situation, Maxwell. What with the expense of hosting at Chequers—and keeping Chartwell, even though we've shut it down for now—we are, I'm afraid, at a loss. Literally. And frankly, I have come here to inquire if we could secure a loan to tide us over until the war is over—or rather, until we win this war and Winston can get back to his writings and sell books again."

Beaverbrook stared hard at Lady Churchill, his bald pate shining in the chiaroscuro of the gilded room. He looks like the portrait of Cosimo de' Medici in the Uffizi, she thought.

"My dear lady, I am afraid my answer is no," said Beaverbrook, looking not at all regretful in Lady Churchill's eyes—in fact, he seemed almost to gloat. She sat stunned, feeling her cheeks flush from the shock.

Seeing her reaction, Beaverbrook went on in as gentle a voice as he could muster. "It has always been my practice to never a lender, nor a borrower be, precepts I learned at the knee of my teachers back in Canada."

"Oh, dear, I'm sorry to have bothered you, then, you are so busy, I must be taking up so much of your time," said Lady Churchill, befuddled and embarrassed, rising to her feet.

Beaverbrook waved a solicitous hand at her. "No, please, Clementine, take your seat. I have a proposition that might satisfy us both."

Taking a deep breath, Lady Churchill sat, her back straight, features hardened in suspicion. "And what might that be?"

"Your memoirs, my lady. If you were to keep a diary of these war years . . ."

"I already do."

"Splendid! Then, you could use that for a book relating your life, your background, your romance with Winston, how you helped him win this war. If you would do that—well, then, we have a deal."

"Really, now?"

"Really."

———

LADY CHURCHILL WAS STILL TREMBLING from contained emotion by the time her chauffeur picked her up at the *Daily Express*. Beaverbrook stood at the front door bidding her goodbye, as the Rolls rolled away from the crowds of the city.

Dear, dear, thought Lady Churchill, forty thousand pounds. That should more than suffice. We'll keep Chartwell shuttered, all the same. And we can finally pay that pesky banker holding Winston's IOUs. But what shall I tell Winston? You know how he wants to be in charge of everything. Every little domestic detail is his purview. How shall I break this to him? How will he react?

CHAPTER THIRTY

THE TABLES at the large hall of the Savoy were all set for the convocation, with flowers from Suffolk and Cornwall and the fanciest china and silverware. The bar was arrayed with the finest liquors that could be procured despite bombing and rationing. Waiters and stewards were at their best in spotless uniforms, wearing their plummiest expressions of servitude, ready to cater a meeting of the most powerful political body in the land, the one that could topple a government, stop a war, and send a prime minister to a lifetime of political banishment: the 1922 Committee.

The doors opened and the hundreds of members of the Committee sauntered into the room, chatting about the latest disasters at home and the battlefront—all attributable to the man many aimed to crucify that day, the eternal bulldog of British politics, the seemingly irradicable figure who for so long had loomed so deviously over English history, from the last clashes of imperial arms in Africa to the current pathetic attempts to bring the war to Hitler.

The object of their contempt at that moment was in an

adjoining room, reviewing his notes for the speech that could save his career—and, in his mind, Western civilization. His aide, Jock Colville, would later write in his memoirs that Churchill did not appear nervous or agitated, but rather was his usual gruff self before speaking in public, wrangling with the language over the precise punctuation and the *mot juste* to the last minute.

Now Churchill looked up from his reading glasses, correction pencil in hand.

"Is Erskine there yet?" he asked Colville.

Coville stepped out of the back room, returned moments later.

"He's just arrived, Prime Minister."

Churchill nodded in quiet satisfaction, and then did something Colville had never seen—he handed him the text, which highlighted his accomplishments and minimized his failures.

"I shan't be needing this today," said Churchill. "They all know what I have done and what has been left undone. Let us walk calmly into the lion's den and see who takes the first bite."

Everyone rose the moment Churchill entered the hall. A few of his supporters clapped and the others, out of politeness —much like the killer apologizing for the bloody mess he's caused—applauded as well.

Thompson walked into the room at that moment, having checked and double-checked the locale, placing trusted officers from Scotland Yard at all the possible entrances, ordering them to pat search every single server coming into the room. He posted himself at the back, behind the smallest farthest table given to an MP from Thompson's own district.

"Thank you, gentlemen," said Churchill, raising his hands to stop the applause. "Thank you. Please, take your seats. I won't be long. Afterward, you'll appreciate the meal and spirits even better."

A few chuckles from the crowd. What is he saying, thought Thompson, this could be the end of his premiership. He glanced at the members, who looked equally intrigued.

"I appreciate greatly the honor you have done me by inviting me to address you today. It's not often done, and I am as grateful as that queen who thanked the guard for a handkerchief to blow her nose before he separated her head from her body."

Nervous laughter and grins from the members, who looked intrigued at Churchill, wondering what political legerdemain he was about to display.

"As I understand it, the moment I walk out of here, you will all take a vote to decide my fate—that is, you would, if all the conditions for such a vote were in place. So now I ask of the Committee President, Major Erskine, are all the letters in order? Has the requisite number of dissensions been tallied?"

Thompson and all the members of the Committee turned to the table where sat Erskine, a short, florid-faced man who looked flustered, his fingers constantly rubbing the edge of the white napkin on his knees.

"Yes, so it appears."

"Then, read it—let us hear the names."

"I'm afraid I cannot do that, Prime Minister. That information is confidential."

"Well, then, what is the exact number of those who filed their request?"

"I say, Major Erskine, with all due respect to the prime minister, this is of no concern of his," said a spindly older member, rising from his seat.

"Cannot a man about to be hanged know what the offenses are that justify such a grievous act of tremendous finality? In my case it is numbers that dictate the sentence, and I demand to know the exact figure," said Churchill.

"Ah, yes," said an increasingly agitated Erskine, "the honorable member from Leeds is incorrect. Whilst we cannot disclose the names, there is nothing in the rules that prohibits disclosing the numbers."

"What is it, then?" asked Churchill, his head low, cheeks flushed as if about to charge at Erskine.

"Sixty-five, Prime Minister."

"Sixty-five out of 435, is that not so?"

"Prime Minister, you know how many members there are in our party, yes."

"Those sixty-five are the votes in favor. You have a majority of one! Have you any who have changed their mind and asked to have his vote withdrawn?"

A hush came over the room. Erskine's cheeks flared a deep red; beads of sweat sprouted on his forehead.

"Yes," he answered feebly.

"How many?" roared Churchill, tearing into Erskine.

"One—we received notice last night. The number now is sixty-four," said Erskine, softly.

The room erupted in clamor and disgust. "Unheard of!" "Unimaginable!" "What the bloody hell!" "Shame!" "Shame!"

Again Churchill raised his hand, seeking to calm the members, who after a few more seconds venting their frustration quieted down.

"It is obvious you cannot proceed—and the name of that individual will never be known. The vote of no confidence cannot go on. But I have something I want to say to you."

The room went still, all eyes fixed on Churchill, who unbuttoned his jacket, revealing its red silk lining. Thompson scanned the room, wanting to make sure there would be no further surprises that day.

"I am a Tory. I always have been, even when I momentarily lapsed from virtue and crossed the floor to join the scallywags on the other side," said Churchill to scattered laughter, refer-ring to the time he'd joined the Liberal Party in 1904.

"But they and that other band of scoundrels are now our allies in our Wartime Cabinet, and this unity government must stay together to defeat the most horrific threat England has faced since the Spanish Armada. I know I was not the utmost choice for many of you, but remember, there were none who would take up the cross at that moment, when all seemed lost. I was called by England to do my duty, and I did so, proudly. A change in our governance now will be seen by the enemy as a sign of weakness, and their efforts will redouble, and the dreaded invasion shall come lightning fast, and we shall see the swastika hanging from Parliament and a puppet king dancing to the strings pulled from Berlin. We must stand together, or we shall surely perish together.

"So I say to you, go ahead, take your vote, do your utmost. If it be the will of the party, I shall resign on the spot, and return like Cincinnatus to plow my fields. Find someone else to lead this nation and preserve this empire, someone else to tame the gathering storm that will surely come to destroy us, someone else to summon the strength to triumph no matter the adversity, if that is your will. And rest assured that when the time comes, which it will, I shall be there, ready to drown in my own blood, fighting an enemy that gives no quarter. I will be doing my duty, as England expects everyone in this room and in this land to do. God save the king and God save England and the empire."

All the members of the Committee that moments before had been clamoring for his neck now stood up, cheering. "Huz-zah! Huzzah!" "Stay, stay!" began the chant, led by Erskine, who also pounded the table along with the rest of the exalted crowd.

Churchill nodded, smiled, and walked back to the adjoining room. Within a minute Erskine entered, beaming.

"The Committee has resolved to continue supporting your government, Prime Minister. It was practically unanimous. Congratulations!"

When Erskine left, Colville whispered to Churchill, "Maybe now you can put the appeasers down for good, sir."

Churchill lit a cigar, pensively, shook his head no. "I can't. It's live and let live. There's too many of them."

He paused, exhaled a cloud of sweet Cuban smoke, smiled. "But I might make a few exceptions."

CHAPTER THIRTY-ONE

THOMPSON WOKE UP WITH A START, drenched in sweat. He glanced around his small room in the basement of 10 Downing Street, still breathing heavily from his nightmare.

In his dream, security in the prime minister's residence had been breached. Assailants had entered the building with machine guns in a suicide mission that left no one alive, countless corpses strewn everywhere in the halls and offices. Thompson had run to Churchill's bedroom but Riley, who somehow had come in with the killers, was already there, waiting for him, a satanic grin on his face, a gun to Churchill's head.

"This one's for you, Walter!" said Riley, firing a bullet into Churchill's temple . . .

With a supreme act of self-control, Thompson regained his normal breathing, got up, looked at his watch. 5:30 a.m.

He recalled that Churchill had gone to bed around 3 a.m., following another tour of bombed-out sites, and after a couple of stiff drinks, giving instructions and processing orders before finally calling it a night. Thompson was so exhausted he had fallen asleep in his clothes. Now he took off his shirt, tie, and pants, put on a clean top, and eased back into bed.

It was obvious what his dream was telling him—he should not stop trying to find Riley, even if Special Services, Scotland Yard, and everyone else believed the worst had passed. The day after he'd been cleared for duty, he'd gone back to Wormwood Scrubs, again dealing with the same supercilious supervisor with the stiff starched shirt, signet ring, and smell of Beefeater and stout.

"I understand your concern, Thompson, but be advised we are doing everything in our power to apprehend this man," said Sir Humbert Hopkins. "God knows he's quite a scoundrel. You saw the papers, did you not? We had a man with a heart attack and a pregnant woman with a broken leg, in addition to the poor chaps working for the railroad. They were sworn to secrecy, spy business and all that, and the papers attributed the entire episode all to a deranged drunkard. Stuff and nonsense, but nowadays people will believe anything they see in print."

"I understand, Sir Humbert," said Thompson impatiently, "but what specifically are you doing to try and find him?"

"Come now, old man. Try and understand our situation. We are a city under siege. Hundreds of buildings are destroyed every night. It's hardly business as usual, is it? In the event, we have distributed flyers with a drawing of the man, a general description, you know the routine. Fortunately, we do have the Home Guard. Mayhap those chaps will spot him, because our own regular forces are stretched to the limit. Now, don't you worry, Thompson, you've done your duty, almost bought the farm, like the Yanks say. So go along, keep an eye on the PM as before. You are his bodyguard, after all. Leave the rest to us. We'll take care of it."

Like hell you will, thought Thompson, remembering the conversation. Again he was assailed by the feeling there was something else going on within MI5 and the Security Branch. Their efforts were slow and unavailing, as if deliberately ratcheting down the pace of the investigation, as if in cahoots with . . . no, that was not possible. No honorable Englishman would stoop that low, not in wartime. He pushed aside his suspicions and, getting up, took a quick bath, changed into fresh clothes, and walked up into the building proper.

Six thirty in the morning and 10 Downing Street was already abuzz with activity—the early shift of aides, secretaries, planners, counselors, military advisors, reporting to work at six thirty to catch up with the enormous, manifold aspects of the grinding, horrific war, as well as to match Churchill's prodigious energy, which seemed inexhaustible in his flood of memos, instructions, orders, and observations about every aspect of government.

Thompson caught up with his second, Brandon Jenkins, getting his morning tea in the staff kitchen. He told him he was going out and to please keep stay close to the PM, even though Churchill was not scheduled for any outside meetings that morning.

"On leave, sir? Medical?" said Jenkins, who, like Thompson, had come up through the ranks of the police and Scotland Yard. Tall, dark, and handsome except for a crooked nose, he was the favorite of the secretaries in the typing pool—and doggedly devoted to Thompson.

"No, just some follow-up on the Waterloo case. Back in the afternoon."

"Anything new? Something I can do?"

Thompson wavered for a moment, wondering if he should confide in him his dream, but instead said, "I will inform you if there's anything new. Eyes on the PM."

"Yes, sir."

Thompson swung by Churchill's office, where Mary was

already at her desk, setting up to deal with the avalanche of paperwork Churchill had issued overnight.

"Hello there, bright eyes!" said Thompson, smiling. His heart lifted at the sight of Mary, so prim, so proper, so well prepared, so warm. His thoughts ran back to the last time they'd spent together, a night at her mother's flat—the taste of her cooking, her kisses, her breasts, her smell of almonds and lilacs . . .

She turned, set her wide brown eyes on him, smiled back. "Good morning to you, Mr. Thompson."

He looked around, made sure there was no one in the immediate vicinity, then gave in to impulse and, bending down, gave her a quick buss on the lips.

"Mr. Thompson!" said Mary, laughing, pushing him away. "Woke up frisky, didn't we?"

"It's the sight of you, my dear," said Thompson, whispering in her ear.

"Ahem."

Thompson and Mary looked back at the door. There stood Churchill, in his Chinese dragon bathrobe, wielding a sheaf of papers.

"If you two lovebirds don't mind, Mis Layton, please correct this speech. I'm due in Commons at fourteen hours."

"Right away, sir," said Mary, blushing as she got up to take the paper from Churchill's hand.

"And Thompson, come here, I need to talk to you," said Churchill.

"Yes, sir," said Thompson, following Churchill into the adjoining bathroom, but not before turning around and winking goodbye at Mary, who rolled her eyes with a smile of pretend desperation.

Churchill waddled into the bathroom, the tub slowly filling with warm water for his morning bath.

"Close the door," said Churchill. Thompson did so. Churchill dropped his robe, sank into the tub.

"Now listen, Thompson. I don't believe the things I'm hearing from MI5 about this fellow Riley. They are trying to hide something, and I want you to get to the bottom of it. I need to know who all is behind this man. I refuse to believe he's a lone mad killer, even if he is Irish. Don't report your findings to anyone but me. Utmost secrecy, understand?"

"I understand, Prime Minister. I've been suspicious myself."

"Good. Now, hand me those rubber duckies over there," said Churchill, pointing at a nearby shelf. "Might as well amuse myself in this bloody war."

CHAPTER THIRTY-TWO

THOMPSON STOOD IN THE SUN, feeling the unusual September warmth penetrate the thick tweed of his jacket, sweat beginning to drip down his back. In front of him, a mountain of rubble of what had been the church of Our Lady and Saint Katherine of Siena in Bow, just a handful of blocks from Mary's flat.

The rubble rose two stories high, a collection of broken masonry, smashed tiles, twisted windows, crumpled metal girders. Next to it, a smaller mountain of debris, the remains of what had been the church's rectory. On that smaller hill a handful of men were digging with spades and picks, as if archaeologists excavating some ancient midden.

Thompson moved closer to one of the men, who wore the distinctive hat and vest of the Home Guard.

"Hallo!" shouted Thompson.

The man turned, waved back. Thompson gestured at him to come down the hill. The man nodded, began to descend. Thompson wondered why the man, in his thirties and seemingly fit, was not in the service, until he noticed the limp and the telltale clanking of an artificial leg as the man negotiated his way down.

"How may I help you?" said the man, coming up to Thompson.

"Inspector Thompson, Scotland Yard," said Thompson, showing his official identification.

"Something wrong, inspector?"

"Nothing out of the ordinary. We're conducting an investigation of the former occupants of this building," said Thompson.

"You mean the church rectory, sir? I'm afraid there's not much to see. Most of the people died when Jerry bombed it. Nasty work, almost as if they were aiming directly at it—passed over the garrison up the road. Good thing that, I suppose."

"Mostly died, you said. Who survived?"

"A young nun, sir. Was in the basement doing laundry. Girl from Brazil, I was told, she's at St. Mary's Hospital right now. I can get you the name, if you care to follow me to headquarters round the block."

"Let's do that. Lead the way."

The Home Guard hobbled ahead of Thompson, his artificial leg clickety-clacketing like the cheese striking the pins in a game of skittles.

"Were you in the war?" said Thompson, gesturing at the leg.

"Oh, no, sir, out in the West Indies. Royal Navy."

"Shark?"

"Nothing that romantic. Jumped off a pier on my day off, didn't see the lines of wire rolled under the water to ward off submarines, cut off my femoral. If not for my mates I would have bled to death—or bitten by the sharks, come to think of it. They pulled me out. By the time I got to hospital I was so far gone, no use keeping the leg so off it went. But it's all right, one gets used to it. That's why we have four limbs, methinks, so the others can do the job of the missing one. Here we are."

Thompson and the Guard entered a small storefront, still bearing the sign Holland & Co.—Spices—to which the badge of the Home Guard had been hastily affixed. The guard waved hello at an elderly woman going over a ledger. She smiled back.

"Mrs. Shaw has been kind enough to lend us the use of her store for the time being," said the Guard.

"Aye, there's hardly any business in spices right now, with the blockade and all, thought it best to do my bit for the war," said the woman, proudly.

"And we are very grateful, ma'am, indeed. This is Inspector Thompson from Scotland Yard. He would like some information on the church rectory blown to bits last week."

"Oh, Our Lady's, bless me. My church, it was. Nice Father O'Riley, poor man. He riled so much about the war, though. Riled, huh? I just made a pun, ha!"

"Did you know him?" said Thompson, not amused.

"Well, yes, Inspector. He was very well liked, even if I personally did not agree with his views on the conflict. I say the Germans started it and we got to give it back to them. But that's all behind us now. The father was very popular. All kinds of high and mighty used to come to his early Mass on Sundays, even!"

"Really? Did you recognize any of them?" asked Thompson.

"There was one such, I used to see him regular at the seven o' clock Mass. Fewer people, get it out of the way, you know? Very tall, this gentleman, with a bad arm. Hung down useless at his side, poor thing. His driver would park his Rolls outside the church and wait for him. I think Father O'Riley, bless his soul, was his confessor."

Thompson nodded, smiled, his mind reeling as he realized

the implications of what the chatty woman had just disclosed. The man in question was probably Lord Fairfax, the current foreign secretary in the War Cabinet. Why would he be coming to Mass in Bow when he could easily attend the Cathedral at Westminster near Belgravia where he lived? And why would he choose as his confessor the cousin of an assassin?

"Here's the name of the nun," said the guard, digging up a handwritten note from a carboard box with loose items. "Sister Maria Braganca. At St. Mary's, like I said. Maybe she can give you more information."

"What's in that box?" said Thompson, moving closer to the guard.

"Things found in the rubble of the rectory. We've been expecting someone from the diocese to come fetch them. Medals, missals, diaries, things of that sort. We thought the Church might want to hand them to relatives and such."

"Yes, of course," said Thompson. "Let's have a look."

"Please, go ahead. We have another couple of boxes. I'll bring them over. Mrs. Shaw, can we get a chair for the Inspector?"

"Most certainly," said the woman. "Here, take mine. I'm done with the little accounting one can do nowadays."

Thompson sat at her desk, a scratched metal castoff from some institution. The guard returned with two full four-by-four cardboard boxes, placed them before Thompson.

"A cuppa tea?" said Mrs. Shaw.

"That would be lovely, thank you."

Thompson rummaged through one of the boxes. St. Anthony medals, crucifixes, rings, devotional cards of saints, a handful of scorched passports. Nothing of importance. Mrs. Shaw set a cup of tepid tea before him.

"Any sugar?" she said.

"This will be fine, thank you," said Thompson, then turned to the guard. "You said there were diaries in here?"

"Yes, sir, in the second box. Let me see," said the guard, rifling through the items. "Found it myself, near where they found the father's body. Poor man, bad injuries, a broken neck. Nasty business. Here it is."

He handed Thompson a small book with mother-of-pearl covers smudged with dirt and dried blood. A tiny lock kept the book closed.

"It's shut tight," said Thompson, examining he book. "Have you a screwdriver?"

"Would an ice pick do?" said Mrs. Shaw, peeking over Thompson's shoulder, eagerly snooping.

"Yes, it will," lifting the book to look closely at the elaborate design on its cover—a cross potent with four smaller crosses potent on each of the cross's quadrants, all enclosed in a ribbon circle. What does this mean, he wondered.

"Here you are," said Mrs. Shaw, handing him the pick. Thompson inserted the point in the small lock, pushed the latch, opened the book.

"It's a devotional," said Mrs. Shaw, peeking once more over Thompson's shoulder. "Look at all the pretty illustrations. That's St. Martin, isn't it?"

"Madam, if you don't mind," said Thompson.

"Of course, of course," said Mrs. Shaw, embarassed, and moving away. "I'll go along and mind my own business."

"Thank you."

The frontispiece had the name of Father Thomas Alonzo Aloysius O'Riley written in flowing script, with the date of his ordination. Thompson spent the next half hour leafing through the book, which apparently had served as both diary and devotional, with quotes from diverse saints and Scripture alongside the day's date atop each otherwise blank page.

There were notations handwritten in the highly stylized curlicued letters of the late nineteenth century, which in an odd way matched the equally outdated precepts for good behavior. Toward the end of the book, by August, Thompson observed that the priest several times was writing Lord F, often alongside the letter C, as well as noting down the time. The final notation stunned him. He re-read it, then pocketed the book. He called over the guard.

"What is your name?"

"Price, Robert Price, sir."

"Mr. Price, I am ordering you not to hand these items to anyone from the Church. They must be preserved intact as they are. I shall send someone to pick them up."

"Yes, sir," said Price. "Anything important?"

"I cannot disclose that. You must ascertain that no one else has access to them. Please seal the boxes immediately. I must be off."

"Yes, sir," said Price, watching Thompson as he walked briskly out of the shop, got into his car, and drove off in a hurry.

"I wonder what he found?" said Mrs. Shaw, peeking out the door at Thompson's car speeding round the corner.

"None of our business, Mrs. Shaw. Top secret, I'm sure," said Price.

CHAPTER THIRTY-THREE

TO THOMPSON'S SURPRISE, the address he had found in Father O'Riley's devotional was still standing when he arrived there. A handful of blocks from the turbid Thames and the nearby Wapping docks, the neighborhood had sustained a brutal direct attack the previous night. Only the brick building housing the Brazen Head pub remained, as if a defiant middle finger to the marauding Nazi bombers.

This was address of the man known as Cypher, as the priest had carelessly written the go-between's name next to it. With any luck, Thompson thought he might be able to use it to trace Riley's whereabouts. It was obvious to Thompson that Riley was not Cypher, for he had taken his place for the meeting at Waterloo—but to what purpose? Thompson could not be certain. Did Riley already have the weapon and was needing the mechanic to make it work? Or was the mechanic going to take him to the weapon? And who else was involved? Lord Fairfax already seemed to be implicated—anyone else?

A handful of firemen were dousing the structure's black-ened brick sides, the roofline wafting clouds of fetid smoke into the clear morning sky. Thompson parked his car, looked at the efforts of the fire crew, instinctively touched his shoulder holster with its revolver, then stepped out and walked up to the smoldering building.

Thompson showed his identification to the crew, who directed him to the captain. A heavyset man with a thin Ronald Coleman mustache, he spoke with a heavy accent Thompson could not place. The man shook his head.

"No, not safe, Inspector, everybody leave last night," said the man.

"I still must go inside," insisted Thompson.

"Okay, Okay, you wait," grunted the man. "I send someone. Roof no good, you be careful."

The captain shouted something in some incomprehensible language. A young man in his twenties stepped away from the crew, nodded.

"Righto," he said and walked up to Thompson with an ax in his hands. "Inspector? Shall we?"

The two entered the pub. The tables had been turned upside down by the force of the blast, smashed bottles littering the floor like a carpet of broken glass, the smell of beer and liquor mixing with the burnt resin stench of charred wood. They went quickly through the place. No one.

"Any other rooms?" asked Thompson.

"Around the back, sir," said the young man. "Offices upstairs."

"Lead me to them."

They stepped out a side door and to the stairwell leading to the building's second story. Thompson glanced at the smudged building directory: "McCarthy & Sons, Import/Export" and "Hamilton Fish, Barrister."

"Best be careful, sir, the roof is very unstable," said the fireman. "One step at a time."

"Understood," said Thompson.

They yanked open the entry door, headed for the set of wet and narrow smoky steps leading up.

"What was that language the captain spoke?" said Thompson.

"Polish, sir. He's my dad. We've been in England for a while, but he's never mastered the language right proper."

"Some people never do. How long have you been here?"

"Ten years, sir. I've been waiting to join the RAF, thought I'd give the old man a hand meanwhile."

"That's good of you . . . careful there!"

A piece of charred timber fell from the rafters and dropped in front of them as they reached the first landing. Everywhere the smell of burnt wood, masonry, and something else—a familiar scent which grew stronger as they walked up to the end of the stairwell. Two office doors—"Hamilton Fish," read one. The other, "McCarthy & Sons."

"Do you smell that?" said Thompson.

"Yes, sir, I think I know what it is," said the fireman.

"It's coming from here," said Thompson, signaling at the second door. He tried the door. Locked.

"Will you break this, please."

"Step aside, sir," said the young fireman. He swung his ax, smashed the top part of the door to splinters, then made quick work of the bottom part. He gave it a kick and the door collapsed with a loud crash.

A cloud of smoke, ashes, and decomposition sailed out of the room, so strong it made Thompson and the fireman cough—then the fireman turned and retched. Thompson felt the bitter bile rise from his stomach to his throat as well, the pungent stench of death filling his nostrils.

Ahead of them, on the floor next to an overturned table and chairs, lay the body of a man, badly charred from the fire.

Gagging, Thompson placed his handkerchief over his nose and approached the corpse.

The man was face down, his hands outstretched as though he'd been trying to seize something and had been badly burnt in the process. Tall, well built, he was wearing the uniform of railroad workers, which hardly fit his massive body.

Thompson turned the man around. His face was disfigured by the fire, charred beyond recognition, as if the man had fallen headfirst into a boiling cauldron of oil.

Thompson looked up, saw the small kitchen and open gas oven door, a spilled vat of an oily liquid on the floor. Holding his breath, he felt the dead man's clothes, found a British passport with the name Henry Howard, bearing the picture of Marcus Riley.

The fireman approached. "Do you know this man, sir?"

Thompson stood, shook his head. "No, I don't. Let's get him out of here, shall we?"

CHAPTER THIRTY-FOUR

THE CALL to Sir Hugh Northrop, the king's physician, came late at night, a not unusual occurrence in wartime London, where it seemed as if no one ever slept.

"We have to be very precise," said the muffled voice. "At no time is the patient to be subjected to obvious extreme measures. Is that understood?"

"Yes," said the doctor.

"One last thing," said the voice from deep in the Foreign Office. "The treatment must be made this weekend. The patient is hosting a dinner party, to which you will receive an invitation. Please respond affirmatively. Conditions will be provided to ensure your success. The fate of Europe, of the world, is in your hands, doctor."

The man clicked off abruptly, stopping Northrop from automatically spouting the Heil Hitler salute he'd so keenly learned in Munich.

The call had come in while the doctor was in his study, reviewing the latest papers on the precise medication he was to impart. Since his activation by the Foreign Office, he'd been alerted to expect the call at any time. He'd had to forswear his usual weekly appointment with his favorite call boy, a long-limbed lad from Bristol whose lovers supplemented his paltry salary as a cutter in Saville Row.

Now, all alone in his Belgravia townhouse, surrounded by the portraits and luxuries of his station, Sir Hugh felt more alone than ever—and yet at the same time even more devoted than ever to the Führer, who had personally chosen him to be his secret weapon against the decadent British Empire. It was worth the sacrifice if at the end the glorious vision of one world, one people, ruled by one man, the Führer, and his subject monarch, King Edward VII, became reality.

Still, he missed his boy, his Orville, who had so quickly surmised the doctor's predilection when measuring him for his bespoke suit. Even dedicated followers of National Socialism are allowed to have feelings, he told himself as he picked up the phone, eager for some words of consolation, even though he knew that regrettably it would be his right hand that would bring him the much-needed relief.

———

WHAT THE DOCTOR did not know was that his boy Orville —born Archibald Leach—at that moment was being interrogated in his flat by a couple of Scotland Yard vice officers, who were very interested in the cutter's long and varied clientele. One of the officers was going through Orville's phone book, replete with notations on what particular sex toy or practice was the favorite of each party.

"Look at this, Thornbill. Marquess of Bloomsbury, the French back twist. What is that, Archie? A variation on open-mouth kissing?"

Orville frowned, shook his head, ran a long, delicate finger through his shiny golden hair. "Something like that, only it's not the mouth."

"Ew!!" said the inspector in disgust. "In the middle of the bloody war, you are still . . ."

"May I have a fag?" said Orville. The second officer, who'd been sitting quietly observing Orville, nodded yes. Orville nervously shook a Turkish cigarette out of his silver holder, lit it with his gold briquet.

"Well, inspector, *de gustibum non disputatum est*," said Orville, exhaling a cloud of smoke out his finely chiseled nostrils.

"Speak the King's English, will you?"

"No accounting for tastes, sir. If I were to tell you all about that, would you consider letting me go?"

"All about what? Your sodomy, which is illegal and an offense against . . ."

"We can discuss that," said the quiet inspector, signaling at the other to be still.

The phone rang. "Pick it up," said the quiet agent.

Orville nodded, placed the receiver to his ear. "James residence. Oh, it's you. Yes, listen, darling, I am quite busy right now. May I give you a ring in a little while? I have some . . . pressing business to attend. Yes, darling, I miss you too. *Mio caro, mais oui.* No, no, you bad boy, leave your willy alone!"

The vice inspector frowned in disgust. Orville shrugged as if saying, what can I do. "Yes, dear, I will call you right promptly. Many kisses."

Orville hung up, turned to the quiet inspector. "There's someone you'd be interested in."

"Who was it?"

"Sir Hugh Northrop. Personal physician to His Majesty, King George. And now to the prime minister."

The inspectors looked at each other, nodded.

"Yes, I believe we would be interested," said the quiet inspector.

"I thought you might," said Orville.

————

"WE'VE MADE SOME CHANGES."

Thompson was again sitting in the office of the director of espionage for MI5, only instead of portly Sir Humbert Hopkins, with his drunkard's nose and stench, in his chair sat a trim and compact man in his early forties. Thomas Wiley looked and sounded like he ran four miles every morning and swam another two in the evening just to let off steam. His gaze was direct, his speech carrying the flat accent of Yorkshire.

"Following the prime minister's directive, we've had a stint of house cleaning, following our move here to St. James," Wiley explained. "Sir Humbert was transferred to another department. I was appointed to take his post. I understand you wish to inquire about the man codenamed Cypher."

"Yes, sir. I have been given to understand that the flat where we found Riley was let by a Malcolm Boyd, who was one of yours, a man known as Cypher. Who was he?"

Wiley removed his glasses, scratched the bridge of his nose, put the glasses back again, which made him look like the eternal inquisitor.

"Cypher was our man, working with Nazi sympathizers like that priest in Bow. We first came in contact with him through his connections with the IRA. He was very helpful with that, then, not so much. We believe he's dead, killed by Riley."

"You say he worked with Nazi sympathizers. Does that include Lord Fairfax?"

Wiley stared at Thompson, his expression deadpan. "As

you know, certain members of government are Catholic, and they partake of the Catholic rite of confession. Sometimes their confessor has lamentable political opinions. These opinions, so far, have not been outlawed, so long as they remain private."

"You haven't answered my question."

"I don't have to. But I will tell you this, everyone's being watched, Thompson. Even you. And I. This is a game where everyone is a player, and everyone is guilty until proven otherwise."

"You have nothing on Fairfax, then."

"Trust me, the moment we have solid workable information, we'll take action. Let us keep it at that. What you should know is that we believe the dead man you found in Cypher's office was Riley. We've sent for his dental records. They might take a while to arrive from Ireland, but we're confident he was your man."

"How certain are you?"

"As certain as I am sitting here. We caught a big break, Thompson. Let's not muck it up. Go back to being the bodyguard, leave the spy business to us."

CHAPTER THIRTY-FIVE

"HEY MATE, time to send off. Six o'clock in the morning."

"What, what?"

Riley opened his eyes, looked around, focusing on the dozens of Londoners who'd also taken refuge in the shelter—men, women, a few children who now bawled, hungry—one little boy pissing against the tile wall at the far end.

"I said, time to go back to your ship, sailor. Cap'n will be sure to have your behind if you're late," said the Home Guard, smiling at Riley.

"Yes, of course, much obliged," said Riley, seeing now the blue serge of his arm sleeves, feeling the broad open collar of his tunic, and remembering, remembering . . . the images coming in a flash, one right after the other, tumbling past in a torrent of mental fatigue from days of killing and running—and why? A tiny voice in his mind echoing, why? Why?

To survive and finish the job, that's why.

"Pardon?" said the Home Guard, who'd turned his back on Riley but now returned, quizzical.

"Nothing, never mind, thank you," muttered Riley, getting

up, feeling his muscles ache from the hours in his cot's narrow confines.

"Well, go on, sailor, off to rule the waves!" said the Home Guard with a smile, then went after the boy, who had finished pissing and was dropping his pants to defecate.

"Oy, little rat, didn't your mum tell you to use the bucket?" shouted the Home Guard.

Riley followed the crowd out of the shelter, into the blinding light of the Indian summer morning—every face on the street haggard from bad sleep or none, walking as if in a trance but determined to last the day and hope for another chance at rest that night, as they dodged the mounds of rubble cluttering the street from the night's destruction.

Limping from the wound left by Thompson's bullet, Riley made his way to Lyons Corner House on Oxford Street, stood in line for a cup of tea, and sat at a small table by a window, observing the crowds and planning his next move. The doubts that had assailed him on waking now began to vanish the more tea he drank and the more he contemplated his options.

It was too late to turn back—he had nowhere to turn back to. Cuba was shot and so was New York. Perhaps somewhere in South America, Brazil, or Argentina, once the job was over. With the four thousand pounds Fairfax had given him, he had more than enough capital to start afresh. Now that he knew how to assemble and break down the weapon, it was safely stashed at the luggage depot at Epping Station. A bit heavy perhaps, but all in all indistinguishable from the thousands of other suitcases stored there for the convenience of people displaced by the bombings.

He smiled recalling the arrogance of the Nazi engineer, who thought he spoke perfect English when he sounded like a drunk schoolteacher on a holiday. How he'd gotten into the country was beyond Riley's grasp, unbelievable if not for the fact that the man was there and obviously knew all about the weapon. Seeing how they were the only ones in the building, the pub having closed hours before, for safety Riley and the German moved the weapon down to the basement, where the German gave him a lesson in ballistics.

It didn't take Riley long to understand the principle behind the weapon, and how to put the thing together correctly. The German insisted on making Riley break it down and assemble it several times, until he could do it in a minute. When the bombing ended at dawn and they returned to the office with the weapon, the German fell asleep, and Riley strangled him.

Riley had a plan for the body, seeing the German was approximately his body type—give him his identity and throw Scotland Yard off his trail. Putting on him the uniform of the railroad worker he'd killed at Waterloo Station was a genius touch, he thought. No, burning him with the oil to make his face and fingerprints unrecognizable, leaving the gas oven door open, and setting the place on fire, that was the master touch.

He did regret somewhat that when he returned to Mrs. Grayson's flat to get some sleep, her nephew Desmond showed up, having just gotten a few days leave from the Navy. But again luck was with him, as he was approximately Riley's height, and Riley had surprise on his side—smashing Desmond's head with an andiron, knocking him unconscious, stripping him of his uniform, and then breaking his neck.

So, he reflected, sitting at his table at Lyons Corner House, how many people had he killed so far in pursuit of his objective? Four, he counted. Cypher, Mrs. Grayson, her nephew, and the German. Not bad. Oh, and the railroad worker. Five. All casualties of war. Think of all those who will be saved when the war ends.

Riley didn't count his cousin, as he had been planning to kill him for years, waiting only for the right moment to carry out his revenge. He flashed back for a moment to that time in the barn when his cousin . . . Riley immediately shut the image out of his mind, not wanting to think that maybe it had been his fault, that maybe he had liked it after all . . .

His eyes drifted to a trio of waitresses standing in a corner, staring at him. One of them, a tall blonde with a toothy grin, nodded at him. Riley smiled back. To the jeers of her friends, the girl walked up to his table.

Riley liked what he saw. A full bosom that strained her uniform across the chest, thick lips, blond hair in ringlets. She should take my mind off my troubles for a while, he thought. She was a few feet from the table, bearing a menu in her hands as a likely excuse for conversation, when . . .

"Marcus O'Riley, how the hell are ya?"

Riley shifted his gaze, looking to his left at a tall, thick man with a baby face and prematurely gray hair smiling at him. The girl, on seeing the stranger, hesitated, then walked back to her coworkers, who chatted excitedly.

Riley debated for a moment whether to deny it was him, but it occurred to him that perhaps this was Fate aiding him for his last step, that this might be just who he needed to accomplish his mission.

"Sean Cassidy," said Riley, offering his hand, "what wind is this that blows you my way?"

"One that will take us both to safe harbor, for certain," said the tall, heavyset man. "Mind if I keep you company for a while, before you go back on ship?"

"Be my guest. Tell me tales of your life and wandering and I will tell you mine."

Cassidy dropped into the chair, which squealed as if it were about to break, but held. He glanced at the waitress, waved at her to step forward. The server walked back to the table, a sly grin on her face.

"How can I help you, sir?"

"You mind another spot of tea and some scones and bacon, dearie?"

"Sorry, no more bacon left. But we do have some tasty ham..."

"Eggs?"

"None, I'm afraid."

"Oh, well, we'll take the ham—or do you have bangers?"

"That we do."

"Two orders, then, one for me and one for my gallivanting friend, who as you can see from his hungry look does not get to chow down proper when sailing the seven seas, isn't that right, Marcus?"

"Right as rain, Sean," said Riley with a sigh.

"Well, off with you, my girl. And we'll take the tea right away, if you please."

Cassidy's plump and placid expression disappeared the moment the waitress walked away. He whispered urgently, in Gaelic:

"Are you still with the friends?"

"Always," replied Riley, also in Gaelic.

"I saw you through the glass as I was walking by, and I told myself he must be here for something. How can I help?"

"Your tea, sir," said the waitress, setting a cup before Cassidy. She looked invitingly at Riley, moved next to him.

"Anything for you, sir?"

Riley grinned back. "Maybe later we can discuss that."

"How much later would that be, sir?"

"What time are you off?"

The waitress blushed, lifted her eyebrows, whispered, "At four. Name is Julie."

"In the back?" whispered Riley. She nodded.

"Thank you, miss, that will be all for now," said Riley, as the girl sashayed back to her circle of giggling friends.

"I see you haven't lost your touch, Marcus," said Cassidy. "I still remember fair Sally from Ballymena."

Riley smiled, shrugged, then shifted in his seat, and asked, as innocently as he could make it, "Have you a car? And could I stay in your flat overnight?"

"All you need do is ask."

CHAPTER THIRTY-SIX

DUE TO ONE of those phenomena that plague even the most efficient of systems, the coroner's report was mixed in with official papers in Churchill's red box. That was the container where top-secret documents were delivered to the prime minister: maps of military engagements, statistics on weapons and aircraft production, numbers of deaths and casualties in the battlefield, the thousand and one details that Churchill received, devoured, and processed at the start of his day. He was sitting in bed, having finished his eggs and bacon, and was sipping his usual morning dram of Johnnie Walker when Thompson walked in.

"You wanted me, Prime Minister?"

"Come in, Thompson. Just wanted to congratulate you again on a job well done on this Riley fellow. I was reviewing the medical examiner's report. Very fortunate you found him."

"Thank you, sir. May I have a look?"

"Of course," said Churchill, handing Thompson the report. "Incidentally, your suspicions about Fairfax are well taken. I have made some changes at MI5."

"I noticed, Prime Minister. Change is good, especially in a place like that. Old habits die hard, people are reluctant to alter their ways."

"Yes, well, I've also a mind for some further changes for our Cunning Fox. I think he would be a wonderful ambassador . . . to America, let's say. Or Argentina. Find a place more congenial for him. Get him away from . . . all this. But more of that later. The dinner at Chequers—evening dress. Do you have it, or shall I make arrangements?"

"I believe I can manage it, Prime Minister."

"Now remember, start with the cutlery on the outside and work your way in—like a good mystery plot!"

"I'm aware, Prime Minister," said Thompson, curtly, mortified by Churchill's assumption about his table manners.

"No offense. I personally don't care, but high muck-a-mucks will be watching. Did I tell you the time I dined with the king of Romania? The man drank the soup from the plate like it was a big bowl, so I and everyone else had to do the same. He was drunk as a skunk—no surprise he lost his throne. Well, be a good man and have Colville come in, please. I have work for him."

Thompson moved to hand the coroner's report back to Churchill but was waved off. "Keep it as a memento of your bravery. Well done."

"Thank you, sir," said Thompson, allowing himself a slight smile of satisfaction.

On his way out, Thompson stepped to see Mary, who was hard at work typing up changes to yet another one of Churchill's speeches. Thompson closed the door to her small office, leaned over her typewriter to kiss her. She pushed him away, laughing.

"Not now, Walter. Wait till the weekend."

"Have you picked out your dress? It's a mighty fancy affair, you know."

"You'll be giving me fashion advice?"

"I might, but only for bedroom attire."

"Oh, hush, you! In any case, I will have you know that I have chosen a creation by Madam Gres. Cost me all of ten quid, it did. But I must say I look fetching in it."

"You'll look even more wonderful out of it, I'm sure."

Mary laughed again. "All right, off with you, we'll have none of that sort of talk. I'll see you tonight."

Thompson headed to his small office next to his improvised bedroom in the basement of 10 Downing Street. He spent the next few hours reviewing security plans for Chequers as well as the new headquarters at Whitehall, where the government was scheduled to move for further protection. A bomb just the day before had blasted the kitchen at 10 Downing and almost killed the prime minister and his guest, the American envoy Harry Hopkins—the building was too old to withstand any more direct hits.

Thompson therefore did not begin reading the coroner's report until the early afternoon, when he finally took some time to eat a cucumber sandwich for lunch. That's when it struck him there was something odd about the report's findings. He stopped, went over the conclusions, jumped to the last pages with their illustrations of the body—a sexless outline with arrows indicating where the major injuries and wounds were located. What he expected to find was not there.

Maybe I missed it, he told himself. He forced himself to reread the entire report, with its stultifying details of the decedent's height—6'1"—weight—210 pounds--complexion—fair, uncircumcised, with scars on arms and legs, most likely from gunshot wounds. The war, thought Thompson. And then the horrific burns he sustained when the vat of hot oil fell on him, disfiguring his face and hands.

Thompson thought it was a strange end to a strange life, not even to be shot in battle or hanged, as he deserved to be, but to die from the odd capriciousness of fate. Yet the more he thought about that death, the more he felt an alarm going off in his head. The wounds, which the report attributed to battle. When had Irish republicans fought in the Great War? Very few had, if any. Well, then, he told himself, maybe during the Irish Civil War in the twenties. Yes, that was a possibility. But a small detail in the notes deeply troubled him. What about the bullet wound during the gunfight at Waterloo Station? Thompson had hit him, for sure, he'd seen the blood. Where was that?

Nowhere.

Thompson picked up the phone, dialed the Metropolitan Office of Greater London's Medical Examiner, and after identifying himself, asked for the doctor who had conducted the autopsy.

"Sorry, sir," said the female attendant, "Dr. Chapman has left the office and joined the Royal Air Force. Is there anyone else who can assist you?"

"Never mind," said Thompson, "is the subject body still there?"

"Hold on, Mr. Thompson, I shall ask the chief examiner."

After a few minutes a raspy voice came on the line. "Dr. Howell here, how may I help you?"

Thompson explained what he wanted. "I see," said the examiner. "Let me check our records. You do know we have a high number of bodies nowadays. It's making the amount of paperwork we do almost impossible to handle. One does what one can, and . . . ah, here it is. Afraid not, it was sent to the crematorium this morning, sir. As you well know . . ."

Thompson cut in before the doctor gave another self-commiserating excuse. "Yes, yes, where is the crematorium?"

"It's at East Tilbury, sir. Terribly sorry about this. Is there anything else we can do for the office of the Prime Minister?"

Thompson did not bother to answer and hung up. Grabbing his coat, he dashed to the nearby office of his second, Jenkins, told him he was off on an investigation and not to let the prime minister out of his sight until he returned.

Once in his car, Thompson drove as fast as he could out of London. He had to see for himself what that so-called symbol was, and why the fresh bullet wound did not appear on the body. He berated himself for not having thought of that detail earlier, but also knew that second-guessing would get him nowhere. What he needed was confirmation that the dead man was in fact Riley, for if not, they had just given him enough time and cover to try again.

———

LONDON'S CREMATORIUM, a late nineteenth-century construction, had been erected by the estuary of the Thames, originally close enough to the metropolis to serve its final purpose for the dead, yet far enough so that the pungent smell of burning bodies and calcinated bones did not disturb the still living. Over the years the growth of the city had reached the location, and rows of cheap housing now surrounded the facility, with its constant spewing of gray clouds and fine ash.

Thompson reached the building by the late afternoon, right around a shift change. It took a while for the evening supervisor to come out and meet him. All the while, Thompson watched trucks wheeling in, filled with bodies from London, the few who died from natural causes and the many killed by German bombs.

The shift supervisor was a short, dour-looking woman in her fifties, Dr. Lilah Graham, who was not too happy to hear Thompson's request.

"Inspector, as you know, we have our hands full nowadays. We hardly have any staff, and . . ."

"I'm aware, but this is a matter of the utmost urgency," said Thompson.

"Have you an order signed by a magistrate?"

For once, Thompson was unable to contain his anger.

"Doctor, we are at war, and this is no time for legal niceties. The subject is dead already, so there won't be any invasion of privacy. Furthermore, I have the full authority of the prime ministers's office. Were your actions to result in an inexcusable delay, you should be made completely responsible for the results!"

Graham glared at Thompson, blinked her thin eyelashes.

"This way," she said, finally.

She led him down the wide hall out a set of stained-glass doors to another, smaller building out back, a nondescript rectangular one-story brick structure without any windows. The parking lot around it was full of transport vans bearing the lettering Coroner's on the side. From one of those vans, two white-uniformed attendants were unloading a stretcher with a body wrapped in tarpaulin.

The attendants nodded at Graham, and, straining under the weight of the corpse, walked up a ramp and entered through a set of folding doors into the building. Thompson and Graham followed. The stretcher bearers veered down a wide hall to the right, while Graham ushered Thompson to the left, into a small office.

"When bodies first arrive, they are identified, stripped, and numbered, then they are placed in refrigerators to await their turn at cremation," said Graham, calling over an assistant behind the wide wooden desk. "We keep good records, in spite of the current chaos," she added with a touch of pride.

"Edward, please hand me today's incoming list." An assistant turned over a clipboard with an inch-thick wad of forms. Graham leafed through the pages, nodded.

"You are in luck, Inspector. The body is still at a locker. Please come with me."

She opened a metal side door and led Thompson down yet another corridor, which opened to a vast hall, its walls full of small refrigerator doors with letters and numbers above each one. The walls extended for over fifty feet, the doors rising twenty feet high. A rolling steel staircase with a lift stood by the side to access the uppermost row.

The heat of the day permeated the room, the strong smell of decomposition, phenol, and disinfectant so strong that Thompson covered his nose with his handkerchief.

"Ripe, isn't it?" said Graham, strutting down the wall, checking the numbers. "One gets used to the smell of death. It becomes kind of pleasant after a while, strange at it may seem. It's the smell of work. But then, in the end, I suppose even hell becomes a place familiar too."

She stopped at small locker at the far end. "This should be it," she said, yanking open the rectangular door and pulling out a metal slab. Thompson craned over Graham to better see the body.

The slab slid out—on it, the naked body of a very fat and very dead woman, her eyes still open.

"Oh, dear, this shouldn't be," muttered Graham, looking over the paperwork, then stepping back to double-check the numbers on the door. She shook her head, then shuttered the woman's eyes.

"Will you excuse me?" said Graham, shutting the door. She

stormed down the hall, shouting, "Ellis! Ellis! Come here at once!"

Out of a narrow passageway that Thompson had not noticed before exited a short, wiry man in a soiled white uniform. He conferred with Graham, who slapped her papers and shook them in his face. The worker shrugged, threw up his hands, and returned to the hallway he'd scurried out from. Controlling herself, Graham rejoined Thompson.

"Mix-up. Come, it was sent to the oven," she said.

Graham took off at a fast clip down the hall to another joining structure, its entrance shut by two giant rolling steel doors. Graham pulled at one of them and dashed inside a high cavern holding a twenty-foot-high steel oven, its round door still open, flames inside burning vivid blue and orange. Two men in dirty overalls were wheeling a cart stacked with two corpses next to a metal ramp with small casters, which debouched into the oven.

The taller of the men had placed the top corpse, a young woman, in a metal gurney atop the ramp when Graham approached him. The man grabbed the corpse by the arm to stop it from sliding into the flames while he conversed with Graham.

The roar of the flame drowned out their conversation. Thompson watched and waited—and for years after, he would occasionally have a recurring nightmare where he was the body in the metal gurney about to be incinerated, only he was still alive but couldn't move or speak.

Graham returned, shaking her head. "I am terribly sorry, Inspector, but the paperwork was incorrect, or rather, it had not been updated. Your man was cremated earlier this day. I do believe we still have his ashes. If you desire, I shall have them sent to you."

"Yes, please, if you don't mind. The teeth survive, don't they?"

"Many times. Most definitely any kind of dental work done, if it's not gold. We'll be sure to send it all to you right away, as soon as we locate them."

"That will be greatly appreciated, Doctor."

"Is there anything else I can do?"

"That will be all, thank you."

The man by the chute looked at Graham, who nodded. The woman's arm was released, and her corpse slid down into the maw of the blazing oven. With a shudder, Thompson walked out of the crematorium.

There was nothing else he could do. He just had to accept that for some strange reason the wound had not been noted, and the dead man was Riley after all. The dental records, when they arrived, would confirm the identity, hopefully. If not . . .

CHAPTER THIRTY-SEVEN

THE NEXT DAY, and thirty miles away, in a rattling Morris Minor already old and creaking well before the war, Riley and Sean Cassidy stopped at The Lamb, an inn in Buckinghamshire. In the back seat, Julie Sayres, the buxom waitress from Lyons Corner House, could hardly contain her excitement. She leaned over the front passenger seat, placed her head next to Riley.

"Are we stopping for the night?" she said, her breath smelling of the apple she'd been munching on during the ride from London. "Or just for a bit of lunch?"

"I don't know, lovie. Should we stay the night, or do you have other plans for tomorrow, Sean?" said Riley. He glanced at Cassidy, who yanked the hand brake tight to halt the car from rolling down the sloping roadway.

"No plans for me, boyo, free as a bird."

"Well, then, let's discuss this over a pint or two, shall we?" said Riley.

"I could use some grub myself," said Cassidy, easing his massive girth out of the tiny car. Julie hooked Riley's arm with hers as they walked to the inn, the trio appearing to any onlooker as young people thrilled to be escaping the horror of wartime London for a while.

That's how The Lamb's innkeeper, Harold Matthews, would later describe them during the investigation—nothing out of the ordinary about them. They took a seat at one of the booths, ordered their pints and kidney pie, and seemed very much happy to be in the countryside, chatting and laughing.

Matthews recalled that at one point the handsome young man with the limp asked if there were rooms to let. Matthews informed him they were all busy that weekend, but that if they drove on to the next village, Aylesbury, perhaps at the Broken Bell, an inn owned by Matthews's cousin, they might find accommodations.

When asked, Matthews stated the trio had not drunk to excess, only a couple of pints per, and that they were all gay and laughing when they took off, that he couldn't see how they could have died like that. Matthews added that nowadays one never knows, everything has changed since the war—a statement investigators believed referred to the current conflict, when in fact Matthews meant the one before, the Great War.

Investigators following the trio's trail noted that after reaching Aylesbury and inquiring at The Broken Bell, where again they were told there were no rooms available, their car was driven through an old sheep enclosure down to the bank of the Thane, as per the tire tracks in the mud.

In their preliminary report, investigators stated that the bodies of one of the men and of the girl were found a few days after by a hiker who had been following the nearby Chilton Hills path but had deviated from it for a spot of lunch by the river. He was accompanied by his dog, an Airedale, which began to bark excitedly at a tall hedge nearby. When the hiker went to investigate, he stumbled upon the corpses and immediately alerted the local constabulary.

The bodies had already begun to smell. An analysis surmised they had been lying there over the previous weekend, whose elevated temperatures had accelerated the natural rate of decomposition. The girl was found face down, her skirt raised, showing her naked lower body. The man nearby was lying face up, his pants undone, in death his face registering an expression of shock or surprise. The second man was nowhere to be found, and neither was the car.

The investigators' theory of the case argued that the trio were inebriated, as evidenced by several empty bottles of ale and one of Scotch found in nearby bushes. On a lark, they decided to go down to the river for a swim or perhaps just to cool off from the sweltering temperatures.

The investigators further surmised that the male and female victims may have been in the midst of sexual inter-course when the second man, who perhaps had fallen asleep from drunkenness, caught them in the act and shot them out of jealousy, the male with a bullet straight to the heart, the female with a round to the back of her head. The female was to be examined for evidence of sexual penetration and the presence of spermatozoa to confirm this hypothesis. Neither of the dece-dents carried any identification and their names and places of residence could not be immediately determined.

As to the second man, the presumed killer, investigators could find no trace of him. The man had never given his name or shown any identification at either of the establishments he visited. Investigators did find a trail of broken branches and a rut in the mud leading away and up to the Chiltern trail from the location of the incident, as if someone or something was being dragged there, but nothing conclusive was determined.

An alert with a description of the man went out to

surrounding towns and villages, but as of the time of the report's writing, the suspect had not been located. It was believed he might have had a second vehicle nearby or perhaps an accomplice to spirit him away, although that detail did not conform with the theory of a crime of passion, but rather of premeditated murder. That last theory was, in the opinion of the investigators, highly unlikely.

CHAPTER THIRTY-EIGHT

RILEY WAS EXHAUSTED.

He set down the heavy canvas bag with the weapon, took out a piece of bread and cheese and a bottle of ale from his knapsack, and leaned against a spindly beech to grab a bite and some rest.

He'd driven Cassidy's Mini Morris around and hidden it among bushes in a hollow near Aylesbury, then carried the weapon for miles through the forest. The journey had been steep and difficult, especially once he went off the Chilton Trail and traipsed through vegetation that hadn't seen the presence of man in years. With the overgrown tree tops at times hiding the sun, Riley had to rely on an old pocket compass to point him the way to the location of his intended target: Chequers.

At first he had hoisted the heavy bag astride his shoulders, then, when the weight grew wearying, on his back, cursing himself for underestimating the toll the heavy apparatus would take on him over the long distance.

Looking at a map back in London, he had calculated it

would only be about five miles from a point south of Aylesbury to Ellesborough, just a stone throw's away from Chequers and Churchill. He knew the prime minister's residence would be heavily guarded, sentries and soldiers posted around the fifteen hundred acres of the estate. But he noted that Chequers was on a plain surrounded on three sides by forests, which the military obviously thought were impenetrable, forgetting what the German army had done in the Ardennes, fast cutting through the woods to achieve an unexpected victory.

Not that security at Chequers was all that smart. The paved entry to the place was a quarter mile long and shaped like an arrow aiming straight at the building. Any German bomber going by, knowing that Churchill was there, could easily blast the residence to smithereens.

Riley had asked himself why the Germans had acted so reluctantly and out of character, sparing the estate so far. But he knew from the papers Fairfax had left him that a directive had finally been given in Berlin. That night, Nazi bombers would be making their presence known over Chequers for the first time—and that was when he, Riley, would strike.

He glanced at his watch. He had another three hours before sunset. The dinner party would be starting right about now, he figured. He didn't have much time left, resting would have to wait. He got up, lifted the sack with the weapon and ammo, and hustled his way forward. A half hour later he peeked through the branches of a laurel and saw for the first time the Gothic turrets of Chequers, where Churchill would have his final date with destiny.

Riley sat down, leaned against the trunk of the tree, and closed his eyes, willing himself to finally take a quick nap and settle his nerves to strengthen his aim. But he couldn't sleep. No matter how hard he tried, the images of all that had happened, the faces of his dead brother and the others in

Ireland, the faces of all he had killed to get to this point, kept surfacing in his mind's eye, so he gave up on resting and opted to assemble the weapon.

The German technician had been tediously thorough, making him assemble and disassemble the weapon dozens of times, so he was able to put it together easily enough in the soft amber light of the English sunset. Still, it was heavy work, as the entire assembly weighed close to thirty pounds.

The technician had been very proud of the weapon, calling it his Puppchen, his little doll. "Eighty-eight-millimeter caliber, can shoot almost a mile, ja? Is good weapon—but must be careful! The smoke, it shoots, and puff!! And the sound—big, big!! Nothing behind, you understand, nothing!"

Of course, Riley had said, understanding only that this tube was the practical solution to the problem. Or part of it—the other, the German's presence in England, he'd disposed of by killing him.

The broken-down weapon, a stack of interlocking reinforced steel tubes, assembled into a slender, four-foot-long cannon designed to be fired from the shoulder. Written on the back tube were the words "Achtung-Feuerstrahl" which Riley assumed meant handle with care. The cannon was outfitted with the special sight that functioned like a fine telescope in the light of day and then, with a twist of the mechanism, as Riley had seen earlier in London, became a night sight—capable of showing objects in the dark distance as though at arm's length.

Riley had trained in the IRA with long-range rifles and knew he had to adjust the angle of the projectile when it came time to fire over the length of the fields surrounding Chequers. He spent a half hour experimenting, placing the weapon in the ground and on a branch, trying to gauge the exact angle of declension that had to be factored in.

He was situated at the edge of the forest, on a low hill abutting the plain that surrounded Chequers a half mile away. The German had said the weapon could strike at a thousand meters, so the target was safely, or rather unsafely, within range. He finally erected a small mound of rocks stable enough and at the appropriate height on which to prop the weapon and account for the necessary angle.

The ammunition was a torpedo-shaped rocket, fed from the rear of the weapon. Ordinarily one man would be feeding the ammo while a second man aimed and fired. Riley had to make up for that by making sure his first shot was the only one he would need.

Sweating, he opened the rucksack that contained the rockets, four in all, each one weighing six pounds. Next to them, the heavy gloves, mask, and poncho the shooter was assigned to wear. He looked at them pensively and opted not to wear the mask—he wouldn't be able to sight the target if he had to look through the mask's glass eye opening—but he would use the gloves.

Riley picked up one of the rockets, which to him resembled nothing other than a bowling pin. He grabbed one, feeling its precisely balanced weight, and, laughing, tossed it into the air and grabbed it as it came down, playing with it as though he were still in the gymnasium of some institution under the benevolent eyes of a good priest. He tried juggling two of them but stopped when one fell on the ground, and he feared it might go off.

He picked up the fallen grenade, wiped it clean with a rag, then sat on the damp ground, staring patiently at Chequers, waiting for his chance to finally rid the world of Winston Churchill . . .

CHAPTER THIRTY-NINE

THOMPSON COULD NOT BELIEVE what he was seeing—
the Prime Minister of Great Britain, the man on whose shoulders rested the fate of freedom and democracy, whose job was
the definition of seriousness and dedication, was dancing a
Scottish jig all by himself like a drunken hussar in fancy dinner
dress, in front of a living room stuffed with the highest digni-
taries in the land.

Thompson knew Churchill had a fondness for military
music, a remnant of his days in the Army during Queen Victoria's reign, but he had never displayed this kind of exuberance
before at any time or place, at least that Thompson had
witnessed.

Mary, at Thompson's side, was laughing and clapping to
the music along with all the other guests—even Lord Fairfax,
the humorless foreign secretary, was smiling and nodding to the
spectacle, while Walter Hopkins, the American envoy, dressed
in a dinner jacket that seemed as rumpled as everything else he
wore, marked time and pumped his fists energetically to the

music while sending off clouds of apple-scented smoke from his pipe.

Still smiling, Mary whispered in Thompson's ear, "Has he gone daft?"

"It's the war," muttered Thompson, "finally got to him."

Having danced the last steps and concluded with a flurry of footwork, a two-step, and a half turn by the imposing fireplace, it was Lady Churchill who finally put an end to the martial display.

"Very nice, dear, but perhaps we should put on some other music so our guests can dance with one another!"

Everyone laughed and Churchill bowed to his wife. "As long as you favor me with one more turn of terpsichore," said Churchill.

"My pleasure," said Clementine, signaling at the butler, who had already slipped a 78 disc onto the record player. Churchill took his tall, slender wife into his arms and the two swayed in a slow foxtrot to the melody of the Glenn Miller Orchestra. Soon everyone followed suit, the thirty or so guests stepping gently to the burnished sounds of the American band.

"That was quite a performance, Pug," whispered Clementine in Churchill's ear, after a while.

"Sometimes our vexing spirits can only be cast out by musical exertion, Puss," said Churchill.

"Or revolution?"

"Meaning?" said a puzzled Churchill.

"I heard about your visit to that Cuban child in the hospital," she said, softly. Churchill stiffened.

"I will remonstrate Thompson!" he threatened.

"It wasn't him. But I often wonder about your time in Cuba. Remember how cross we were with each other?"

Churchill relaxed, nodded. "Yes, there were some things

then that . . . what is that music?" he asked as another record, a burnished tropical melody, came on.

"'Green Eyes,' Tommy Dorsey. I thought it might make you remember how close we were to ending it all."

"Yes, well, dear, there is something I must confess. It's been a heavy burden all these years, and I hope you will forgive me. You see, that boy . . ."

"No, Pug dear, there is nothing to confess or forgive. That boy found his mother. And his father. And you saved him. No matter what all may have happened in Cuba, that was long ago and in another country."

"You are most . . . magnanimous, my dear."

"In that case, I hope you will be the same with me."

"How do you mean?"

"Well, you see, dear, you know how strapped we are for funds, and . . . I approached Beaverbrook for a loan."

"You did not!"

"Well, he didn't give me one. But he did make an offer, which I accepted."

"Is fidelity involved?" said Churchill, archly.

"Only the literary kind. He wants to publish my memoirs. And he is going to pay us forty thousand pounds."

"Oh!" said Churchill, quietly. Concerned, Clementine took a step backward, looked Churchill in his deep blue eyes.

"I was hoping you would find it in your heart to forgive me, for not asking your permission beforehand."

Churchill glared at her, then broke into a smile. "As you said, there is nothing to forgive. But you will let me edit the thing, will you not?"

"I wouldn't have it any other way," she said, and they danced on, in quiet satisfaction.

At the other end of the living room, Thompson was dancing with Mary, basking in the momentary peace and beauty of the surroundings. It seemed to him that at least for that moment, the war and everything that went with it—the bombings, the rations, the fear, the deaths—all were ghosts, bad memories from another world.

"I don't think I've told you before," whispered Thompson, "but you are quite fetching tonight."

"Just tonight, hmm?" answered Mary, coquettishly. "Is it me or my Madame Gres dress?"

"Must be the dress," said Thompson playfully. "Otherwise you're just . . ."

"Just what?" said Mary, eyes shining with feigned indignation.

"Just adorable," said Thompson, hugging her close.

"Well, Inspector, I shall let you adore me. For a price. A shilling for a dance, a guinea for a kiss. Other favors to be negotiated."

"Small prices to pay," said Thompson, intoxicated by Mary's smell, her warmth, her spirit. He held her tight and closed his eyes, and then he recognized the music and for a moment found himself spinning back into the past.

'Green Eyes,' he thought. Remembering how the band at the nightclub had played it the last night he'd spent with his wife, trying to patch things up with her, making amends for his repeated absences by taking her to the fanciest place in Manchester—and how the night ended in recriminations, complaints, a long silent drive home and Eleanor announcing she wanted a divorce and him out of the house.

"Something wrong?" said Mary, seeing Thompson frown, his expression cold and distant. He looked down and his heart melted, as he held this precious young beauty who was willing to give his heart a new chance at life. He smiled tenderly.

"Nothing much, only that this song brings back unwanted memories."

"Then let them go, dear," she said, softly, and they danced silently until the song ended. While everyone else returned to the living room for refreshments, Thompson led Mary out to the terrace adjoining the ballroom.

A scent of blooming lilacs filled the air, still warm from the day's summery sun, crickets chirping their usual melody, a nightingale spinning its nightly song. The hills around Chequers were dark and deep, in contrast to the soft yellow of the plowed fields around the building. A gibbous moon in the clear sky seemed full of promise to Thompson and Mary, who leaned on the stone balustrade.

"It's so lovely," said Mary. "I see why the PM comes here as often as he can."

"Yes, far from the madding crowd," said Thompson.

"Well, I don't know about that, he seems to bring along his own mad cast of characters," riposted Mary. They laughed.

"He does, doesn't he?" said Thompson. Then, hesitantly: "Mary, there's something I've been meaning to ask you."

"Yes, Walter?" said Mary, looking up at Thompson with eyes so wide and bright he thought he'd drown in them.

"Will you . . ." Thompson stopped, his ears picking up the familiar, hateful sound of throbbing engines.

"Yes, Walter, will I what?" said Mary, a desperate tone to her words, fearing that a slim chance of a beginning for them had been truncated by Thompson's dogged devotion to duty—and Winston Churchill.

"I say, Thompson, what's that I hear?" came Churchill's voice behind them.

They looked at the newly darkened sky, where a constellation of stars was obliterated by a squadron of German bombers noisily drilling through the velvet night. Dozens, hundreds of them on death's errand, were crossing over the hills, heading north to the industrial cities of Liverpool and Coventry to drop their deadly cargo.

All the guests streamed out of the ballroom and onto the terrace, watching with varying degrees of horror the incipient disaster above them.

"Really, Winston, there must be something we can do at night about these fellows," said Fairfax, now at Churchill's elbow.

"Our planes cannot fight at night," grumbled Churchill. "It would be a suicide mission to send them up."

Fairfax shrugged. "Well, then, I know how you are opposed to civilian bombing, but I do believe it's time we give the enemy a taste of their own medicine."

"Fine, we'll discuss it tomorrow. I've reached the end of my patience—one bad turn deserves another."

"Glad to hear that," said Fairfax. Nervously, he put a cigarette to his lips, took out his gold lighter and struck it once, two, three times. "Blasted thing, wind must be putting it out. Come, dear," he said to his wife behind him, "let me have a smoke inside."

Thompson, next to Churchill, glanced at Fairfax hurrying into the building. Odd, he thought, there is no wind, what the devil is he talking about?

Just then Thompson heard a familiar whistling piercing the air. They wouldn't dare, he thought still, as he glanced up. The bomber squad was close enough to be seen and heard yet still some distance away, there was no aircraft near enough to drop a bomb—and in that split second he swiveled and looked at the forest nearest, where a flash of lightning had lit up a giant cloud of smoke, pierced with tongues of flame. That was where the whistling and the projectile were hailing from—inconceivable but undeniably true—somehow a cannon had been transported to the hills and now was firing at them—all these thoughts running together in a whirlwind of impressions as the whistling ended in seconds.

Thompson instantly jumped on Mary and grabbed Churchill's sleeve to force him down—but Churchill instinctively broke free and began to say, "Thompson, how many times do I have to tell you . . ."

He did not finish his sentence as the rocket slammed into the balustrade, which burst into pieces, shattering windows, destroying the gargoyles on the roof, the force of the blast driving everyone to the floor. In the confusion following the blast, in the smoke and heat, some of the guests began getting up, stumbling around in a daze.

"Down, down!" shouted Thompson, "there might be a second one! Down on your knees and crawl back into the building! Stay down!"

He turned to Mary. "Are you all right?" She looked up, nodded yes, her dress smeared with pulverized bits of stone, her face smudged. She jerked her chin at Churchill.

"He's not," she said.

Thompson looked at Churchill, lying on the pavers a few feet away, unconscious. He crawled next to him.

"Prime Minister! Prime Minister!" No response. A bloody gash on his forehead. "Prime Minister!" he repeated. He quickly took his pulse. Still alive.

Summoning all his strength, Thompson got to his feet, swept up Churchill, and, carrying him in his arms, dashed across the terrace back into the hall.

"Here, here!" said a helpful voice. Thompson turned around—Sir Hugh Northrop, Churchill's physician. "Let us have a look at him. Is he alive?"

"Yes, but I can't tell the extent of his injuries . . ."

"I'll take care of him," said Northrop, calling over two servants.

"Please do, I've to go get those buggers," said Thompson, placing Churchill on a chaise far from the terrace.

Lady Clementine stepped in, her dress torn and dusty.

"Bring him to our bedroom!" she ordered. Northrop looked around in anxious desperation, but then nodded and followed the servants and the prime minister's wife to the bedroom wing.

Thompson rushed out of the ballroom, out to the terrace again, glanced at the hills. Already the sentries and soldiers posted about the estate had come alive, turning on the searchlights. A rattle of machine guns fired aimlessly at the hills. Fools, thought Thompson, bloody good that's going to do.

He looked at the forest, where he could still see the cloud the rocket had left behind dissipating in the shadowy gloom. Why hasn't there been a second shot? Damn it, they're moving! They're preparing to fire from somewhere else!!

Then the thought finally came to him.

Riley! He's still alive!! That's what the Germans were here to do—a portable cannon from miles away. Good Lord, what's next?

He glanced down at the grounds around the building, saw the soldiers out in formation, spreading around the grounds. There's the answer—the motorcycles of Churchill's escort! He shouted down at Jenkins, already ordering men about.

"Guard the perimeter! No one in or out!"

Thompson ran to the stairs, not waiting for a response. Once down at the entrance, he jumped on one of the Triumph motorcycles and headed out to the hills to stop Riley before he could fire again.

CHAPTER FORTY

IN THE HILLS of Chiltern Forest, Riley came to.

Dazzled, disconcerted, he slowly he began to regain his senses, his memory of who he was and where he was, and then he remembered the German's warning. The smoke, it shoots, and puff!! And the sound—big, big!! Nothing behind, you understand, nothing!

He'd been knocked unconscious by the force of the blast, which had dislodged the rocks on which he'd balanced the front of the launcher. The explosion had sent half the rocks hurling straight at his head, even as the flames surging out of the back of the cannon struck the trunk of the beech tree behind him, reflecting the heat of the explosion back at him.

He touched the back of his head—a bloody mess, his flesh oozing from the burning gases, his hair scorched, his ears ringing. His head hurt and throbbed as if a thousand-pound weight had fallen on it.

The gloves had protected his hands, so he could still move the cannon. Pushing it aside, he got up, wobbly from the impact. He removed the sight from the launcher, focused on the target. He spotted the confusion, with all the guards milling around, Thompson lifting Churchill up, a few of the wounded guests traipsing around the terrace. He smiled. I've got him! I finally got the bloody bastard! He sat down on the ground, basking in the glory of his accomplishment. Finally! This one's for you, Danny boy!!

But it wasn't over, not yet. Looking down at the fields and Chequers, Riley spotted a lone motorcycle racing his way—with Thompson on it. No time to waste, thought Riley, calmly. Better get out of here. Or not.

He could try to run away, scurrying through the forest back to his car a couple of miles away, but in his weakened condition he knew he wouldn't get far, and Thompson would quickly overtake him. He could stay and try to fight Thompson, but again, he was in no condition for a long struggle.

Stumbling in the shadows, Riley searched his bag, found Cypher's Luger.

Only one bullet left.

He looked down at the pistol, blood from his scalp dripping down his neck. He could hear the varoom of Thompson's motorcycle coming near, already at the foot of the hill. It would only be a handful of minutes before Thompson and all the security swarmed the area looking for him. If Thompson didn't kill him, the others certainly would.

For a moment he contemplated turning himself in, exposing Fairfax, bringing down the whole edifice of the British government. But no, he had done his job, there was no need to be a turncoat—and after all, maybe now Fairfax would return Ulster to Eire. Wasn't that what everyone fought for and died for?

He went over the details once more, seeking a way to escape what seemed an unavoidable fate. There was only one way out—he'd have to do it. Yes, this was the way to end this.

Riley lifted his gun.

————

THOMPSON HEARD the shot over the hubbub of the motorcycle. He killed the engine, sat motionless on the seat, controlling his breath, straining his ears. Nothing. He had ridden the Triumph hard, up a narrow path in between the trees, and now he looked up. The gun blast had come from a copse about two hundred feet up the hill. In the pallid light of the moon, he detected the clearing, traces of the rocket's fiery cloud still clinging to the treetops, like a raised curtain to a nightmare.

Thompson took out his revolver, dismounted, advanced quickly through the vegetation, crouching and darting, not certain of how many people Riley had brought with him. No, probably not, he decided, this was a one-man mission, otherwise he would have had others helping him at Waterloo Station.

Thompson momentarily regretted acting so rashly and coming out all by himself, instead of leading a search party to properly rake the area. It wasn't like him to act so impulsively, but the sight of the wounded Churchill, the danger Mary had been exposed to, and the sheer surprise of the attack had shattered his usual caution. He hoped that Jenkins would send a party out to follow him, should there be others with Riley after all. That was why one could never let emotions guide one's actions—must keep a tight rein—steady, always steady. Now, where is this man?

Thompson crept up the hill, stopped at the edge of the clearing, the stench of scorched vegetation and gunpowder in the air. He heard a scurrying in the bushes. He whipped around, finger on the trigger—in the shadows, a small fox dashed away. Grateful he'd held his fire, he slowly advanced up the hill and, crouching, stopped at the edge of the clearing.

On the ground he saw an array of materiel—a long cannon by the side of a half-built rock tower, a sack with a handful of rockets by the weapon, and next to that, the body of a man face down, his left arm outstretched, right arm under his body, a pool of liquid underneath him.

Riley, thought Thompson. He killed himself rather than be captured.

Thompson approached slowly, gun pointed at the man on the ground. In the half-light he could see the back of the man's head, a glutinous blub where the scalp had been. The weapon must have malfunctioned, thought Thompson, that's why it was fired only once—he was grievously injured and chose to end it all. He went the way of all fanatics, like the Thuggees, would rather kill himself than face just retribution. The coward's way out. Like Mueller. Cowards one and all.

Full of contempt, he walked up to the prone body, kicked it, like with a shot deer. No response. Dead.

Just then, something caught his eye—the liquid under Riley wasn't blood—what was it? The smell—he pocketed his gun, placed both hands on Riley to turn him over. Just at that moment, when he realized the liquid was ale, Riley whipped around and, Luger in hand, struck Thompson on the chin, knocking him down.

Riley sprang to his feet, easing a knife out of his waistband and into his hand, just as Thompson, still down, grabbed one of the rockets and sprang to his feet. With surprising agility Riley thrust the knife at Thompson, who swung the rocket at Riley, who in turn stepped back to avoid being struck.

Thompson transferred the rocket to his left hand and with his right reached in his shoulder holster for his revolver. Riley dashed forward, slashed Thompson's left hand, making him drop the rocket, and kicked him in the chest, sending him reeling into a tree. By the time Thompson drew his gun, Riley had already run into the forest, losing himself in the vegetation.

Thompson hurried after him, following the noise of the breaking branches and bushes as Riley raced down the hill. Thompson heard the faraway hubbub of cars and motorcycles nearing the edge of the forest—the soldiers, and police from Chequers.

He can't get out that way, thought Thompson. But then came a closer sound, the thrumming of Thompson's Triumph being kicked on, then taking off. He's going to run up the hill and lose us, we can't let that happen!

Thompson raced desperately down, trying to intercept the Triumph, judging by the racket of the motorcycle, which swept up ahead, darting here and there, swerving wildly. The throbbing of the engine headed up the hill, trampling through the vegetation, with Thompson, almost out of breath, giving chase —until the Triumph reached the crest of the hill and then plunged three hundred feet into a steep rocky ravine, at the bottom of which ran the dark Thane river.

In the half light of the moon, Thompson stood silently on the hillcrest, looking down at the crumbled remains of the motorcycle, smashed up against the rocks. Gone, thought Thompson. No one could survive that impact, much less someone in his condition. Good riddance. We'll go look for him in the morning.

Thompson was traipsing down the hill, in the half shadows, when he heard the search party ahead of him.

"Thompson? Thompson, where are you?"

"Here!" he answered, the beams of the search crew's torches shining through the dappled shadows of the trees. Thompson failed to see Riley, hidden behind a massive oak, knife in hand, a few feet away, within striking distance.

Riley was preparing to jump him, when Jenkins burst forth, shining his light on the bleeding Thompson.

"Are you all right?" asked Jenkins.

"I'm fine. It was Riley. His bike went over the cliff. No way he could have survived. Let's return to Chequers. We'll send a search party at daybreak."

It worked, they believe I'm dead, thought Riley, stepping away carefully from the scene. But it's not over yet, Thompson, not for you or for Churchill. I'll come back for you some other day, when you least expect it, Riley promised to himself, as he scurried away noiselessly through the brush to the Morris hidden in the valley miles away.

———

ONCE AT CHEQUERS, Thompson was heading to Mary's room when one of the staff approached him.

"Call for you, sir. It's urgent."

"Who is it?"

"Whitehall, sir."

Thompson took the call at the small vestibule by the entrance.

"Thompson here."

"This is Wiley, MI5. We have received compromising information about Sir Hugh Northrop. We want you to detain him immediately. Take whatever measures are necessary."

"The prime minister's physician? Why?"

"We have reason to believe he's a Nazi agent."

CHAPTER FORTY-ONE

CHURCHILL LAY FLAT, unconscious, on the wheeled stretcher of the infirmary at Chequers.

Long before the estate was gifted to the British government for the rest and relaxation of future prime ministers, a previous owner had set up a rudimentary clinic in the basement. A wealthy American businessman with many interests in Britain, the owner had married a noblewoman with a weak heart, so he'd outfitted a proper doctor's office in the basement in case her condition suddenly worsened, and she couldn't travel the fifty miles to the nearest hospital.

The infirmary had never been used before. And now England's prime minister, himself the child of an American and British union, was the first, unexpected beneficiary of the industrialist's largesse—even if the attending physician had something other than Churchill's welfare in mind.

Sir Hugh Northrop was all nerves. He had wasted precious minutes convincing Lady Clementine to bring Churchill from his bedroom down to the infirmary to treat him, knowing that

Thompson would soon be coming back to guard him with his life. The success of Northrop's mission, his long-awaited intervention, required swift action, the sooner the better.

Northrop had ushered everyone out and locked the door after Churchill was brought in, claiming he couldn't risk any kind of infection from present company, all of whom were dirty and smudged from the rocket blast. Now he bent over Churchill, examining him quickly.

Churchill had suffered a concussion, the skin on his forehead split open, nothing that some sutures and a few days of bed rest wouldn't cure. He had suffered a far worse clash in New York when that taxi had plowed into him at thirty miles an hour, so Northrop was confident he'd ride out this one without too many aftereffects. Churchill seemed to have a lucky star, a guardian angel who protected him no matter how many times he wandered into danger.

But not this time, thought Northrop.

Before cleansing the wound, he gave Churchill a dose of phenobarbital to make sure he wouldn't come to during the unorthodox procedure Northrop was about to undertake.

Berlin had been quite insistent—at no time should Churchill be killed. Der Führer did not want to make him a martyr. That would only make the next head of state even more obdurate in the war against the Reich. No, the aim was to disable him, leaving him alive but useless for office, so that his stranglehold on the British people would be broken and reasonable men, like Chamberlain, Fairfax, and Lloyd George, would see the virtues of a negotiated peace.

Yet, how to do that? Simple. Make him shut up.

More than any other politician, Churchill had made his political career not so much on his judgment as on his voice. Churchill's speeches, defiant, cultured, patriotic, drawing on English history and customs, were the glue that held Great

Britain together. Once he could no longer give a speech, he could no longer lead—for what is a written speech but a piece of political folderol no one bothers to read? No, Churchill had to be deprived of his faculty of speech, and that was what Northrop was about to do.

Northrop had been expecting this moment. He knew ahead of time that there would be an apparent attempt on Churchill's life, that it would not be successful as the ammunition would be faulty, and that it would give him the excuse to silence Churchill once and for all, blaming his malady on the aftereffects of the attempted assassination by the IRA.

He took out the vial of pancuronium, a powerful neuro-muscular blocking agent similar to curare that had recently been developed by German laboratories following experimentations on concentration camp inmates. Ordinarily used for surgeries, pancuronium, at an elevated dose and combined with benzodiazepine, when injected into vocal cords, made a person unable to utter even the simplest sounds. Permanently. It was his own brilliant contribution to the order he had received from Germany.

Churchill would be as mute as the walls of Parliament, where he would never triumph again. Northrop wasn't certain who exactly would take Churchill's place, but it was no matter. This simple injection would assure the triumph of the Aryan race and the rebirth of a virile, manly England.

He had drawn the 30 cc of pancuronium when Churchill stirred. The man has the constitution of an ox, thought Northrop; the phenobarbital should have put him away for a while.

Churchill flopped around, moved his arms, attempted to sit up. Northrop put down the syringe with pancuronium, moved quickly to Churchill's side.

"There, there, Prime Minister, easy, easy," said Northrop, gently pushing Churchill back down. "Lie down, sir, please."

"Where am I, Hugh?" said Churchill, his eyes glazed, the effect of the sedative not strong enough to quiet him down, yet enough to make his world a vague vision of shadows and glass jars. "What happened?"

"You've been severely injured in the attack, Prime Minister," said Northrop. "You will require further intervention. Please be still, I must administer this sedative to allow me to proceed."

"What? What happened? What was broken? I don't feel any pain," said Churchill.

"That's the sedative, Prime Minister. I'm about to give you another dose so you can be safely transported to hospital," said Northrop, and before Churchill could object further, he inserted a syringe full of phenobarbital into his exposed arm.

"But I don't feel anything, Hugh, just a headache, a tremendous headache," said Churchill, lying down, eyes closed.

"There, there, sir, all will be well," said Northrop, soothingly. He stood for a minute next to Churchill, making sure he fell back into a stupor.

Northrop took a deep breath. I'd best hurry, someone's bound to come down. He returned to the side table and picked up the syringe with the pancuronium. He bent over Churchill, snoring, the sedative had taken effect. Churchill mumbled a few words, as if in deep sleep at Chartwell.

Northrop pushed down Churchill's jaw to administer the shot, but Churchill's jaw snapped back every time he attempted to pry it open. The sedative had activated the sympathetic nerve—he needed something to keep it open.

Growing more impatient by the minute and cursing himself for not having thought of it previously, he searched frantically for a block of some sort to insert into Churchill's

mouth. He opened drawers, vitrines, all full of medical implements but nothing like the wedge of solid rubber dentists use
during oral surgery. He finally found a length of rubber tubing
used to wrap around people's arms during injections. He tied it
into several knots, making a ball out of it with just enough
width to keep Churchill's jaws open. He jammed it into
Churchill's mouth. It held.

Finally! thought Northrop. He returned to his table, picked
up the syringe of pancuronium, headed back to Churchill.

A click at the door.

Northrop turned, saw the door handle being jostled.

"Open up, Doctor!"

Thompson! I cannot let anyone interfere with this! I must
complete my mission!

Northrop grabbed a chair, pushed it against the door. He
returned to Churchill.

"Open up, Northrop! Open this door immediately!"

Northrop grabbed the syringe—30 cc, enough to render
him speechless for life. But wait, there's air in the needle, that
could kill him, I must empty . . .

The door flew open from Thompson's kick—behind him,
three soldiers.

Thompson took in Northrop holding his needle on high,
squirting drops of pancuronium into the air—Churchill lying
on the stretcher, mouth gagged open, unconscious—instinctively, automatically, Thompson drew his gun.

Northrop stepped forward to Churchill's prostrate body.

"Stop or I'll shoot!" said Thompson.

Northrop bent over Churchill, the needle moving down to
his open mouth when the shot rang out. Northrop gave a jump,
startled, as the bullet pierced his lungs and blood filled his
mouth.

He turned, looked at Thompson, then in a last frantic

move, brought his arm down as Thompson's last shot shattered the syringe in midair. Northrop dropped his hand down on Churchill's chest and collapsed on the floor, next to the snoring prime minister.

CHAPTER FORTY-TWO

CHURCHILL'S VOICE, hoarse and still strained after his hushed-up recovery from the Chequers attack, blared through the radio in Mary's flat:

"We must regard the next week or so as a very important period in our history. It ranks with the days when the Spanish Armada was approaching the Channel, and Drake was finishing his game of bowls; or when Nelson stood between us and Napoleon's Grand Army at Boulogne. We have read all about this in the history books; but what is happening now is on a far greater scale and of far more consequence to the life and future of the world and its civilization than these brave old days of the past.

"Every man and woman will therefore prepare himself to do his duty, whatever it may be, with special pride and care. Our fleets and flotillas are very powerful and numerous; our Air Force is at the highest strength it has ever reached, and it is conscious of its proved superiority, not indeed in numbers, but in men and machines. Our shores are well fortified and strongly manned, and behind them, ready to attack the invaders, we have a far larger and better-equipped mobile Army than we have ever had before.

"Besides this, we have more than a million and a half men of the Home Guard, who are just as much soldiers of the Regular Army as the Grenadier Guards, and who are determined to fight for every inch of the ground in every village and in every street.

"It is with devout but sure confidence that I say: Let God defend the Right."

His speech went on for a few more minutes, and when it was over, Mary dialed off the radio and turned to Thompson.

"Well, I must say, that was quite stirring. Do you really think we can win this war?"

Thompson leaned back against the bed's wooden headboard. "We have to. The whole world depends on us."

Mary got up from her chair, sat on the edge of the bed. She gently tousled Thompson's thinning hair. "And Churchill and I on you."

"And I on you, Mrs. Thompson. Now give your brand-new old husband another kiss."

"Gladly," she said, bending down, and kissed him.

THE END

A NOTE FROM THE AUTHOR

Dear Reader,

Thank you for reading *Mission Churchill*, I hope you enjoyed it!

I love hearing from my readers, so please, leave a review on Goodreads. They greatly help in getting my books out into the world and are hugely appreciated.

Warmest regards,
Alex

ACKNOWLEDGMENTS

No author stands alone—they are always guided by the previous generation that opened the road, breached the wall, and carried the standard triumphant into battle. So it is for me, as this book would not have been possible without the stunning creativity and thorough research of Warren Adler and James C. Hume. They were the first to bring to life the wondrous story of Winston Churchill and his prize bodyguard, Walter Thompson, in their novel Target Churchill, allowing me to fashion another chapter in the saga they created. My thanks to Adler's sons, Jonathan and Michael, for choosing me to carry on the legacy of their father, a writer whose equal has yet to be found in American literature.

Finally, an enormous debt of gratitude to my family—my wife Armeen, my solace and joy, and my children, Christian, Nicolas and Veronica, whose love and support light my life and inspire my work.

ABOUT THE AUTHOR

Alex Abella is a *New York Times Notable Book* novelist, screenwriter, *Emmy award* winning news writer and reporter.

Alex's legal thriller, *The Killing of the Saints* (Crown), was a *New York Times Notable Book,* and was translated into twelve foreign languages. Its sequels, *Dead of Night* and *Final Acts* (Simon & Schuster) were published in quick succession. The trilogy won praise from critics and prominent writers such as Michael Connelly, T. Jefferson Parker, and Robert Ferrigno. *Paramount Pictures* optioned *The Killing of the Saints* and commissioned Alex to write the screenplay. Alex has developed original series for Warner Bros. and The Disney Channel. Alex's two-act play, *Camelia,* was staged Off Broadway at the Actors Ensemble Theater in New York City.

Alex also wrote *The Great American* (Simon & Schuster), a historical novel set in 1950s Cuba based on the life of William Morgan, a real-life, Ohio-born Marine who became one of the leaders of the Castro revolution. For years Alex has conducted dozens of interviews of prominent Cubans and Cuban Americans for an on-going project on the influence of Cuba in the U.S., *A DARKER MIRROR.*

Alex's last non-fiction book, *Soldiers of Reason: The Rand Corporation and the Rise of the American Empire* (Harcourt), a study of the world's most influential think tank, was long listed for the *National Book Award.* Alex's other non-fiction books include *Shadow Enemies* (Lyons Press) a narrative account of a plot by Adolf Hitler to start a wave of terror and destruction in the United States. Alex has been a contributing writer to the Los Angeles Times, TIME Magazine, and a number of publications.

Born in Cuba, Alex's family migrated to the United States when Alex was 10. Alex grew up in New York City, winning a Pulitzer Scholarship to Columbia University, earning a B.A. in Comparative Literature. Moving to California, Alex was a reporter for The San Francisco Chronicle. Switching over to broadcast media at KTVU-TV, Channel 2 News, Alex became producer, writer, and reporter, won a *News writing Emmy (Group)* and was nominated for an *Emmy for Best Breaking News Story*. Alex was a foreign correspondent in Central America and received a commendation from The San Francisco Press Club for his reporting.

Alex speaks five languages and has traveled extensively through Latin America and Europe. Alex is married and lives in the suburbs of Los Angeles.

MORE FROM WARREN ADLER

This work was inspired by the novel *Target Churchill*, written by Warren Adler and James C. Humes. This is the prequel.

For complete catalogue of Warren Adlers works, including novels, plays, and short stories visit: www.warrenadler.com

Inquiries: Customerservice@warrenadler.com

Facebook—facebook.com/warrenadler
Twitter—twitter.com/warrenadler

ALSO BY ALEX ABELLA

Soldiers of Reason: The RAND Corporation and the Rise of the American Empire

More Than A Woman

Shanghai

The Total Banana

Shadow Enemies: Hitler's Secret Terrorist Plot Against the United States

The Great American

CHARLIE MORELL SERIES

1. The Killing of the Saints

2. Dead of Night: A Novel

3. Final Acts: A Novel

ALSO BY WARREN ADLER

FICTION

Banquet Before Dawn

Beneath the Ivory Tower

Blood Ties

Cult

Empty Treasures

Flanagan's Dolls

Funny Boys

Madeline's Miracles

Mother Nile

Mourning Glory

Natural Enemies

Private Lies

Random Hearts

Residue

Target Churchill

The Casanova Embrace

The David Embrace

The Henderson Equation

The Housewife Blues

The Serpent's Bite

The War of the Roses

The War of the Roses: The Children

Trans-Siberian Express

Treadmill

Twilight Child

Undertow

We Are Holding the President Hostage

THE FIONA FITZGERALD MYSTERY SERIES

American Quartet

American Sextet

Death of a Washington Madame

Immaculate Deception

Senator Love

The Ties That Bind

The Witch of Watergate

Washington Masquerade

SHORT STORY COLLECTIONS

Jackson Hole: Uneasy Eden

Never Too Late For Love

New York Echoes

New York Echoes 2

New York Echoes 3

The Sunset Gang

PLAYS

Dead in the Water

Libido

The Sunset Gang: The Musical

The War of the Roses

Windmills